PENGUIN BOOKS

Kate le Vann was born in Doncaster. She writes
and newspapers, and is calling herself a columnist these days. She lives
in London and is easily led.

kate le vann
bad timing

PENGUIN BOOKS

PENGUIN BOOKS

Penguin Books Ltd, 80 Strand, London WC2R 0RL, England
Penguin Putnam Inc., 375 Hudson Street, New York, New York 10014, USA
Penguin Books Australia Ltd, Ringwood, Victoria, Australia
Penguin Books Canada Ltd, 10 Alcorn Avenue, Toronto, Ontario, Canada M4V 3B2
Penguin Books India (P) Ltd, 11 Community Centre,
Panchsheel Park, New Delhi – 110 017, India
Penguin Books (NZ) Ltd, Cnr Rosedale and Airborne Roads,
Albany, Auckland, New Zealand
Penguin Books (South Africa) (Pty) Ltd, 24 Sturdee Avenue,
Rosebank 2196, South Africa

Penguin Books Ltd, Registered Offices: 80 Strand, London WC2R 0RL, England

www.penguin.com

First published by Viking 2000
Published in Penguin Books 2001
1

Set in Monotype Sabon
Printed in England by Clays Ltd, St Ives plc

acknowledgements

Thanks to my agent, Judith Murray, for making it happen; to everyone at Penguin, for making it easy; and to my editor, Hannah Robson, for making it better.

1

you haven't met
ivan yet

Fifteen-year-olds give the best parties. It's only fair, because they have the worst of it everywhere else. Whether you're the girl who spends all night crying in the bathroom, or the one who makes her cry – and half the joy is that there's no knowing which you'll be when you set off, shiny and hopeful, with your Special Brew or your alcopops – they're the last place on earth where everything you do matters. You can have your hopes spat at, you can poison yourself in the first two hours or embarrass yourself so badly that suicide starts looking sensible, but you'll always stay to the end because part of you knows you're making history.

It's downhill after that. When buying booze is easy, when buying drugs is lazy, when there is such a thing as bad sex, when people don't know all the words to all the songs any more and wouldn't sing them even if they did, when tears in public aren't given due respect, when not a damn thing you do will be remembered in the morning (except by you), parties stop being fun. It takes quite a few years of disappointment for this to sink in. In a basement in Fulham, a short, slight girl who had seen about enough was just beginning to catch on. Lainey, her back to one wall and her eyes on another, let her face relax into plainness and went to look for her coat. She found her friend to kiss goodbye in the middle of a group of tall, loud people.

'Lainey – you're not going?' Chrissie said.

'Yeah. Sorry. You don't mind, do you?'

'Well you haven't met Ivan yet.'

'Ohhh. Next time?'

'Why are you rushing off?'

She was tired, physically. Tired of not knowing anyone, and of being ignored and hoping something would happen. Optimism was draining.

'I'm too old for loud parties,' Lainey said.

'God, and I'm not? Think how you'll feel at thirty, though. In a few years it's going to be dinner for eight at eight for eight-thirty. We should do this while we can.'

Chrissie was a great one for landmark ages, but nothing ever changed her. She added a five or rounded up to ten, moved the goalposts all the time, but never altered her belief that oldness was just a few heartbeats away. As senility was always impending, it stood to reason that wherever she was was the last gasp of youth, and she behaved like someone reprieved, throwing herself into action with breathless vigour and urgency. The clock consciousness was a feature of their generation, and its root cause was the persistent deterioration of parties, which were the most complete expression of leisure. Although maturity had brought all the independence it promised, they couldn't enjoy the view: they spent too much time questioning whether they really had fun any more.

No debate this evening. It was the opposite of fun. It was standing. Lainey and Chrissie, who could speak for hours on the phone, often had little to say to each other in public. They gave it their best shot, but were both relieved when someone joined them: his hair glistened like freshly laid tarmac and he seemed to know Chrissie.

'It's Chrissie, isn't it?'

Chrissie stood straighter while she assessed him.

'We both did subsid French at Edinburgh. You used to know Dan Fuller? I lived with him. I'm Peter. Beck.'

The decorative furrowing of Chrissie's brow smoothed. She nodded, moving closer to Lainey as Peter Beck filled her in on the missing years, as if she knew who he was, as if she cared. He was dropping names the way a teenager drags his feet, and the girls were grateful to have something to laugh at together. Their shoulders touched, pushing slightly because elbowing would have been rude. Outsiders calcified their friendship, reminding them that they were more like each other than other people.

'Are you in advertising too?' Peter Beck asked Lainey, after running through Chrissie's CV. He had to know more to see if they were worth being interested in. It was that kind of party. And Lainey's looks were the non-conclusive sort: alone they weren't enough. She could take him on or lose him with the next few words.

'I work in a supermarket. Check-out.'

His pleasure opened like a rose, the edges curling over into condescension.

'Really? How cool.'

'It may be cool, but it's not true. She writes for magazines,' Chrissie said evenly, managing to make it an accusation that lived up to Lainey's embarrassment. 'She used to write for *Panic*.'

'Really.' Peter Beck's voice was deep this time.

'Not any more,' Lainey said, and was so anxious to broadcast her annoyance that she made herself believe in it, and trembled with the force of insisting. 'That was just a –'

'Well, you will again,' Chrissie said, with fuck-you nonchalance.

'Oh Chrissie, I won't. Shut up. I don't want to do this.'

Cat fights were well and good, but bickering was never sexy, and Peter Beck had stopped listening. Later Chrissie would tell her off for being rude to him, but Lainey didn't care; more than that, she was proud of not caring. She found a phone and called a cab.

'Yes, leave *me* with him,' Chrissie said behind her as Lainey hung up.

'Come on, does it matter if I go? You only live round the corner. Ivan'll know where you are if he doesn't find you here.' She felt strange using the name of someone she'd never met, making assumptions about a third person.

'He's never been to my flat.'

'I've ordered a cab now. You were talking to some people earlier . . .'

'I've talked to them enough,' Chrissie said. 'I don't really know them anyway.'

'What are you saying?' Lainey said. 'Do you want me to stay?'

'I wanted you to meet Ivan.'

Since Ivan, Lainey had noticed a new vulnerability in Chrissie that suited her so well she couldn't believe it hadn't always been there. Sometimes she looked lost and alone, even scared. She did a timid thing with her eyes now that Lainey had never seen before in years of friendship. She seemed smaller, and crushable like choux pastry. It was undeniably becoming: novelty was always charming – and it was nice to see Chrissie take a break from being strenuously arch – but it bothered Lainey, as if she were somehow expected to change too before she was ready.

'I didn't know he'd never been to your flat.'

'I've been to his.'

'Yes, you told me that. You said he's got a corduroy sofa and he lives with a comic.'

'Sort of a comic. John. He's just starting out. He hasn't given up the day job and I'm not sure he will. He's getting on a bit to be making it, I think. He's a sweetie, though, you'd like him.'

'You said. How many times have you seen Ivan now?' Lainey's interest, though real, sounded false, which pleased her.

'I don't know. Three weeks, so . . . I'm not sure. If you mean when am I going to sleep with him . . . ?'

'Obviously that's what I mean –'

'Why do you think I want you to meet him?'

Lainey laughed. 'You're waiting for me to approve him.'

'I just want to see what you think.'

'What's with you? Since when would you listen to a word I'd have to say about a man?'

Chrissie did it again, the kittenish look, the shrinking thing. It was easier to see tonight because the music was so loud, and she had to make up with facial expression what Lainey couldn't hear.

'This is an unprecedented situation, if you think about it. You've never seen anyone I've been interested in. So it's not like I don't normally ask you. It just hasn't come up yet. Maybe this is what I do.'

Through the window, Lainey saw a cab pulling up.

'That's probably mine.'

'Don't go,' Chrissie pleaded, but with pantomime humility. She could cope. Smiling and shrugging, Lainey was already pushing open the door.

By the time the cab's leather seat had begun to feel a little warmer and kinder to the backs of her thighs, she was depressed. The empty feeling twisted inside her like a hunger pang: Chrissie was growing, and she was still the same. Already she was regretting leaving so soon; she always did. She had started believing that rejection was an inevitable part of any encounter, that it was just a question of who got to be unimpressed first; but the problem with pre-empting was that you missed all your chances. And, in fact, she'd very much wanted to meet Ivan. Ivan, the first visible man to make it over Chrissie's criteria, if not her threshold.

Chrissie made her affairs semi-mythological by having them out of the country. At sixth-form college she'd been too weird to attract anyone: a trombone-playing freak with a Nordic bone structure and a proclivity for deadpan that meant no one knew when she was joking. She reported the loss of her virginity in Boston, where she'd spent the summer after A levels, to a Jewish art student called Damon. It had been a flawless realization: as painful and empty as in all the right literature. She didn't come up with a sequel until she was abroad again, this time for her course, a year in France, where she had an extended affair with a tutor – but not hers – at the conservatoire. Aside from these, Chrissie seemed content to be picky and alone, but she felt she'd gained enough insight to entitle her to advise Lainey on *her* sex life. Lainey sometimes wondered if Chrissie had invented the romances, or at least had them only in order to contribute to discussions on the matter – otherwise, perpetually single, Chrissie would only have been able to listen, and there was nothing she hated more. She had a wonderfully giving nature, but was especially generous with her opinion, and if hers was not the best opinion around, she was lost, and she was narky.

So it shouldn't have surprised Lainey that Ivan hadn't been to the flat because Chrissie would have said: it would have been an event. None the less, it was strange that Chrissie could still do all that, even in today's world, all that *waiting*, because Lainey never could. It wasn't anything to do with what the men wanted – she didn't feel she had to go along at their pace – it was that their pace was her pace, and when she was with a man, even if she wasn't sure about his soul, sleeping with him was always a temptation; nothing else gave away as much about someone. You didn't get to know a man *before* having sex, but *by* having sex. It always felt right at the time, even if it felt dumb later. Sometimes, she just needed to know she was exactly what someone wanted, to feel the soft strength of heavy arms holding her close. Sometimes she fell in love with the nearness of a square shoulder in a leather jacket, or the crease of an unexpected smile: she was a bit like a man, she supposed, in her ability to become so susceptible so quickly, so objectively. Chrissie often told Lainey off for insinuating that she had a higher sex drive – Chrissie said her own behaviour was rational, not frigid; she just didn't see the sense in being intimate with a man you couldn't see yourself having a future with. This only proved that Chrissie had a lower sex drive, because as far as Lainey was concerned, being rational wasn't much of a distraction when there was a man breathing into your throat, saying all the right things. Perhaps the major difference between them, then, was that Chrissie made such a big deal about what was *going* to happen that she didn't give a shit

8

about what was happening now, whereas now was the only thing that Lainey cared about. That was also why Lainey always had so many problems and Chrissie never had any, even though that didn't seem to stop her getting pissed off a lot.

She got in, found her lens case in the bottom of the shower and took out her lenses. Her eyes felt like a stomach just released from stays. She made toast. Other ways Chrissie had changed since Ivan: she called more. Not less, more. The difference was barely measurable because Chrissie called all the time anyway, but change had definitely been an increase, not a decrease. Surely that wasn't right. The thing was, she didn't even just call to talk about Ivan, although he was always there, in her mind, in her mouth; Lainey could hear his presence, she could hear Chrissie chewing his name even as she talked about something else, like bubblegum in the classroom. She didn't push it, she waited to be asked – *so* like Chrissie – and Lainey didn't always ask, but Chrissie kept calling, apparently happy to talk about anything. The whole point of having a new boyfriend was the luxury of being able to call friends less. The phone was just the phone. You could be aloof, absent-minded, busy. But Chrissie wasn't: she was desperate to talk. She was just desperate-sounding all the time now. Desperation had an appeal all of its own; there was something attractive about needing to the exclusion of critical function. But because Chrissie was her best friend, Lainey wondered whether she should be concerned. What kind of person was Ivan, that he could seduce, and then subvert her friend? Lainey went to bed in her make-up, and dreamed about fairies.

one is plenty

The Numskulls were a dozen or so little balding
middle-aged men who lived in a big balding middle-aged man's
head, and engineered his neurological functions. They gave him
ideas through the suggestion box, moved his eyes, operated his
teeth and his tongue: they were his brain. When John was small,
he read their stories in the *Beezer* annuals his granny gave him
and, like everyone else who read them, wondered if he had
Numskulls in his head. Then he wondered if the Numskulls had
Numskulls in their heads. He'd teeter on the brink of infinity, and
then he'd turn the page and read 'Pop, Dick and Harry'.

Two decades on, John had just taken the bins out. His chest
was a bit tight from the three flights of stairs – he still had a
cough after last Saturday's skunk and Silk Cut binge – and he
gave the Ventolin a quick suck and listened to his breath
scratching the silence. Ivan had gone out to a party; without him
the flat was somehow more alive, sentient. The walls had ears.
The fact was, John could see, he'd been looking the wrong way:
inwards – and actually he was becoming the flat's Numskull. It
was the bigger living organism for which he did all the dirty
work. He brought in colourful bags of fragrant food, and took
out stinking black ones. John stood at the window and looked
out along the street at all the black bags, then he closed the flat's
eyes. He was moving slowly, deliberately wasting time. He was
supposed to write some new material. The felt-tip rings on the

television page were staring, compelling him to skive. His only option was to take a break and try to eat himself to death.

Boredom began with television and ended with food. He had already enjoyed a well-balanced microwave meal earlier in the evening. He certainly didn't *need* anything else. But television had a habit of being not enough; it made interesting things dull. In the real world fountains were interesting: people stood and stared at them for hours, hypnotized by the magic of physics. Love affairs and wars on television couldn't compete with fountains off television. Half an inch behind the glass of his specs, John was removed from the screen's bluey spatter: conscious of only seeing a refraction. Without contact lenses he was hardly involved, he might have left the glasses on the table to watch for him. He knew it would only be a matter of time before he had to find something for the rest of him to do. So. Just have one. You *can* eat just one. One is plenty. He was thinking so loudly that it felt like speaking. Perhaps he even raised his eyebrows. When he was being this amiable to himself, it was a sign that he was losing control.

He went and got a chocolate egg and ate it carefully, lying on the sofa, trying to notice the pleasure but essentially faking it. That was fine, John told himself, like a soft parent. You don't have to eat anything else. But he'd made the first move, his willpower's part was over for the night. Still bored: can't just sit here. He went back for another and brought in both of the last chocolate eggs, one of which he started on before he sat again, swallowing lumps, hardly chewed, to make a point to himself, but the self-abuse felt fairly stupid. He let a packet of crisps breathe and pinched as many as he could in one go, hurting the sides of his mouth as he pushed them in.

John wasn't fat at all, but he always seemed to be getting there. There were parts of him that he considered surplus to requirements. Actual fatness would be achievable with a week or two of serious eating. The fact that his weight had never changed much didn't matter. He wanted to be in the safe zone, so he could grow old thinly, like Bowie. He was young, still only in his twenties, but felt closer to middle age than nightclubs now, and when he went to nightclubs, he knew his fears were justified. His eating was no worse, really, than it had been five years ago, but back then, when there were never visible effects the next morning, he'd thought he was immune to weight gain and believed that the received equation of food and fat wasn't the whole story. Fat, he thought then, was another thing that happened to other people, like death and dyslexia. But, these days, whenever he tangled with calories there were tangible consequences. His clothes squeezed: he loosened buttons and softened the stiff holes at the further end of his belts. Proof: that was what brought the dimension of panic to his eating.

Mars bar. More crisps. Ham sandwich – he ate it with a sad flourish of surrender, an admission that he had exceeded snack boundaries. After throwing the plate into the sink he stared into the fridge, bent over, holding the door. There were processed cheese slices, a packet of butter, some bruised, clammy mushrooms, two yellow apples; all untempting enough to restore a little order. But that was enough. All he'd wanted was some real protein. He should have eaten the ham sandwich in the first place because that was what he'd wanted. If he just had some fruit now, that would be it; he wouldn't eat again. One yellow apple. He sat and waited, persuading himself, letting go. An hour later he was up again: he managed to find a Mars bar. It was beginning to hurt. He lay back on the sofa, changed the channel, watched the first half of a comedy, ran the side of his thumb tenderly over his stomach. When the ad break began, he thought: There's some bagels in the freezer, and went to find them. 'You're such a fucking *woman*,' he said aloud, as he told the microwave to defrost.

In the morning John dressed in navy blue fleece and went for a run in the park. The last few nights had been warm and bloated and the winos were back on the corner of his street; two grey beards with three legs, and an old woman who sat in a wheelchair and pissed through it all day long. What the fuck did alcoholics do with their legs? The pavement was dark and tacky with the old woman's old urine; today's new streams criss-crossed yesterday's. He'd hoped the winter might have killed her off, but she'd survived: soon the warmer air would shimmer with her fumes. He didn't hold his breath soon enough as he passed them and tasted the stale brown cloud of Tennent's piss and rotting wool; involuntarily he imagined the hot prickle of urine on cold, pickled buttocks. He moved quickly, skittish as a nettled cat, over the fresher patches and at the bottom of Queensway remembered to stop frowning. For the first few yards of park, as always, he forgot why he'd come here, felt stiff and reluctant and lethargic; and then he entered the recall zone. There was a point where the traffic behind him went soft and cottonwool quiet, and the air the trees breathed came gently from all sides, like the first distant strains of a brass band playing, and he was suddenly there, completely within the park and wondering how he'd ever be able to leave it again.

There was no question of jogging when the morning was so gentle and sweet – exercise was something he could only do on cold days, when the punishment factor was already there. Instead, he walked around the large pond, played chicken with the geese, then sat on a bench, watching young fathers with buggies go by. Without a buggy and child, John had to rely on the sporty look to distance himself from the seedier element of the park. Men needed an excuse; they couldn't just wander, like women. The suspicion was deserved. John watched as a late-middle-aged man sat down next to the twenty-something girl on the bench opposite. She didn't look up from her book. He was half-naked and suntanned, wearing only a Day-Glo orange vest and short shorts, several bumbags strapped in several directions all over him; he looked like a tourist, a foreigner. He was making conversation. She turned her head and nodded without smiling, then turned back to her book. The man spread his legs and crossed his hands behind his head. She closed her book and picked up her bag, walking away without looking back. He took his hands down and put them on his knees.

The little sketch should have provided a moment of pleasure –
smug xenophobia, the usual fun – but other men had a habit of
drawing him in. They made him an accessory, a co-conspirator;
shared out their shame by being so readable. It was their
transparency that made him empathize, against his will. And
when he most wanted to sneer at them, that was the moment his
brain chose to point out everything they had in common.
Pick-ups in parks were not John's style, but visible desperation
was universal. For John, monogamy was currently the main
attraction. He was grown up enough (proof of this being the
realization that every new emotion he experienced had already
been covered in a record played on Radio 2), he wasn't getting
any better now; it was time. But the business of finding a
relationship was too taxing: he wanted to be *in* one already, to be
at the point beyond excitement and lying, to be bored and
complacent. Safe. Getting there was the hard part. Clearly, the
teak Lothario on the opposite bench was wrong, presumptuous
to the point of harassment, but John didn't know where to place
himself on the same scale. The fear wasn't in the quick sting of
rejection, but coiled in the long, drawn-out squeeze of
embarrassment that followed, the knowledge that his efforts had
been unwanted and he hadn't noticed in time. It was, in the end,
a problem of etiquette as much as anything.

John was still not quite old enough to repulse teenage girls,
displayed no features that suggested he might be a carrier of
unacceptable genes, and had been told, often, by women's
magazines that a sense of humour was worth more in real terms
than wealth or handsomeness. But tallness still bullied comedy
into second place, and he was not tall. He had the nous to take
the edicts of women's magazines with a pinch of salt, but, in
common with all of their readers, didn't. He found fault with
himself in more ways than he had time for, but what stood in the
way of finding The One (who started that whole The One thing
anyway? what if it was true?) was the fact that so many women,
although no doubt the gentler, fairer and better sex, turned out to
be nightmares once he had any kind of sustained contact with

them. They felt too much, they wanted to understand everything. Girls who weren't neurotic knew how rare they were; their eyes held true, level and sane, their voices were clever and steady. Those girls were too good for him, and he sabotaged things while he still had some dignity. He was petty, needy, aloof. He lost his temper and his cool. He lost them. Every one.

In another life, Chrissie might have been one. It would have taken no special effort to conceive of Chrissie as being The One. When Ivan had turned up with her a few weeks ago John had occupied the foolhardy area of showing off obviously enough for his friend to notice, but being too nervous to be impressive. Already he had talked himself out of Chrissie, not because he wouldn't have shat on his best friend, but because *she* so obviously wouldn't. He could see that the road to Chrissie was paved with obsession, and usually he liked to think he was in with a chance before he got very obsessive. Otherwise it was just stalking.

tomorrow would be convenient

'You're a bossy little thing, aren't you?' Uncle Peter said, as he dandled Lainey on a half-hearted erection. 'A very bossy little girl. I bet you're going to be a teacher, like your mummy, when you grow up. Aren't you?'

Thoughts of Uncle Peter had long been displaced to her subconscious as a source of unspecific guilt and shiftiness, but his predictions, breeding as they did with the pronouncements of others, were fixed prominently into her psyche. Character assessments of six-year-olds had a habit of sticking around. Universities might as well consult primary school reports for references, as nothing really changed. The only things adults still found use for long after they'd grown up were their perversions and emotional deficiencies. There should have been something that was the opposite of therapy available. Cosmetic lobotomy. Americans'd got it wrong; by talking about problems you just relived them, and the more you heard something, the truer it became. If you could forget for ever everything that shaped you, the opinions misheard or misinterpreted or understood only too well, the shit that lived with you and made you do everything you did, only then might you start getting better. What Lainey had to contend with was the knowledge that, come what may, she'd be a teacher, because she'd been told she was bossy, because she'd been told she was good at learning, and because both her parents were teachers, although, as they liked to remind her, this was her time, her world, and she could be anything she wanted to be.

Lainey grabbed her denim apron and put her hair up for the supermarket: too much hair, too little time to tame it. She crossed the road recklessly, smiling apologies at the men who braked. Some days, when she clocked in, she found it hard to believe she was really here doing this. There must have been a mistake somewhere – she was supposed to have a proper job by now, not a real job. The most underrated enemy of opportunity was choice. It could ruin young women; it was the teenage pregnancy of the middle classes. Whatever mess of conceits cluttered their consciousness, the hardest to let go was the one that said they should keep their options open. Lainey had made the retention of choice her motivation and her excuse, and now felt her options all passing their sell-by dates at once. Her life, she realized, would have been better if she'd just relinquished some of that choice and thought about actually doing something while there was still time. Freedom and change had danced like sugar plums in front of her: Lainey had dithered, and slid into teaching.

It didn't last.

Teaching was bad from all angles, bad in a thousand different ways, which all grew out of the one thing that made her do it: it was expected. And whereas following in one parent's footsteps is excusable, if predictable, imitating both looks like mindlessness. Still living at home in Hounslow, she woke before dawn on the morning of her first day and spent the last hours of being a kid looking out at the grass behind her house, the small square patch of green that she'd seen her father mow for twenty years, that was exactly the same as the small square patches of green on either side next door, the same as the small square patches of green behind the houses over the road and along the road. This was what being an adult was about: abducting a little piece of the world and taming it, domesticating it like a pussycat. Lainey didn't want to keep a little piece of the world, she wanted to live in it. All of it. She wanted to lose herself out there while she found herself. She wanted it to abduct her.

She tried to summon the spirit of Julie Andrews in *The Sound of Music* when she got to the school gates, but the first sight of her class crushed it. This was too much like her first day at the local comprehensive, ten years ago. They were no more impressed now that she was a grown-up. She knew straight away that the cool girls didn't like her, but felt contemptuous of the blatant sympathy from the sad speccy girls who sat at the front, despising their eagerness to please. There were no boys here, which was just as well, because she would probably have been preoccupied with whether her breasts were too small, and too scared to teach them anything in case she sounded stuck up or swotty. The days were Scandinavian; she glanced at the clock so many times that it was scored on to her retinas and projected its negative on the inside of her eyelids. She held blinks longer and longer, the way one does when driving great stretches of motorway. On the fourth day, every time she opened her mouth she heard her mother talking – the phrases, the intonation, the telephone voice. This was alarming: meaning one thing and being someone else. It was getting harder to dress in the mornings; she fancied she heard the trendy little bitches laughing at her sensible skirts. She'd begun to leave her bedroom with an empty wardrobe and an invisible bed.

On the twelfth day Lainey came in, dropped her shabby, shapeless bag, and stood for a moment, looking at twenty glassy-eyed girls who only wanted her to not be there, and she knew she had to go. It wasn't that she was finding real life too much to take, but that the rest of the world actually wasn't this bad. There were places where you could work with humans, people who didn't click their tongues when you started to speak, and laugh behind your back while you were still in the room. (And that was just the other teachers – ba-dum-bum.) That day she decided there was still time to explore another option. There was always time to make a new choice.

In fact, she stuck it out for four weeks before an excuse came.

She had answered a newspaper ad for a freelance writer, which requested applications in the form of a hundred words about whisky, but no experience. Lainey faxed an overwritten parody of alcoholic degradation and forgot about it. Weeks later the editor phoned: he'd liked the piece and offered her regular work, and she called in sick for a week and then gave up teacher training. The money wasn't enough to live on but it was enough of a something else to take her out of teaching. She told her parents she couldn't devote enough time to both, because when she wasn't writing her four articles a month she was applying to other publications. And although the magazine, called *Panic*, was papery and blowsy and chiefly a forum for promoting nightclubs she'd never been to, it was something to wave at her parents when she asked them for money. She spent a lot of time in her bedroom, writing affected, unglamorous articles about sex that the editor assured her the young nightclub-going population was burning to read.

Around that time, Chrissie bought a flat in Battersea, and strongly recommended it as a good thing to do. She didn't offer to put Lainey up, but she talked a lot about freedom and room to breathe. Lainey, in the pink bedroom of her parents' house, scribbling Morrissey-angst and sex tips on to curly-edged paper, made a decision: she needed space. So she found some – but not much – a tiny flat at the rough end of Ladbroke Grove, owned by a mad old lady who knew her father and didn't seem to care too much about the rent being paid on time as long as Lainey wasn't a freemason, and kept the noise down. The shower was in the kitchen, but Lainey could afford it. She took a part-time job at the organic supermarket over the road because she'd read that movie stars shopped there and spent her free time writing.

A few months on, the editor called to tell her the publishers had pulled the plug on *Panic*, and it was all over. At the check-out, where she'd taken more hours, Lainey tried to drop hints to the healthily undernourished customers, as she packed up their mung beans and rice milk, that she was more than this, more than the check-out. What had felt like a quirky sideline was now looking like what she did. She hardly ever wrote. Sometimes, if she'd submitted some unsolicited pieces, a big magazine would call her to their offices to say they liked the work she'd sent, and ask her to provide ten ideas and write something on spec. And then just never call again. Her feet had been – briefly – in too many doors to fall back on the not-what-you-know-but-who-you-know defence, but she was still sceptical about people who'd made it: making enemies was always more satisfying than making sense. Steady rejection stoked her paranoia but fuelled despair, not determination.

She liked working at the supermarket, that was the worst thing – the fear that it wasn't terrible enough to push her into something else. Inertia brought a new kind of confidence: it's easy to be cool when you know all the moves. She liked being a model of efficiency at the check-out and forcing the environmentally responsible customers to take brand-new carrier bags by packing their groceries while they looked for their credit cards. She liked teasing the flash young suits who paid double figures for haddock that they believed swam in a more organic sea. On her breaks the in-house florist talked about his girlfriend and she jabbed the Kombucha mushroom with a cocktail stick, tilting her ear close to hear if it winced or screamed. Life was fine. No stress, no thinking, no decisions, no teenage girls. And if, when she spoke to the friends who were now teaching, and touching lives – and having lives – her soul choked on the dust of regret; and if, as she lay next to her bed looking up at the tiny ceiling, she remembered the salad-freshness of her parents' lawn on summer mornings and felt so, so thirsty; and if she woke sometimes and remembered with a jolt that she'd probably thrown away her only chance of a decent life; if these things got to her, the freshly squeezed mango and bramble juice that hadn't been sold by closing time still tasted as sweet as a gambling win, and the denim pinny still looked good.

Wednesday morning shift. Personal shopping. The best part of Lainey's week. It felt something like a trolley dash, something like snooping, mostly like shopping (ah yes! she remembered shopping). She picked the nicest fruit for the delivery customers, packed it as carefully as china, enclosed spunky little notes with the invoices. And she finished early, which left the day for her. She took a hard rye loaf, some soya milk, apple juice and a carton of white-bean soup from the not-sold-by box left for staff. Health had been forced on her since she'd started working there. After a while she found that if she only thought of taste as a privilege, not a right, she hardly had to pay for food at all. When she got the food home she made toast and anti-oxidant tea and read the paper. The phone rang. The man on the other end had a high, grating voice and sounded gay.

'Could I speak to Elaine Mackerras? Good morning, it's CK Cromwell from *Brazen* magazine. We liked the letter you sent us and we'd like you to work for us. Would you still be interested in coming in?'

'*Jesus*, yes,' Lainey said. 'Excuse me, overexcited. I mean, yes, I'd be very interested in coming in. When can I?'

'Would tomorrow be convenient?'

'Tomorrow would be convenient, yes.'

'Fine. It's the address in the magazine. Could you manage twelve o'clock? Good. I'll see you tomorrow at twelve, then.'

Lainey always allowed hanging up to be done before she knew all the facts. First, she had no idea who *Brazen* magazine were, or what she'd said in the letter, or what the job was. Please, not one of the porn ones. She applied to so many and received so few replies that she no longer took them seriously. There was a big pile of torn-out newspaper squares that she had to go through before discovering that *Brazen* was the name of the official *When Voyager?* fan magazine, named after the show's main character, Harry Brazen. Then she wasn't sure if CK Cromwell had said he wanted to interview her, because it had sounded like he had pretty much said the job was hers – unless that had just been a suggestion, dependent on her performance in an interview. Lainey didn't want to assume, so she took out her interview suit anyway, because no one gives anyone a job without interviewing them.

She only had the one interview suit, which meant she couldn't afford to think of it as her unlucky suit, even though she'd never had any success in it. The best thing about being superstitious was the enormous scope for creativity. When making up her own hoodoo Lainey started at the outside and moved inward, so that blaming herself remained an unlikely last resort – she held things like shoes and Tuesdays accountable when things went wrong. The men she knew tended to work the opposite way, inside-out, believing, for instance, that the timing of their urination directly led to their football team conceding a goal, then moving outward via lucky pants but hardly ever reaching as far as accessories. She drank some orange juice and a little organic vodka and set off for her new job.

new products

One of the great modern fears is discontinuation. It may not match up to death in terms of all-out flashy scariness, but it has a comparable impact on buying habits. There's a Damien Hirst work called *I want to spend the rest of my life everywhere, with everyone, one to one, always for ever, now*. As well as expressing the collective dread of mortality and futile bids for its defiance, the sculpture incorporates the discontinuation anxiety, a fear that can only exist when people already have everything they need. Death remains the only absolute worst consequence, but a life without that Ramones record you had as a kid, or the first novel you ever finished, the one you lent to someone who never gave it back, or your favourite Marks & Spencer teacakes, isn't much of a life.

When he discovered that VO5 had stopped making Flexible Hold Liquigel, John felt sick and depressed – right there in the middle of Superdrug he decided that maybe he would never have another truly good hair day again and his life would always be shit. As he got on top of it he considered the possibility of using this experience in his act, but then he couldn't really see anything funny about it, so he gave up and bought two new brands, feeling so self-consciously vain at the check-out that he mugged a bit for the pretty black girl who couldn't have cared less, trying to convey without speaking the sentiment: God, don't girlfriends use a lot of crap on their hair? At the last moment he threw a couple of Crunchies into his basket as well. When he got home, John squeezed a little of one of the new products into his palm and swept it through his hair. The effect wasn't reassuring, but he'd have to try it on wet hair before he really knew: this midday fumble wasn't a reliable test. As he sat with a Crunchie, sucking to soften it, he ran his other hand kindly along his parting, feeling the smooth hair slide under his fingers.

John's barnet: pleasure and pain, a privilege and a responsibility. Realistically, John probably spent no more time worrying about his hair than most men. Baldness was not in his genes – the pattern of hairiness on the rest of his body and in the rest of his family sent good messages about the future of his crown. But if his thoughts were mostly untroubled by his head, the hair demanded a greater share of actual physical time, although this was now so much a routine as to be automatic. He had honed to an art the combinations of product and blow to make his do commercial-perfect. It was short, very thick – not too thick – lying close to his head with the insinuation of a quiff at the front, barber-shop smooth all round, clipped with precision every three to five weeks, and naturally blue-black, like Clark Kent's. In the past, several hairdressers had admired it without embarrassment, telling him they could do anything with hair like this. By which they meant they could do anything *to* it, but secretly, they were thinking: with it. Now he stayed faithful to Italian Barry in Kentish Town, because they communicated minimally and the cut was just right. The difference between genetic advantage and really good hair was, as the late Roy Castle would have said, dedication; but upkeep was costly and knowing he had to make the most of it was onerous. So when they pulled his favourite product without the notice that would have enabled him to make Blitz-like stockpiles, his concern was understandable. John was not consistently confident, but he always had his hair. When things affected that, they screwed with his psyche.

John tried the second of the new products, combing it through, looking with mild irritation at a cowlick that sprang impudently from his temple. That was when he saw his first grey hair. He pulled it out and shivered. From the pain.

a full quota

When Lainey turned up at the address in the magazine she was starchily overdressed, a well-baked potato in the middle of a limp leafy salad. Her clothing suited the date – April – but the weather, without warning, had taken on the airs and graces of June. The boy who answered the door and brought her in was wearing shorts, and there was an older man, who barely looked at her, dressed in a T-shirt and old faded jeans. This office was in fact someone's home, a flat: partly open plan and quite tiny, looking something like a kitchen that was temporarily providing storage space for the rest of the furniture from a large house. One corner was marked off as office area; two computers elbowed each other on the same busy desk as the fax machine and several piles of letters and papers. Behind them, a few shelves of back issues, more papers, lever-arch and box files, reference books and floppy disks. Inches away, the living room area: a royal blue sofa that showed some signs of fatigue but no sign of softening, a long coffee table, an armchair and an impressive bookcase. Lainey sat neatly on the sofa with her legs crossed at the ankles and waited to be spoken to.

'You're early,' said CK Cromwell.

The thing about CK Cromwell, the main thing, was that she was fat. If there could be another thing, though, it was that she was a woman. Having received no hint of either of these facts on the phone, Lainey was thrown. Generally she liked women more than men, when it came to beginnings, unlike Chrissie who got on better with men – Chrissie thought of herself as both spontaneous and profound, and believed that most women were neither. It was an incompatibility thing, not a competition thing, Chrissie said. She didn't believe that women started out as rivals – that was a male fantasy, because men liked the idea of women fighting over them (in fact, just the idea of women fighting usually did it for them, which was why they put it in films whenever they could). It was certainly the case that Chrissie didn't have many female friends – but then she didn't have many male friends either, if any – so, like everything else she said, it was just theory. Here and now, for whatever reason, whether it was competition or incompatible levels of spontaneity, or just the fact that Lainey had rung the doorbell at nine minutes to twelve, the two women did not hit it off.

The fatness mattered. It made one of them shocked and the other shocking. Lainey didn't really want to look. It was like being confronted by a prominent wart or birthmark on a stranger's face – having to respect the period of not looking at them at all before you could make your face blank and ungaping enough to seem normal. Her first instinct had been to maintain eye contact – there was no such thing as fat eyes. But as her new employer was on the phone and the two men were making no attempts to include her, Lainey was able to take in the fascinating reality of that flesh. In her college days, fat had been a feminist issue. The boy students she'd known were rude about fat people; the fat were also oppressed by television and movies and magazines, dismissed by society, humiliated by doctors. Lainey and her girlfriends, like all young women, were idly insecure, afflicted by the strains of eating disorders that demanded the least physical sacrifice and allowed the greatest public exposure. They knew about food and all its implications, they worried aloud and complained a lot. They protested like victims when fat people were mocked, their response to body fascism was Pavlovian and violent. They believed that being fat was not the crime but the sentence of a twentieth-century tyranny, and they turned on

27

anyone who disagreed. Not one of them ever had trouble zipping up a pair of size-twelve jeans.

Principles were fine things, but she couldn't do anything about her thoughts. To CK Cromwell, who was maybe twenty stone overweight, her gut response was: Good God, how *can* you? Haven't you heard of self-control, woman? Some people were so fat that feminism coughed and looked away. Andrea Dworkin had never received the following among modern women that she might have attracted if she'd looked even halfway capable of refusing that third helping of grits. Some states of obesity could not have been achieved by mere laziness, or disregard for the pressures of society, or even gluttony; there was fat that looked like a career, where nothing short of hard work and determination could have brought about the result. People who upheld those dimensions gave every impression of having surrendered all peripheral considerations in favour of amassing and retaining weight. Aggression and defeat existed side by side in mountainous sloping shoulders, all-consuming buttocks and friction-toasted thighs, in the sheer magnitude of their inexorably tolerant backs. They lumbered, lolloped, struggled, and, above all, they scowled, asthmatic tracheas compressed into permanent martyrdom, every organ tortured by the pressure of its insulation.

CK hung up and sat down, her body reshaping gradually on the sofa like setting blancmange, and she sighed, scratching a tier of her neck with a long painted fingernail. Her cleavage capillaried to the neckline, squashy and solid as the gap between white leather sofa cushions where people in the 1970s lost small change. She looked at her watch and Lainey couldn't help doing the same. It was twenty past twelve now. Lainey had been mostly ignored for nearly half an hour. CK pulled the telephone closer to her and dialled another number. As she waited to speak, she covered the receiver with a fat hand and turned to the office.

'Is anyone ready for lunch?' she asked them. Muted affirmative response. 'Elaine, you can go with Dominic to the sandwich shop.' She turned back to the phone and didn't look up again.

Lainey waited for one of the men to identify himself, hoping that Dominic was the boy who'd answered the door and not the older man, who sat with his legs wrapped around each other. The boy got up and brushed himself down. Standing, it became plainly visible that he only occupied his clothes to a lesser extent, but they suited him, the unbleached cotton barely a tone away from his own skin colour and that of his floppy translucent hair. He looked like his body had never heard of melanin, and Lainey wondered how it was going to react to the rays outside: would he turn a dangerous red or vaporize? They set off together.

Dominic was maybe Lainey's age, certainly no more than twenty-five, and, up close, taller than she'd initially thought. He seemed unaffected by the heat, cool within the breathing space his long loose shorts gave him, while Lainey, still in full interview suit, thought she was going to die. She'd taken off the jacket, but the sun was insistent and she could feel sweat collecting under her eyes and prickling her upper lip.

'Wow. I wasn't expecting it to be so hot,' Lainey said.

'Yes, it's nice,' Dominic said, then softly added, 'You must be very warm. Your bag looks heavy. Do you want me to carry something for you?' He seemed almost surprised by his own sensitivity; with each addition he sounded puzzled, and he turned his head away from her. He was ordinary-looking but extraordinarily sweet, the kind of boy she'd say was 'too nice' when she was telling him no. The niceness was never the reason, always the face, but at such times it seemed like a good thing to mention.

'Oh. No, it's not so heavy. Just big, for paper. I thought I might have to take notes. Was that everyone?'

'Was that . . . ? You mean was that the entire editorial staff of *Brazen*? I'm afraid it was, really. But there are other people who work for the magazine. We've got an adman, Scott, he's in most of the time, and a couple of freelancers help us with subbing and layout closer to publication. It can be busier than you just saw.' He spoke as if there was a time limit, efficient rather than flustered. 'It's a bit unsettling, isn't it, expecting to turn up to work somewhere and finding yourself in a domestic kitchen.'

'How long have you worked in the kitchen?'

'Two, two and a half years. I joined not long after graduating; this is all I've done, in fact.'

'And what's the relevance of this sandwich –'

'This sandwich reconnoitre?' He smiled. 'This is your job, I'm afraid. And not just part of it – most of it. You're sort of taking over from me.'

'If I get it.'

'You've got it. Well, as far as I know. Clare isn't interviewing, anyway; she liked your letter, she liked the fact that you live close. She was thinking in terms of travel expenses.' Lainey, relieved to hear this, was still put out to learn that her best qualification was geography. Also, it seemed too easy, and she was suspicious, *Brazen*'s accessibility undermining its status as a real magazine. She had bought a copy when she wrote her application, from WH Smith's, which was respectable. All the same, that strange little flat, the scarceness of people, the largeness of people, all a bit dodgy. Dominic was reassuringly not dodgy.

'Really?'

'As far as I know. Then again, what do I know?'

'You said I was taking over from you. Meaning, you're leaving?'

He laughed to himself. 'Good God, no. Leave *Brazen*, with all its promise and camaraderie? No, I've been promoted. Which is just another way of saying that Clare accepted there was too much for me to do, and agreed to get someone else to do the photocopying and the sandwiches.'

They crossed over to the sunny side of the street. 'Is there much further to go?'

'No. It's just round the corner.'

Dominic introduced her to the owner of the sandwich shop (Tony), explained that *Brazen* had an account there, so at least there was such a thing as a free lunch, and made her choose a sandwich to prove it.

It was never easy to gauge a stranger's opinion of another stranger, and on the way back, Lainey forced herself not to talk about CK. Although she wanted to know more, it was sensible to wait. Instead, she asked Dominic where he lived, where he'd come from, where he'd gone to college, and in return he answered. When they got back, she was surprised to see that CK wasn't there. Devoid of its focal point, the room was filled with a horrible overcompensation of reticence. The older man sat alone, drinking tea from a Harry Brazen mug. He put it down and picked up each of the wrapped sandwiches in turn to establish which one was his. By weight, maybe, or a sort of dowsing?

'I think it's bloody rude of Clare to just leave you like this. Thanks, Dom,' he said, unfolding brie and grapes. 'But then that's her for you. I was waiting for her to introduce you before, but I suppose even such minimal politeness is beyond her. I didn't even really know who you were until she sent you out with Dom. I'm Theo. You're Elaine.' He sounded actually angry, as if the editor's rudeness inconvenienced him. He suffered from the kind of shyness that overlapped with crossness, the kind that came with being stiffly brought up and having confidence expected of you that you could only fake by snapping.

'Hello. People call me Lainey.'

'Sure,' Theo said. 'Lainey.'

'Isn't, um, CK going to have lunch with us?' Lainey said.

'Clare doesn't eat,' Dominic said. He underplayed the private joke disgracefully, not raising his eyes from his sturdy ham roll. Theo sniffed – that was how he laughed – to show his support for the oblique slur, but he didn't stop frowning.

'Clare takes lunch in her office,' Theo said. 'She often finds she has a lot of work to get through during lunch.'

'And you're . . . deputy editor, is it?' she asked Theo.

'Deputy editor, assistant editor,' Theo said, pointing to himself, then Dominic. 'We're all editors here.'

'Except me,' Lainey said.

'No, you're actually a full editor,' Dominic said.

'Sandwich editor?'

Dominic laughed. 'Picture editor. That's the other thing you do – you get our pictures. Although you'll forgive us for placing greater importance on lunch occasionally. You're in charge of acquiring, filing, maintaining photographs for the magazine. So, picture editor.'

'Still, the title sounds a little scary. Couldn't I just be something else first and work my way up?'

'There are no other positions,' Theo said. 'As you probably, probably worked out by now. What do you think you should be?'

'Oh, I don't know. Picture girl?' Lainey said.

'Picture girl,' Theo repeated, more or less laughing. 'We can't, can't call you picture *girl*!'

'I don't think it's sexist any more,' Lainey said. 'I think there was a change in the law.'

'All the same, Clare wouldn't like it,' Theo said, reminding himself to be annoyed and scornful, and for a while none of them spoke. The sound of their collective chewing swelled to exacerbate the break in conversation. Theo came back with a few questions that were all covered by Lainey's CV, and she was relieved when he gave up and left her alone, switching to shop talk and asking Dominic technical questions about the current issue. With the strain of Theo's politeness removed, she didn't speak again until they'd finished eating.

'Do you have a biggish readership, then?' Lainey said, watching them both to see what she should do with the paper sandwich wrapper.

'We're called *Brazen* but it's not just about *When Voyager*?' Theo said, and hesitated to make way for a silent belch, which happened behind his fist, but was still infectiously embarrassing. 'We cover most – er – cult – er – programmes, particularly other shows with a time-travel element: *Crime Traveller*, *Dr Who*, et cetera. We tend to favour British productions because you'll find the, the American programmes are well covered in other magazines. And most British science fiction followers have a rather, rather patriotic attachment to home-produced shows, so it's reasonably demand-led. But we've done features on, for instance, the *Time Tunnel* and *The X Files*, so we get a fairly, fairly broad readership. I mean broad within the sci-fi community, of course. Which is broader than you might think.'

'*Star Trek*?' Lainey said.

Both men laughed and cleared their throats.

'No, we try not to mention the Trekkers. We rather sneer at them,' Dominic said, sweetly self-mocking. 'We think they're somewhat anal and immature, and our readers tend to agree.' The revelation of wit recategorized the appeal of his asymmetrical smile.

'Yes, we don't believe in all that harmonic mingling with other civilizations business. It's just too easy,' Theo said.

'So, you're all big fans of the programme and that's why you work here, or you got the job and had to like it?'

'The programme's our life,' Theo deadpanned, but then, apparently worried that his straight face might have been too convincing, he cleared his throat and sniffed to explain that he'd made a joke. 'No, not really. I started the magazine with Clare when we were both working at the *Radio Times* and it just took off. Well, you know. Took off a bit.' He remembered something – she saw it in his eyes, before he turned away and found a paperclip to play with. 'But you are a fan? You said you were in your letter.' Suddenly alarmed and imagining tests and accusations and sackings, Lainey spluttered and came clean.

'I wouldn't call myself a fan. I'm not *not* a fan, I'm just not a *fan* fan. I'll start again. I mean, I like the show but I don't have cable so I can't watch it now, and there was a whole series on normal television I missed, but I did like it when I saw it, and I know who everyone is and what's going on and I'm prepared to get videos and read up on it. I exaggerated a bit. Do you want me to go?'

'It's okay,' Theo said. 'The last thing we wanted was a Sci-Fi Pub Quiz obsessive with no external life.'

'We already have a full quota,' Dominic said quietly, looking out the window.

Theo took about three seconds to interpret this, and sniffed.

'Hmm, yes. No, you sounded well-organized and bright in your letter and that's, that's what we need, more than anything.' She must have looked unconvinced because he said, 'Relax, you'll enjoy it,' but every muscle in his face tensed around the assurance.

CK/Clare – Lainey had been around long enough to notice that it was CK on the phone, CK on paper and Clare in the flesh, as if she were trying to put one over on strangers – came back down to the office about an hour after they'd eaten and made hard work out of telling Theo she'd had to call an associate in New York. She needed an excuse for her disappearance, and Lainey guessed it was for her benefit. Clare explained the job to Lainey, who was more interested in examining the contours of her editor's behind-the-neck fat; her tiny, lipless mouth, like a slow puncture in her round face. She wore silvery eyeshadow in crescents above small dark eyes that were being devoured by surrounding flesh – she *did* have fat eyes.

'. . . and we won't be able to pay you, of course.'

Lainey woke up.

'Not anything at all?' she said.

'Well, your expenses, of course: travel, although I think you live quite close, don't you? We buy you lunch. You can still claim benefit. Is that going to prove unsuitable?'

'No, I can do that. I can . . .' she trailed away, counting supermarket hours against rent cheques. 'Yes, that's fine.'

'You can make money by writing articles for us. That's how Dominic gets by.'

They both turned to Dominic, who had only heard his name, and looked startled and uncomfortable.

'He started out doing what you're doing; he's one of the main contributors now,' Clare said. 'Anyway, I don't suppose it's worth you making a start today. You don't actually need to put in full days; you'll find you've finished most things by the early afternoon. So officially, you are available for job seeking. I think that's how it's explained to the benefit office. Well, thank you for

34

coming in. We'll see you at ten? Tomorrow?' The breezy invitation doubled as a dismissal.

'You really should meet John,' Chrissie said, in the middle of Lainey's rant about how she wasn't being paid. When Chrissie came out with non-sequiturs it meant that she was bored.

'He's Ivan's flatmate?'

'Yes. We think you're very alike, actually. Ivan said it first, but he's actually right. You're both very dry, and self-deprecating. You'd probably really get on.'

'How would Ivan know?'

'I've told him about you, of course. I talk about you all the time.'

'I see,' Lainey said. She didn't feel flattered, she felt nervous, even a little hurt. But it was something she also did when she met new men. She liked to make references to friends, so that she'd seem popular and nice, and she liked to build Chrissie up impossibly – the idea being that when the new man finally got round to meeting her he'd be less overwhelmed, less dazzled. Maybe even disappointed. 'So what do you say about me? That you have a sad single friend who needs to be fixed up?'

'God, no,' Chrissie said. 'I'm not trying to fix you up. Not with John.' She stopped, but held on to the silence. 'John fancies me, actually.'

'Does Ivan know this?'

'We haven't talked about it, but I don't see how he could have not noticed. It's no big deal, is it? John's single, I'm tolerable. I'd be pretty offended if he didn't fancy me at all.'

'*Is* he single?'

'Yes.'

'Well, if he fancies you he's not going to be interested in me, is he?'

'Why?' Chrissie sounded genuinely curious.

'Well, how many people can he fancy at once?'

'Oh, I see.' Now she sounded disappointed, as if she had been expecting a compliment. 'Well, for a start, he can change his mind when he sees you. And for another thing, he can like as many people as he wants to. Blokes do, you know. They like all girls who don't do something to put them off. I know that sounds obvious, but with women it's the opposite; they need to be persuaded to find a man interesting. But a perfectly ordinary member of the opposite sex is presumed attractive to a man and presumed unattractive to a woman until proved otherwise. That's how it works. That's the difference between the sexes.'

Lainey wondered how many people had heard this theory before. 'There are plenty of ways I could put him off,' she said quietly.

'Don't start. Anyway, you have to meet Ivan and tell me if I should be sleeping with him, as you pissed off early from the party the other day.'

'I can't wait to meet him. But don't make a big deal about this John thing. I'm not really looking, right now.'

'That's when you're at your weakest. You stop looking out for bullshit too, and you stop referring to your checklist, and before you know it, you've fallen in love with someone who's all wrong for you.'

'Is that what you did?'

For the shortest time, Chrissie looked miffed. Blink/miss. 'Probably,' she said, smiling.

chrissie likes to give
people nice surprises

Ivan had slept with Chrissie for the first time two days ago; John knew this because he'd asked and Ivan had smiled. Today he was re-alphabetizing his record collection.

'When did you buy Kylie?' John asked him.

'It was Jane's. I really should give it back to her. She brought it round once to prove that it wasn't crap. It is crap, though.'

Ivan's last girlfriend Jane still came out with them from time to time. Ivan ended relationships amicably, but never explained how it was done. Or why. The likeliest answer was unfaithfulness: sometimes when Ivan was seeing a girl and he spent nights away from the flat, the girl would call and ask to speak to him – which meant he was somewhere else. His work entailed a lot of schmoozing with colleagues, but all night? Still, if the splits were caused by infidelity his exes took it well, because many of them kept in touch. John usually got on with Ivan's girlfriends, who tended to be very good-looking, at worst dull and pretty, at best quite dull and very pretty. When he first met Chrissie, still acclimatized to Ivan's taste for more user-friendly beauty, John had thought her unremarkable, even plain. Everything about her face had seemed too big all at once – the long, widely spaced grey eyes, the intimidating proudness of her curious upper lip with its silvery feline scar, a repaired cleft palate; the lunar paleness of her blonde hair. Then, through the soft focus of alcohol, everything became clear, and the next time they met, stone cold sober, she had even improved. Now, the idea that he could have used a word like plain anywhere near her seemed comical. She was not so much an acquired taste as a maths problem that had to be solved: an exquisite integration of slow poise and clear blue logic. Now that he knew her, now that he had solved her, he couldn't imagine any face comparing. In his dreams, he had already tasted her scar.

She'd been to their flat several times and although John couldn't unremember falling for her, he had learned to react to her face as merely Chrissie now, to make familiarity work for him in lessening the blow. He knew he might never be desensitized to her brain, though: she was sharp, and nastily funny, and she had theories about everything. Sometimes he deliberately fished for them because the tilt of her head when she delivered something she believed to be original was particularly fetching. If this was unrequited love, though, he couldn't see what the fuss was about. He loved Chrissie – who wouldn't? – but not in a way that caused him pain. Just pleasure. He loved her when he saw her, and he loved seeing her. She was like Beatles music. Occasionally, listening to 'Eleanor Rigby' hurt just a little in your side, because you knew you could never create anything as lovely, even if you lived for ever, but mostly it was enough just to hear it. When Ivan talked about her, John's pulse slowed down.

'Chrissie wants me to meet her best friend. Can I bring her along to your gig on Wednesday?'

'Chrissie wants to come?' He tried to make it sound neutral, but he was worried about doing stand-up in front of her. Mostly he wanted her to see him, because usually when she was there he tried too hard and couldn't relax, and wasn't funny, and if she saw his set she'd know him better, and see him at his best. Unless he died. 'Who's her friend?'

'I still haven't met her. Chrissie says she's a bit weird but pretty cool. She's her best mate; she's going to say nice things about her.'

'She's her best mate but she said she was weird? That's the nicest thing she can think of?'

'That's not the *nicest* thing she can think of. She's only saying she's weird to talk her down before we meet. Chrissie likes to give people nice surprises. That's her thing. She's always non-committal or dismissive so things end up being better than you expect them to be. You're getting some grey hair there.'

'Jesus, how much is there?' John said, forgetting to come back with jokes about Ivan's receding hairline. He went into the hall to look in the mirror.

'Anyway, I'm not asking you to fancy Lainey. It's not a double-date. I just don't want to be judged, and if you're there you're a diversion.'

'What does she do if something's really bad?'

'What?'

'Chrissie. If she likes to give you nice surprises, how does she prepare you for bad stuff?'

'I'm not sure. Tells me it's weird?'

feel free

The girl bus conductor wore a little woolly hat and the nylon flak jacket that came with the job. A tiny, skinny thing, she'd developed a sure-footed swagger for collecting fares so she could keep her balance without holding on, even as the bus reared and coughed over the roadworks on Oxford Street. When she called out the landmarks her boredom wasn't entirely convincing. And then she swung all the way out of the bus when they went around Marble Arch, a hundred per cent outside, fifty per cent flying. Watching her, Lainey could almost feel the pleasure too and held her breath to prolong it. The conductor closed her eyes and leaned into the breeze and gambled her grip on the pole with a reckless two fingers, in one moment both athlete and schoolgirl show-off. Right there and then, she liked her life. The point, Lainey could see, was that the minimum requirement of job satisfaction was whether it allowed you, even if for the briefest, slimmest moment, to feel free.

She wasn't enjoying *Brazen*. In theory it was a good job, even taking into account the lack of pay and the work: calling agencies and cinema distributors for photographs they could use, fetching sandwiches. The great Holy Grail of media work that they all pursued blindly, without question, like it was the only thing that mattered – a whole generation of overqualified graduates fetching cappuccinos and sending faxes for pocket money, and feeling proud that they'd been asked. So it wasn't what she had to do that disappointed – she could have sharpened pencils all day and still been happy. Dealing with Clare's rudeness was harder. Clare wasn't directly unpleasant, but she never took time off from maintaining herself; with Lainey she always had to play the boss, rigid and old-fashioned. In the context of the unconventional office, with its benign domesticity, the effect was heightened and scary, and Clare *was* scary. She had taken the parts of a woman's body that men had traditionally used for their own entertainment: breasts, hair, walk – and she had made them fierce. She was petty and patronizing, and disguised the combination as thoroughness.

Clare would have won Lainey's sulky respect if she'd just been a cold bitch, but her softer side undermined it. When she remembered to, she used any one of a repertoire of feminine clichés, but in such a formidable package they were grotesque, as with old-fashioned woman-hating drag queens. She had aspirations to cute: at thirtyish, fortyish – it was hard to tell, because all very fat women looked forty-nine – she wore little-girl hairstyles with bows and pretty barrettes and little-girl rings on her little fat fingers, but missing the grubby sex appeal that other grown women who wore those things used to claim irony as a defence. Worst of all was the marked shift in her behaviour when she was dealing with someone she liked. Like Elizabeth the First, Clare had favourites.

Scott Flynn, head of advertising, topped the list, being the only one who came into the office regularly. Lainey was used to hearing Clare's IQ plummet as she flirted with journalists over the phone, but she hadn't actually seen a recipient before. Scott Flynn arrived at the beginning of Lainey's second week, and was sitting in her place on the sofa, next to Clare, when she came in. He didn't look at her, and neither did Clare, which was to be expected – but they were blocking Lainey's use of the phone and her files, and she was forced to hover uselessly and talk to the other staff members. Theo was always eager to talk, although she couldn't think why, when it seemed to cause him real pain. His sense of humour had a time-lapse mechanism, and until it

41

clicked, the confusion was edgy. Also, he obviously liked her, and he could see that it *was* obvious and tried to rein it back, only this, too, was obvious, and the fact that he was trying so much made everything worse. So the person who liked her most in the office was also the hardest to speak to, because he invested everything with palpable, feverish self-consciousness. Right now, he talked about foreign films to her – never about *When Voyager?* because that was work. He seemed, fortunately, unaware that Lainey wasn't listening to more than one word in three, because the new boy on the couch was so magnetically charming.

Lainey herself was not charmed. The charming was happening to Clare, but it was none the less enthralling, a professional job, prompting the fat controller to produce a greatest hits version of her annoying affectations. She tittered, was flummoxed, fraudulently claimed to be mistaken, or to misunderstand technical points. Theo and Dominic were not now, if they ever had been, worthy of such hard work. The new boy was. He might have enhanced the older woman's self-confidence just by being there, but he made an effort as well. From time to time Clare broke out of their conversation to randomly belittle Theo, or bully Dominic. Dominic bore Clare's attention with quiet grace, but Theo always took it badly, breathing heavily and trying to catch Lainey's eye. She had learned not to let him.

'Are you all right, Elaine?' Clare said, as if Lainey's hovering was wanton time-wasting.

'I just need to get to the phone,' she said.

'Oh, so *this* is Elaine,' said Scott, and stood up to shake her hand. He was a pretty delicious proposition, and knew it. Younger-looking, even, than her, he none the less had all the moves down already, legs apart, Manchester-cocky. There was a hint of dreading in his long, messy fringe. 'How do you like us so far?' His voice was as warm as Ovaltine but his smile had an agenda. He had a firm handshake; she tried not to be overwhelmed. 'Good God, you've got a good grip there. Remind me not to arm-wrestle with you,' he said.

'You'll have to keep on my good side,' she said, embarrassed that he had brought attention to her body publicly. She felt clumsy.

'*Now* I'm afraid,' he said, and threw Clare a look that made her laugh. There was something Oedipal about their conspiracy.

At lunchtime, Clare went off to work on articles for other newspapers as usual. Although the scheduling of her commitments was an obvious eating alibi, the work was real enough. She wrote freelance for one or two national broadsheets. *Brazen* apparently didn't provide a proper income for any of its staff, but it kept them in sandwiches. There was something civilized about that, that they valued small comfort above salary. Lainey took a list of requests.

'What are *you* having?' Scott said, when she came to ask him.

'I haven't decided yet,' she said.

'Yeeees. Well, I'm feeling like taking a risk today. Bring me whatever you're having, when you decide.'

'Could you tell me now? I don't want to take responsibility for your lunch.'

'Whatever happened to initiative?' he said. 'Anyway, I like to be surprised.'

'Yeah, I bet you do. What if I felt like tongue today?'

'I'd say steady on, I hardly know you,' Scott said.

She had meant to come up with something vile, off-putting, old-fashioned, something that he couldn't have liked. Now, cranberry-sharp embarrassment spilled across her cheeks; she knew she'd have to drop her cool and melt into his joke; being in on a joke was better than being the punchline. Lainey waited until he'd enjoyed her enough, and went for lunch. She walked quickly. Scott had shared an hour of office space with her and already she had lost her balance. He'd thrown everything out of whack, and while she'd pretty much seen every side of Theo and Dom now – there weren't many sides, truth be told – Scott was dangerous. She couldn't work out if he was actually quite nice or if he was only making fun of her, or both; or worse, whether he'd say bad things behind her back. It was possible that the effect he had was entirely deliberate, that he kept this two-tone charm with its shady uncertainty because he liked being unknowable.

When she told Chrissie about Scott, Chrissie, unsurprisingly, had advice on hand.

'Oh, I know his sort; they're usually a lot of fun, easy to fuck with if you know what you're doing,' she said. 'The formula for enjoying them doesn't change. Pretend they're too good for you, but make sure they see you're pretending.'

'He *is* too good for me,' Lainey said.

'Don't be silly. He ignored you, you said, when you first came in.'

'Yes?'

'You had him then.' Chrissie knew just how much to give away, to irritate and enthral in equal measures, to be preposterous but always just inside believable. She promised. She let you down just as often, but that didn't matter.

'Because he ignored me.'

'Of course because he ignored you. He saw you, you said it's a tiny office. He had to have seen you and he ignored you. You say he's pretty flash, so presumably he knows how to be polite and he definitely isn't shy. But he ignored you because he wanted to show Clare that your prettiness was less important than her conversation. Which meant he was aware of your prettiness. Which meant he was acting the ignoring, which meant he was trying. And if he was trying, you've already won.'

'Oh God, Chrissie, you do talk crap.' The way that junk food is crap: moreish. That was why she'd been her best friend since they were sixteen. Lainey wondered, sometimes, why Chrissie kept it going. She was Chrissie's only close girlfriend. She didn't know if that explained things or made them more puzzling. 'Do you honestly think in these terms?'

'You'll see. Just don't be a dick with him. Oh, and don't do that thing you do with your mouth. You're doing it now, I can tell. Anyway, the reason I phoned is, Ivan and I are going to see one of John's gigs tonight. You feel like coming along?'

'One of his comedy gigs? What's he like?'

'I haven't seen one. Do you mean his act? Or him? He'll be funny.'

'But you know I never laugh.'

'What are you talking about? You laugh all the time.'

'With you I do.'

'He's funnier than me. He's professional.'

'That doesn't mean anything. Anyway it's not how funny he is. I just don't always do it with men, I get uptight. And it's a problem if you don't. It's how they work out whether they're in with a chance. I wish it was like the old days, where they only told you how much they earned.'

'Oh, they still do that. And it's every bit as obnoxious as quoting Monty Python,' Chrissie said.

'Maybe. But it's easier to fake being impressed than being amused.'

'True. But John won't try to make you laugh, because that's his job, so he must hate it by now. Like a doctor having to make diagnoses at parties. So what are you worrying about?'

'Are you expecting us to fancy each other? Because I don't know if I –'

'Lainey, do you wanna come? You don't have to sleep with John. You don't even have to smile at him. You don't have to come.'

'I'll come.'

only nearly seen

John had crapped about one and a half times his own weight since lunchtime, and his stomach still felt unsettled. The staff toilet at the Fanny Adams was just behind the bar, and a capable, sympathetic barmaid stood in front of the door. He knew he had to ask her to move out of the way again to let him through, and it was the last thing on earth he wanted to do.

'I'm feeling a bit sick,' he explained. Vomiting was never going to impress the ladies, but it was a better bet than diarrhoea.

'You don't look well,' she said, and pressed her mouth into a kind smile before turning to pull a pint. Be my mother, right now, right here, John thought, and his eyes went puppyish to her back. She was serving a young student who was thinking much the same, with his Radiohead T-shirt and the 'I'm A Virgin' sign that throbbed with the vein in his temple. Although she was slight and boyish, there was something warm and protective about her: girls like that brought out the worst in men. In the toilets he stared at himself in the mirror, ran cold water over his hands and cold hands over his body. The tremor had started in his left leg and showed every sign of staying and spreading. He sat down, couldn't crap, washed his hands again, and this time took the cold water through his hair, to refresh the styling wax. It had been weeks since he had been frightened like this. Some gigs were nothing; just like going for a pint with his mates. He let his material do the work and sat back into it. Then other times, like tonight, it would suddenly occur to him what he was doing, and how unsuited he was to it, and it felt like waking up the day after something bad had happened, and remembering.

'I thought Chrissie was coming,' John said to Ivan, when he got back out.

'She is. With the friend.'

'She's gonna have to be quick. I'm on after this bloke. How is he?'

'He's okay.'

'How's he going down?'

Ivan shrugged. 'You feeling okay?'

'I'll be all right in half an hour.'

The compère, a sexy, heavy girl who couldn't tell a joke to save her life, was already nearly finished. He felt one last red-hot sigh somewhere in the centre of his bowels, and made his legs walk up to the stage. As he passed the compère, she squeezed his arse. His insides lurched and reached for her sympathy so hungrily he could have cried.

He died at first, and barely pulled things around as he went on. Just as he was picking up, just as the sexy compère threw him a wink, just as Ivan started a three-man applause at one of his best lines, he caught sight of Chrissie standing at the back. With her friend. Who was really pretty. And he couldn't remember where he was or where he was going. He laughed and raked his hair and shrugged a shoulder, and improvised, and, amazingly, it seemed to work, and even though he wasn't funny again, the audience vibe was warmer now, he could actually feel it, them wanting to like him. As he came off, one of the blokes at the front patted him on the arm.

'You were fine,' Ivan said, nodding thoughtfully. 'You were fine.'

'Oh just . . . I lost it, mate. Never mind. It's all good . . . you know, whatever.'

'You were fine. Shut up, forget it, come and meet Chrissie's girlfriend and take her mind off thinking up ways to destroy me later.'

47

'She's nice.'

'She looks all right, doesn't she? Come on.'

What Lainey looked was anachronistic. Not deliberately: she hadn't succumbed to the cute retro shit so many girls thought witty. It was just her: she belonged to the sixties. John saw it straight away. The top half of her face was very English – to say English rose would probably be pushing it, but it was delicate; her complexion glowed like the sun through china. She'd made a mess of her eyes, which were pretty but caked with old black mascara, giving her a few fat thorns where there should have been lashes. She held his gaze longer than she needed to, like it was an endurance test, like she was rising to a challenge. He wasn't fond of that: it felt aggressive, but also demanding, even desperate. Another thing about her eyes – they seemed not to understand. Even when she was looking right at him, he felt himself being only nearly seen. If she'd just had her eyes, John could have looked away . . . but there was her mouth, her lips: wide, fat, almost ugly, almost pornographically sensual. It was the dirtiest mouth John had ever seen, it redeemed everything. Whereas the north of her face was smooth and shockable, the south had seen it all before. The contradiction put her in the sixties. She was Julie Christie and Sarah Miles and Susan George and a thousand pre-teen erections on dull, slow Sundays, with her tawny bedroom hair and her tatty jumper. Oh God, let her be normal, he thought.

Even by the time they'd found a table in the snug of the bar, away from the next comic, who was sadistically proving that, actually, it was a pretty good crowd, John was still shaky from being on. He said little at first, afraid that he wouldn't be able to stop. Exhausted by the self-induced rigours of stand-up, his normal conversational restraint slackened, went all incontinent: he couldn't be responsible for what came out, and knew from experience that it could be stupid. He was shy, but usually that shyness manifested itself in a blundering loudness. Shyness was a concealment, not a facet of personality – it could come in any form and anything could exist underneath it. Sometimes it was safer to leave it there. He wanted Chrissie to stop talking about how they got there, and to tell him what she thought of his act. When she didn't, he knew she hadn't for a reason, but that wasn't good enough. He still had to make her say something, he still needed to hear her talk about him. So, hating himself, he said, 'Did you catch any of it?'

'Oh, just the end really, lovey,' Chrissie said. 'The bit we saw was good, but you know we couldn't *really* get into it because we didn't get the whole thing. You know what the Circle line's like, though . . .' Why couldn't girls lie better? Because they didn't have to.

'We came in at the part about the flat and the colostomy bag,' Chrissie's friend said, and looked frightened.

'Yes. We did. Yes, we thought that was very funny.'

They'd seen nearly everything, then. He made an effort to shut up and stop exposing himself.

It was a difficult evening. Chrissie knew everyone, Ivan knew John and Chrissie, and Lainey and John only knew who'd brought them. The pressure was on Chrissie, mostly, to integrate them all successfully, but for some reason she was pretending to be ditzy, making Ivan finish all of her anecdotes. It was almost gallant of Chrissie to be so annoying when John was supposed to be noticing her friend, but her friend wasn't making the most of it. Lainey sat and smiled when she was supposed to – she waited for a cue to smile, like a little kid – and when she spoke, spoke to Chrissie, and when she didn't, looked bored. Boredom wasn't a bad thing: John used to have a crush on a girl who worked in his office, even though every time he spoke to her she looked out of the window or transferred her weight to one foot as if she were falling asleep standing up. The excuses she made to end conversations with him were borderline insulting and he couldn't get enough of it. He went off her when he saw that she was the same with other people. Somehow, it had only been alluring when she was just too good for him. Being curt and aloof with everyone else cheapened the effect: it became a promiscuity of indifference.

'Chrissie tells me you just got a new job, Lainey,' Ivan said.

'Well, I don't get paid, but I go there every day. You could call it a job.'

'Where do you work?' John said.

'*Brazen* magazine. You won't have heard of it.'

'Is it like a feminist thing or has it got something to do with *When Voyager?*' John asked her.

'Yes!' Lainey said, leaning forward. She looked enthusiastic for the first time. Up to now, they had all sat round and watched Chrissie being coquettish, which John supposed was more attractive than irritating, although he couldn't see why. Lainey's voice was low and spare, contrasting with Chrissie's new pseudo-bimbo turn. 'Don't tell me you've seen a copy?'

'Lucky guess, I think. Unless I have seen it and I knew subconsciously. Are you a real *Voyager*head, then?'

'Oh, hell no. Well, I watch it, but I'm not . . . Are you?'

'I've seen a fair few. It's all right, isn't it? Harry Brazen's cool. It's a good name, actually. Most fanzines –'

'It isn't a fanzine. It's a real magazine. You can buy it at WH Smith.'

'I just used the generic because it's a cult magazine. I didn't mean to belittle it. And you said they didn't pay you.'

'Well, they don't.' Now she looked like it was his fault that they didn't pay her. He felt responsible for the brief silence that followed. Her prickliness was a strain, and she hadn't convinced him she wasn't stupid. But she was pretty.

'Do you two live together?' he said to neither of them in particular.

'Good grief, no. I can't live with anyone,' Chrissie said.

'They both live alone,' Ivan said.

'Why can't you live with anyone?' John asked Chrissie.

'I appear easy to live with, but inside . . .'

'Inside you're burning with rage and resentment, writing lists of what you hate about your flatmate and imagining them dead,' John finished.

'Yes, that's about the size of it. Is there, er, is there something

Ivan should know, John?' Chrissie said, and Ivan and John laughed.

'Why do you live alone, Lainey?' Ivan said, softly, as if the answer might be painful.

'Oh, I just copy everything Chrissie does,' she said, and smiled painfully.

how do you stop being
self-obsessed?

The call came the next day. Lainey had spent a stressful
morning trying to talk the picture library at the BBC into letting
them use a still of Dr Who in an article that belittled the Time
Lord. The lady at the BBC had specifically asked about content,
and Lainey knew that if she lied she might be found out. She
came clean about the article, but improvised something about
how sci-fi fans who were able to look at their favourite
programmes on a kitsch level, as well as a serious one, found it
easier to buy the videos, their intellectual vanity satiated. The
sense of superiority mollified the shame of the obsessive, she
explained. It was a neat argument, but it didn't work. She was
given agents' numbers and short shrift.

Clare hadn't been in all morning. The office without her was
loose and easy, with the slightly hysterical spin that
impermanence puts on fun – like a teacherless classroom. At
times like this, Lainey was one of the boys; with Clare, she had to
respect a tacit sisterhood. She was beginning to understand them.
Originally she'd thought Dominic and Theo were the same
person at different stages of life – points on a nerd trajectory –
but now their characters were clearer: Theo smouldered with
bitterness almost daily, whereas Dominic, who gave every
outward appearance of tightly coiled anxiety, was never mean or

moody. When things went wrong, Dom would just shrug and type harder, but Theo would go for a walk. She sensed Theo was trying to confide in her quite often, and did everything she could to discourage it. Not because she didn't want to know what was going on, but because Theo was too intense: she was afraid he might burn her.

That morning, in Clare's absence, Theo had already emptied his in-tray of grudges. They were all having an easy day. Lainey picked up the phone and didn't recognize John's voice. His first name wasn't enough, he had to feed her more information: John from the night before, Ivan's friend.

'God, of course, I'm sorry, it's because I'm at work – no one has ever called me here before.'

'It's okay, isn't it? You can take calls?'

'Oh, of course I can,' she said, knowing she wouldn't have been as cool if Clare had been around. 'So, how are you, John?'

'Good. I'm good. The reason I . . . oh, how are you?'

His nervousness was making her bolder. 'Fine,' she said, suspiciously.

'The reason I called here – I'm sorry to call you at work, but I didn't want Ivan and Chrissie . . .' He stopped and laughed. He seemed to gain strength from somewhere. 'Look, this is the deal, Lainey. I had a really good time last night when we went out, and I wanted to ask you out, but the whole thing's pretty, you know, sort of smug or sick or something, the fact that we're all friends, or at the very least it could be difficult, so I just thought, maybe we could keep it a secret.' He waited for a response. She wasn't ready. 'I mean, I know how stupid that sounds and you may not want to go out anyway, in which case you have my permission to put the phone down and call Chrissie. Of course, you could do that anyway. You don't need my permission or anything . . . Any time you want to join in and stop me speaking, that would be good.'

By now she was won over, but not so he could hear. 'Oh my God. I didn't think I, I didn't think you, I didn't expect this at all. My God. Well, okay. What did you have in mind?'

'Whatever you wanted, if you wanted to. No, that's not right, is it? Girls hate having to make the decisions. A drink. Like sometime this week. If you wanted.'

'And you're not going to tell Ivan?'

'No.'

'And you think there's a chance I won't tell Chrissie?'

'Of course I don't.'

She inhaled loudly through her nostrils. 'Suppose we do this and it turns out okay. When do we tell them?' This was all as funny as it was unexpected, but she kept her voice steady and serious, and heard him smile.

'Oh, what are the odds on that happening?' he said. They were both doing it, the grave, quiet deadpan. They had a private joke already.

'D'you know, John, I like this idea. In fact, the not-telling-Chrissie part is, really, half of what's doing it for me. So you're on. I should go now, I'm at work. Call me at home?'

She gave him her number and hung up, pink and pulsey and happy, wishing someone would ask her about the call, but they were men, so nobody did. Dominic was typing so quickly his hands blurred. She looked properly at his face, his anaemic complexion and cleverly lined forehead; he was straight and stiff, like cardboard. She was beginning to find him quite charming, because he would go the whole day without looking at her, and then if she spoke to him, or he happened to look up when she was glancing his way, he jumped a little and blinked, as if she was sunlight. He made her shy; he made her feel shiny.

Scott Flynn came in well after lunch, and Clare got back about an hour later, looking stern and solid, like suet. The sight of Scott lightened her.

'Scott,' she said, taking a good half-minute to pronounce the syllable. 'How are we doing?'

'We sold a full page yesterday to BBH, and a couple of halves.'

'That sounds all right,' she said, playing with an earring. 'So do you think we might manage twelve this month?'

'I hope so,' he said. 'Oh, did you hear about Stephen Winger? He's been taken on by Emap.'

'*Has* he?' Clare said. 'I always thought our Stephen would do well. Do you still see him?'

Their conversations, both warm and self-aware, were impossible not to listen to, even though Lainey had no idea who they were discussing. She couldn't be sure what went through their minds; there was artificiality on both sides. When Clare went away to write in her room, Scott made fun of her, but to a point just short of being quotable. He was all innuendo and no articulation; he enjoyed being seen to be wicked. Lainey warmed to him as she hid from him. She knew that his duplicity was a sure thing, but there was an honesty about it, and his presentation was faultless. She remembered one time when he'd needed to send a back issue to one of his clients.

'You'll have to ask Lainey about that,' Theo was saying, and Lainey started listening without looking up.

'I'm not asking her: she scares me,' Scott had said loudly, and Lainey lifted her head to see him grinning at her.

'Lainey does?' Theo said, astonished.

'Yeah, she's sharp. I have to watch myself with her.'

'Are you talking about me?' Lainey said.

'Look,' Scott said. 'There's a real toughie behind those big doe eyes.'

It was nice to have her eyes looked at by everyone: she knew they were her best feature.

Chrissie had said, when she knew the facts, that this was elemental flirtation.

'You weren't paying him attention so he had to force you to consider him,' she said. 'And what outrageous flattery. I have to say, actually, I think I like the sound of him. He does it well.'

'Do you think he fancies me, then? He doesn't.'

'I don't think he does or he doesn't. Only you know that. I'm saying –'

'I don't know that. How do I know that? Do you always know if a man fancies you?'

'Usually. I just assume they do anyway. Saves time. I don't mean,' Chrissie said, in response to Lainey's intake of breath, 'that they all fancy me, it's just that you have nothing to lose by assuming they do.'

'You could make a fool of yourself.'

'Why does this rule your life? Why are you so bothered about making a fool of yourself?'

'I just worry about what people think of me.'

'And what is this obsession with yourself? Just enjoy it, don't analyse it. If you spent less time thinking about what everyone thought of you . . .'

When Chrissie picked on her, which was too often, she liked to tell Lainey that she was obsessed with herself. The more Lainey thought about this, the more it looked true, the more it became true. But how do you stop being self-obsessed? Impossible to do it consciously – experience showed it wasn't going to happen naturally. Were other people really not as self-obsessed?

'What picks you out as especially self-obsessed,' Chrissie had said once, 'is that I know you are. You don't just think about yourself, you talk about yourself too.'

'So doesn't everyone?'

'You talk about your internal struggle. Everyone doesn't do that. They give the facts but not the analysis. I know everything you think about everything, but especially what you think about you. You share your every thought. All of it.'

'I know I do,' Lainey said. 'But I thought you might be a bit interested. I'm always interested in yours. Or I used to be. If you're just going to get at me . . .'

'See, it always comes down to this, me getting at you,' Chrissie said. 'It's always what's happening to you, not what's happening out there.'

'How can I think about things without putting them into relation with myself?'

'Some people do.'

Perhaps they were hardly friends. They understood each other and could be themselves, which was the whole point. All the ground work had been done; it would be difficult starting again with someone else, explaining away the things that they could take for granted – that they could say socially unacceptable things and it would be understood that they didn't mean them (or did), no names but watch my eyes, be mean to each other, be normal. Sometimes, though, Lainey wondered if being yourself really was the best thing. Certainly, it was a good thing, but she had better times elsewhere when she wasn't being herself.

touched in soho

John hung up and breathed out for a long time. He looked behind him, a sudden panicky twist, as if he sensed someone there, laughing. He wasn't sure why he'd asked Lainey out. She'd sounded much cooler on the phone. He'd been so pleasantly startled that he wondered now what he'd been expecting and why he'd wanted to embarrass himself with someone he expected so little of. The easy answer was that she had seemed terribly sexy all along, having a kind of dishevelled vacancy. The difficult answer was that 'dishevelled vacancy' had to be a euphemism for 'kind of stupid', but it was the kind of stupid that relaxed him. He didn't prefer thick girls, but they made things easier. Easier to impress. Not so much of a personal criticism if you didn't pull it off. The night before, Lainey had said very little, and her eyes had looked to Chrissie for permission. Now, on the phone, she was quicker, sharper. It could have been illusory: the phone did that. Somewhere along the wires wit could be added, like static, or taken away, like bass. But even allowing for this, he had a horrible feeling that he'd just made a date with a girl who was out of his league.

By day, John was a mild-mannered clerk in a large management consultancy. He rotted in hell with men who wore dull suits and shiny ties and spoke in up-to-the-minute clichés. Mostly, he kept his head down and tried to remember the dialogue for later use in his screenplay. He tried to be inspired, not intolerant. John was working on a comedy film that would revitalize the spirit of Ealing, while embracing the sex and violence of the new millennium. So far, he had some good jokes but only one character. Because he worked nine to five and hated most of the people he worked with, he spent much more time at home than Ivan, who went out most nights with clients and contacts. Ivan worked freelance in advertising, which was how he'd met Chrissie: he was doing some work for her agency. Now that the stand-up seemed to be going somewhere, though, John was escaping the post-work throb of the silent house more often, exchanging it for the cardiovascular workout of tiny, smoky comedy clubs. He was considering giving up the day job – he wasn't really making enough money to cope, but he had some saved. But when it came down to quitting, he didn't want to take the step without proof that it wasn't lunacy. He wanted a sign.

He got off the tube at High Street Kensington so he could walk through the park. He wasn't used to the later evening light yet: it felt new and luxurious. Free daytime. A middle-aged woman was hiding behind a tree to worry her two spaniels. John realized why she was doing it, for the relief on their faces when she reappeared, and he was touched by how sad she was. He wanted to know if other people could see when he was needy. If it showed. But he was in a good mood and it would take more than identifying with a mad old lady to shake it, because he'd asked a pretty girl out and she'd said yes, and usually it didn't happen that way. Women so took for granted their roles as the generally-asked that they didn't worry too much about the condition of the askers after they'd wiped their hands of them. There was some sensitivity about, some pity, but just as often, an approach was treated as an attack or an aggression, a liberty-taking insult, and women behaved as if they had a right to not just refuse, but to put the suggestion firmly in its place. Your skin got thicker, of course, but there was never a physical seasoning against embarrassment, no matter how long you lived, no matter how many rejections you took on the chin. That kind of indifference seemed available only to the irredeemably ugly or genuinely offensive men, the ones whose advances were underpinned with a hostility that justified the cruel refusals. John walked with his hands in his pockets and tried to remember Lainey's face, with little success.

Ivan was in by the time he got home, frying pork fillets in mustard and crème fraîche. Ivan was every woman's dream: he lived on the cusp of creativity and wealth, dressed like a gay man and cooked like Harry Palmer. He cooked for himself – they didn't share. John put his prick-and-heat microwave curry on the table, tried not to look pleased to see him, and they made the usual abbreviations.

'You not out tonight?' John said.

'No, I've been tired today. Might just go to bed early.'

'You, er . . .' Don't ask if he's spoken to Chrissie. If Ivan knew about Lainey he'd say. Leave it, *leave* it. Shut the fuck up, in fact, about it. 'You, er, had a good day?' he said, and Ivan looked faintly perplexed and ignited his Noilly-Prat.

The reason they got on so well was they were both cool, the definition of cool being 'able to legitimately sneer at other people'. (The definition of grace was not exercising that right.) But the difference between them was that Ivan was hip as well. He listened to the right bands, wore the right shoes, drank in the right places. These trappings of style were a short cut to cool, but not the essence of it, and Ivan was independently cool as well, able to recognize that John, for all his chainstore T-shirts and M&S underpants, was more than on his wavelength: a lot of the time John tuned him in. They'd been living together for years now – since university, longer than some marriages. It felt like a marriage in that it was beyond misunderstanding, beyond apology, but not quite beyond jealousy. Unlike a marriage, its strength grew out of compromise, not insistence on what was right. They didn't judge each other, or keep score. It was the sort of relationship that never existed sexually, where not working hard gave the best results.

'There's a girl at work wants to sleep with me,' Ivan said.

'How do you know?'

'I just know.'

'And what, you're tempted?'

'Obviously.'

'What about Chrissie?'

'That's it, isn't it? I'm worried about Chrissie. It's just a weird feeling, knowing it's serious this time.'

'You're such an arrogant bastard, Ivan. What makes you think she's not just flirting? What makes you think she's even flirting?'

'She's made it very obvious.'

'She's touched you, has she?'

'Mm.'

No big deal to Ivan, being touched by a girl who wanted to sleep with him, even though he had a girlfriend who made commitment look like Christmas.

'She's *touched* you? Where?'

'Oh, in a bar after work yesterday, in Soho, in public. Does it matter?'

John blinked away the possibility that Ivan had understood and was playing with him. Ivan had stopped what he was doing and was looking hard at John, concentrating, as if he'd need to translate the answer. He seemed unusually serious; possibly monogamy was starting to hit him hard, because he didn't have any real experience of it. Maybe for the first time Ivan was really trying to do the right thing, and wasn't finding it so easy.

'And she's what, she's nice, is she?'

'She's nice.'

What did he want – permission? encouragement? admiration?

'Well, it's all right for some, isn't it?' he said, and managed to do camp, passably.

start as you mean to go on

When John called her at home to set a date, Lainey put on perfume almost unconsciously, while she spoke to him. She needed to feel partly artificial while she was speaking to him: start as you mean to go on. This stage was the easiest, when you didn't know each other but knew you weren't making a fool of yourself. Yet. He wasn't afraid to sound interested. There was a lot of information to swap in these last crucial minutes: the *mise en scène* was more important than the actual plot. So Lainey made sure John knew about her possibilities, and he turned her head with hints of himself. New people were inherently exciting to her now. At university they'd been everywhere: she'd binged and purged and taken them for granted. In the outside world they were harder to find, running into them really took a lot of planning. The haphazard destiny of youth was no longer available to her.

Making a date was encouragingly difficult. John had quite a few late gigs on for a few weeks, and Lainey worked five mornings at the magazine, and two earlies at the supermarket, along with three or four evenings: there were few periods where their free time coincided. They were comforted by their mutual busyness. In fact, although she was working so much now, there was still time off. Only less, so that it felt strange, like the rough hush of motorway bridges on a rainy drive. She'd be checking-out, confident and noisy, or calling United International for press releases, letting the speed of it all carry her through, and then later she'd be at home, feeling a cold gust of loneliness hit her when she put the phone down. She was working on an article to show to Clare and she played Tetris on her Gameboy. Lots of Tetris. The blocks kept falling when she closed her eyes.

She called Chrissie as soon as they'd hung up, because she needed to talk about it. But she also wanted to play along with John's desire to keep it a secret, and thought it important that he trusted her. Having a secret from Chrissie made her feel powerful. It felt like rebellion: Lainey was normally the one who offered everything – every worry, every twitch of pride, every barely moulded thought. The effort of even thinking about keeping this a secret was physical; she felt it fluttering inside her ribs, a caged bird; she felt as if she were holding her breath.

'How's work?' Chrissie said.

'Actually, it gets better all the time. I'm really beginning to love it. And I like the people more.'

There was a silence.

'Good,' Chrissie said, with gusto. 'I told you you'd settle down. What about the boy you didn't like? The sexy cocky one.'

'Scott. It's not that I didn't like him, it's just that I didn't know what he was thinking. I still don't. But he's a real smoothie and I can cope with it now. Actually, I really look forward to him coming in.'

Another silence.

'I told you it was easy to handle his sort,' Chrissie said, but this time the gusto was scuffed. 'What about the horrible fat boss?'

'She's not so horrible,' Lainey said. 'It's weird. I think I just didn't understand it at first, I didn't get them, really. They're a bit strange. But it's their strangeness that I like. I do like it. I'm having such a good time.'

'Oh good,' Chrissie said, sort of sternly, as if Lainey had begun following her advice at last. 'Well, I told you you would.' Her smooth coldness invited insolence: Lainey wanted to kick it about, like newly fallen snow. She had the John thing in reserve, but she had to keep it there because, in this mood, Chrissie was as likely as not to say something irreparably diminishing about it all. Lainey changed the subject instead.

the suddenness of
the tube

'Did you tell Ivan?'

She was wearing a big jumper and loose black jeans, neither of which disguised how thin she was. Nice thin, though. Too much mascara, he'd forgotten she did that, but her lips were bare. She looked pretty good, like a girlfriend more than a first date.

'I haven't seen him today,' he said. He worried that it sounded like a lie, even though it wasn't. He felt like a liar today. He had mental flashes of needle-thin fibre-points going berserk on lie detectors.

'But you'll come home and he'll be there and you'll say what?'

'I'll tell him I had a gig.' They were walking, and he slowed down to look at her; her face was glowy with emotion, he didn't know which.

'And will I tell Chrissie?' Her voice was soft and pensive, as if she was speaking to herself.

'Will you?'

'I suppose that depends on you. And how we get on. At the very least you should try to make sure I give you a good review.'

Part of him was enjoying this, another part accepted that it was what was keeping them from talking about the weather now, and part of him was beginning to be irritated – she was being provocative because someone had once told her it was sexy. The last part had the loudest voice. 'For fuck's sake, if you want to tell her, tell her. I don't care,' he said churlishly. The rest of him made him feel bad. 'I mean, I don't mind if Ivan knows, I just didn't want him to, you know, know.'

She rode out the silence and he respected her for it.

'Have you been at work today?' he said.

'I've been at *every* work today. Supermarket from half six, then *Brazen* from ten.'

He made her explain about the supermarket while he made appropriate observations, and they found the bar and he bought her cider, which she drank from the bottle.

'So why do you do stand-up?' she said, picking off the label with short unpainted fingernails.

'Attention,' he said too quickly.

She pulled a face. 'No, God, don't say that. It's kind of wanky.'

'What should I have said?'

'Well, the truth, I suppose. Unless the truth is wanky. In which case you should make something up.'

'You want me to say I was bullied at school for being the short kid, and laughter was my only defence?'

'Still a bit wanky.'

'Why do you work in a supermarket?'

'Because I love groceries. The money, would you believe?'

'Would you believe I do comedy for the money?'

'No.'

'Well, I do. I think there's a slight chance I may be good enough to make it, whereas I know I'm never going to get rich with Hilditch-Sinclair.'

'You really think you're going to –'

'I don't think,' John said impatiently. 'But there'd be little point doing it if I thought I wouldn't. You must, I suppose, think you're going to make it in magazines. Or else you wouldn't be pushing lentils in your spare time. You know, maybe we're both fooling ourselves.'

They weren't joking; there was no light teasing here, nor was it manipulation of arousal through barbed challenge. As far as John could tell, they were really trying to piss each other off, and no longer cared what kind of impression they were making. He couldn't remember ever being like this with a girl, like he didn't have to avoid offending her. His stage persona was espresso-black, but off-stage he was a nice cup of tea, milky-bland, two lumps. He was eager to please, and changed personality to suit whoever he was bumping against. But Lainey brought out something he hardly ever experienced: apathy. He felt more or less immune to her opinion of him, and to what she said or thought, now or later. She was apparently feeling the same way. Unexpected recognition connected them; but if it was chemistry, it was ominous, and bubbling.

'I thought you'd be would-be funnier,' she said, carelessly. He made a noiseless, gaspy laugh. 'I mean, I thought you'd be *on* all the time. I thought that was what comedians were meant to be like. Like Norman Wisdom on chat shows.'

'No . . . *no*, they're the most miserable bunch of introspective self-hating losers you could ever hope to avoid.'

'Tell me more, you're turning me on,' she said. John sort of double-taked, because she was suddenly saying the right things. It still just wasn't working for him, though he couldn't decide why. He felt something at the back of his mind stopping him really liking her. As if he'd written it down somewhere before, so he could remember it later.

'Like the delusional fixational paranoia, Oedipal complexes, fear of commitment and conviction that we're all the most original and brilliant person who ever lived? You want to hear that sort of thing?'

'Oh.' She wrinkled her nose in disappointment. 'You *are* just like normal men, then.'

The best thing about living in London was the suddenness of the tube. You could pretend, and John always did, that it all came as a surprise. Oh, my train's here. Oh, this is my stop. You could leap on or off without summing up, without making excuses, without making plans. When the doors slammed, you were safe. At Paddington, John watched Lainey getting ready to move, and prepared himself to be surprised the station had come up so soon – curious thing: sometimes you could sit on the tube and really feel that the train was standing still and the stations were spinning round, like the lands at the top of Enid Blyton's Faraway Tree. She gave him a shy, crooked smile, as if her mouth was shrugging, and got up. It was the first time since seeing her come up the road at the beginning of the evening that he'd thought about how pretty she was.

'Thanks for coming out,' he said.

'No, it was my pleasure.'

'No. Well, anyway . . .' He didn't want to make any suggestions he had no intention of living up to.

'Yes, right. Okay, then. Good night.'

The doors cut her off.

Well, here was a strange thing. He couldn't see himself calling this girl, who he fancied quite a lot, because he didn't really like her very much. Although he didn't not like her in a bad kind of way: she hadn't been vacant or dull, and she hadn't been a nightmare, she'd just been hard work, and a bit . . . in fact, what she'd been was not all over him, which was normally a good sign. Usually, he found a light seasoning of revulsion a big turn-on. But she hadn't been not all over him in the right way; she'd just been impatient and fierce. He only wanted to see her again for the chance of sleeping with her, and yet she'd given no hint of being prepared to sleep with him, and plenty of attitude to suggest it was the last thing on her mind. Or even that it was the first thing on her mind, and that as a possibility it sucked profoundly. None of this would normally have prevented him from calling: he liked to take things right up to the brush-off. Further than that, even; all the way to selfish sex followed by weeks of animosity, and the vanity of pretending that breaking things off was hard for either of them. This time he didn't want to take it further, because there was something difficult about her, and he didn't feel strong enough to deal with it. It was . . . it was not that he expected rejection, not *only* that – but that he expected her to judge him as well. He didn't want that. He didn't even want to talk about it to Ivan now. He'd just wait until Chrissie said something and pretend to be easy about it all, by which time he genuinely would be.

When he got in, Ivan was on the phone to Chrissie, laughing, and John's stomach turned paranoia-cold while his bowels blushed panic-hot. His body's jumpy reflex to emotional change showed no sign of improving as he got older. A hint of confrontation made his voice splinter and die; guilt brought on dizziness and sweating. The sporadic quasi-viral symptoms of stage-fright kept resetting his life expectancy, and he ate like a maniac when he was lonely. Sometimes he tried to make his mind override it all, he practised breathing and willpower until his head hurt, but it didn't work. He'd tried diazepam but he couldn't feel it enough, and he couldn't take it with drink. No matter how valiant the adventures and conquests of his brain, from day to day his body was a loud, wet thug, there to make him suffer.

'Yeah, he's just back now,' Ivan said. 'Dunno, he's just back now. Where've you been, John?'

'Ahh.'

'Anyway, pussycat, I'm going to make myself some cornflakes. I'll e-mail you tomorrow about the play. Yep. Bye.'

John took a little time out to admire the way they ended their conversation so quickly and neatly. Fuss-free girlfriend.

'Where *have* you been, John?'

'Gig turned up unexpectedly, at the King's Head in Chinatown. I stood in for Jim Feltz at the last minute.' John was a terrible liar because he lacked confidence. He braced himself, not daring to speak again until the lie had been approved or exposed. Fortunately, Ivan hadn't caught on to his tell. He'd started looking through a stack of videos, and didn't make eye contact as he carried on talking. John got himself a Mars bar, because it was easier to tell lies behind a cover of glucose and thick, thick chocolate.

'All right, was it?' Ivan said.

'Zokay.'

'Good.'

'That was Chrissie, then?'

'Yeah.'

'You didn't see her tonight, then?'

'No, I went for a drink with some clients from DBD. Do you know what we taped *The Likely Lads* on?'

Did Ivan know where he'd been? The tension was actually reassuring. The anxiety of furtive dating seemed to make up for spending time with the wrong girl. He liked things this way: harder. He spent the next ten minutes trying to interpret everything Ivan said as a jeer. Ivan was talking a lot, this evening. Normally, they didn't say all that much to each other, particularly if they were watching television and Ivan was eating cornflakes. Unless one of them was telling a story or something, few situations really required speech now; routine had trimmed off the unnecessary fat. John would have put this talkiness down to a little whizz or whatever with the clients from DBD, but Ivan was sucking down his cornflakes at a very unspeedy rate. Speedily. Uppers took away his appetite. Of course, he might have been saying something interesting, but John wasn't really listening: he was trying to catch the subtext, waiting to be found out.

'Where did you go, anyway?' John said.

Ivan paused. Just before John repeated the question, he said, 'Oh. Well. A few places. Started at Quo Vadis and worked our way along.' He still wasn't looking up, but now John had a weird feeling that he was really looking down, avoiding him. Like, *also* lying. It crossed his mind that Ivan wasn't as brilliantly committed as he pretended to be these days. Maybe he'd decided it wouldn't hurt anyone if he just went for it with one of the women who'd let him. If that was happening, wouldn't it be great if they could both now winkingly acknowledge, the way Robert Redford and Paul Newman might, that they were both hiding something, and laugh, and talk about it like men? Wouldn't it be great if they were both like that, and they could open a couple of cans of lager and compare the size of their fibs. A couple of men laughing about women, the way men do.

'Try the tape with *Top of the Pops* on it,' John said.

i ~~could always not~~ tell her

Lainey had dialled Chrissie's number before she took her coat off, before she put her keys away, before she sat down and kicked her shoes across the room and peeled off her socks with her feet and took out her painful earrings and heard the engaged tone. She hung up. Dialled again. Still engaged. I could always, she thought, not tell her about this . . . no, *no*. She lay back on the bed, feet flat on the cold lino floor, and picked up the receiver by its cord, letting it dangle and bounce for a moment. Right, then, that's the plan. I won't tell her, I'll wait for her to talk about it, and then everyone will know how cool I am. She sat up and made an ungodly mess of her cuticles with a safety pin while the magnetic draw of the phone peaked.

It had been a fairly shitty evening: she'd actually decided John didn't like her, she'd actually got that impression, and although at first this had been hurtful and frightening, almost frightening, the top of her mind had been so relentlessly bombarded with the thought, Fuck you, then, that it had been an almighty struggle not saying it aloud, and the internal conflict had given her an outer strength, an emotional Scotchguard. At times, she'd almost felt sorry for him for not liking her, because there'd been moments when he looked sad and apologetic, as if it hurt him to be so cold and indifferent. Perhaps she should get some feedback from Chrissie . . . It was important that he called in the next couple of days to validate her attractiveness. Even so, she almost wanted him not to, almost believed she could cope with him not wanting to see her again, if it meant she was let off the hook of having to speak to him on the phone.

She took a shower to get the cigarette smoke from the pub out of her hair, and here the rejection hit hard. She started to cry. She kept thinking, God, he didn't like me, he really didn't like me at all. The thing was, she'd quite liked John at first, when they'd met with their friends and he'd been jumpy and raw and talked a lot; and she'd liked him on the phone when he'd called her at work, and he'd mumbled and stuff, and made her smile; and when they'd met early in the evening and his face seemed to lighten and grow when he saw her coming up to him, she'd liked him. And then straight away he'd been anal and cross and deliberately a dick, and worst of all, he had actually not liked her. There were few more life-draining places to be in the world than disliked by someone when you couldn't think of a single other reason to dislike them back. Lainey realized that she couldn't possibly call Chrissie about it, because she was really ashamed of herself, and she didn't want to share this with her golden, confident friend, who she knew would convince her with theories and statistics and golden lies, while being unconvinced herself and feeling saintly for being such a good confidante. Tonight, Lainey really didn't want Chrissie to be feeling good about herself: she couldn't spare the vibe, even if the vibe was making *her* feel like shit. Her tears seemed melodramatic, so she had some hummus and went to bed.

a benchmark

Whatever stand-up was doing to the pigment in John's hair follicles, there was no denying the benefits it offered his waistline. He found this crumb of consolation at the bottom of a sack of kettle chips as he waited, bored and alone, for Ivan to come home. They'd gone out together, Ivan and Chrissie, to a fashionable new East End restaurant. Maybe they were discussing him, laughing at whatever Lainey had said about him. He put on a Bill Hicks video and tried to analyse it while he had a modest toss, upon which the American funnyman intruded as little as possible. His masturbatory stimulus recently had been more than usually mundane: Chrissie and Lainey. Not that sex with either of them was on the cards in any space-time continuum of any of his lives across all parallel universes, but it passed the time. Chrissie was a marvel, garish and blonde; Lainey was silent, dark and disturbing, and it was under her shadowy influence that he chose to lurk now. He was beginning to think he could see the advantages in this sort of relationship, a library of images without consequences. But when push came to shove, he was still the wanker at home while his friend was out, eating.

At half past midnight, Ivan came back with Chrissie. She was drunk and pink and smiling secretively, spectral hair mussed from throwing her head back with laughter and no doubt having sex in taxicabs and against brick walls off Brick Lane.

'John,' she hissed, the lingering sweetness of Cosmopolitans on her breath, 'what are you doing all alone tonight by yourself?'

'Nice place, was it?' he said, ignoring her question because he didn't feel up to lying.

'The place was nice, but it was full of losers. New restaurant trainspotters,' she said, flappily, and flopped on to the sofa next to him. She slapped his knee. 'What's going on with you, then?'

Ivan stretched all over the reclining chair and yawned. 'You been in all night?'

They could ask the same question as many times as they liked, he wasn't going to answer it. Ivan put on a Bob Dylan CD and rolled a joint: John took it as a hint.

'Well, I'm going to turn in,' he said, putting a bit of top spin on the last two words, so they'd have a measure of his thoughtfulness, maybe feel they were inconveniencing him too.

'No, don't go, John, stay up. We're not trying to make you go to bed,' Chrissie said. 'Is that a joint, Ivan?'

'No,' Ivan said. 'It's herbal. It's an organic cigarette.'

'Oh come on, do you have to?'

'No,' he said.

'I just think you're a bit old to be smoking pot,' she said, properly. She put her head on John's shoulder. 'Tell him only schoolchildren smoke pot now.'

'Only schoolchildren *call* it pot,' John said, nodding.

She didn't take her head from his shoulder. He was somewhat surprised, and in equal measures flattered and insulted by the ease of her intimacy.

'I ate veal,' Chrissie said. 'Can you believe it? I'd never eat veal, but it said scaloppine and the menu was in Italian and I thought it meant scallops.'

'Rather than little escalopes,' Ivan said.

'Well, you didn't stop me.'

'I thought you wanted veal. I even respected you for it. I was very disappointed to find out you just can't read Italian.'

'You respect cruelty?' said Chrissie.

'I respect disdain for the random edicts of what's cruel in society.'

'They're not all that random, though, are they? Anyway, I wouldn't eat veal because of mad cow disease, not cruelty. No, it *is* the cruelty. I don't like eating mammals. They know what's going on.'

'You eat bacon. Parma ham bagels. You had *bunny rabbit* on Saturday.'

'I know. I'm horrible. But it's like there's a collective abhorrence of veal – like a solidarity thing, almost as if we could wipe it out. I won't make a difference by not eating pigs. I don't *like* doing it. God, it's not as if I'm killing them.'

'Of course you're killing them. You're having them killed. You're ordering their deaths,' John said.

'It's not the same, though, is it, on a scale of evilness.'

'Yes, it is,' John said. 'Their blood is on your hands.'

'No, it's not the same,' Chrissie said, and her face was tranquil with validity. 'I may exploit the cruelty of other people, but it doesn't make me cruel. Like when Diana died and all the newspapers turned around and said we were responsible because we bought the papers. There's a difference between buying a newspaper and hounding a real person with real emotions who's crying in front of you. There's a difference between standing in front of a living, quivering animal with a big stick or whatever it is they kill them with, and eating a bacon sandwich.'

'There's no difference. If you're not cruel, then you're at least callous,' John said.

'Who would you rather have a pint with? Get stuck in a lift with? The bacon-sandwich eater, or the pig killer? Who would you rather married your daughter?'

'Sure, on a *pers*onal level –'

'The personal level matters most,' Chrissie said.

'Not to the pig,' Ivan said.

'More to the pig than anyone,' she said.

Chrissie went home that night: she called for a cab, and kissed them both in the same way and went home.

'Did we piss her off?' John said.

'No,' Ivan said, sounding surprised by the question. 'What makes you think that?'

'Well, at one point I called her callous, I think. And she went home.' John didn't explain his fears: that he'd gone too far. He'd gone too far, in fact, for all the bad reasons. Because he'd seen too many films in which people got angry with each other before falling in love, or at least into bed. Because he enjoyed her emotions the way other people enjoyed fine burgundies and he wanted to get drunk on them. Because he was frustrated and he wanted to affect her. Because he wanted to touch her.

'Yeah, she went home. She has a home.' Ivan didn't sound remotely concerned. 'Chrissie's cool, isn't she?'

'She's a bit naïve, maybe.'

'Isn't she?' Ivan smiled, as if John had just said, She's a bit fantastically beautiful, maybe. 'Wilfully naïve, though.'

'So, have you been touched again lately by that other girl?'

'Not touched, no.'

John had forgotten all about Lainey when Chrissie was there, but while he failed to fall asleep he remembered again and tried to look for signs in things Chrissie had said. The cruelty thing – was that a sly dig? . . . of course not. He was beginning to think that Lainey hadn't said anything about him, improbable as that might be. And he'd even been disappointed in Chrissie; with her meat and Diana rant she'd sounded like every other girl, more or less, and he'd thought, once, that she was outside all of that.

Her hair had smelled of marzipan.

It was no good him trying to rationally find fault with her personality when she came on like confectionery. She was delicious. And it wasn't that he was trying to get her, even – he thought of her as Ivan's girlfriend in every way, and the semi-fraternal thing they had put her simply, painlessly, out of consideration – it was that she was there as a benchmark. The wan sultriness of her pretty friend just didn't measure up, and the girls were too close not to force comparison. That was why he hadn't gone crazy over Lainey. She was Chrissie's friend and Chrissie's direct competition.

it's my football

Theo wanted a favour, and Lainey knew, and she knew what he wanted, and was trying to let him know this so that he could finish his sentence and the misery would end.

'. . . so I thought, if you weren't all that busy, would it be too much of a hassle, too much, you know, to go through these old copies?' Finally something to reply to.

'No problem. Sure,' she said. She took a pile of back issues from him and started to leaf through them. 'Isn't it all on computer now?'

'It should be, shouldn't it? But with the early ones we just didn't have that, all that sophisticated a set-up. We were producing it all with two overdrafts and as much equipment as we could steal from the *Radio Times*, and as many favours as we could get from, from people we knew.'

'It's very brave, setting up your own magazine,' Lainey said. 'Really exciting. Risky. Did you both give up work together?'

'Initially no. We did it in our spare time. Well, actually, Clare had gone freelance, really, by then.'

'So how did you decide who was going to be the editor? Fist fight? Kerplunk?' Lainey had thought this was a highly amusing thing to say at the time, but then as she watched the clouds gathering over Theo's head she regretted the flippancy.

'Ha ha,' Theo said, and his face was straight again before the end of the second ha. 'No, she, er, she, er, she, she was always

very good at organizing and arguing and we talked about it and
were going to do it jointly – that was the original idea – and then
in the end, to get backing and things, it just seemed more
straightforward to have one editor, and anyway we were doing it
in her flat so it proved more successful to do it this way.'

'You have to be the goalie because it's *my* football?'

'Mmm.'

She wished she hadn't asked, but then again she was pleased
that she had found something out. There was something
cryptically shoddy about them all, with their serial-killer secrecy.
In newsagents she always checked to see whether they really
stocked *Brazen*, because all too often she felt she was doing
something private and illegitimate, like the clerk in the Sherlock
Holmes mystery *The Red-headed League*, who scrupulously
copied out dictionaries, unknowingly diverting attention from a
sinister crime.

For Theo, there was clearly catharsis in spilling the beans. He
went on, 'We used to be good friends, actually. She was a lot of
fun once. She'd have these parties and . . . she's very witty, when
she wants, very sharp. But you know, when you start spending a
lot of time with someone and you're, you're, you're doing
something pretty stressful, you don't then want to stop work and
keep doing, well, whatever, the same thing with the same people.
So we're not as, as close as we used to be. But then again, we're
closer, I suppose. We're practically married now.'

Theo was uglier than he looked. He wore glasses and
cardigans and had an unintentionally fashionable bookishness
that was not unsexy, but as she came closer to him, Lainey could
see that without his accessories he would be very weird-looking,
with the face of someone who divided his free time between being
aghast and being contrite. Which, together with his allergy to
Clare, made her wonder whether they'd had any kind of sexual
thing, ever. To the casual observer it seemed impossible, but the
more she knew, the less impossible it felt. A new theory: they'd
slept with each other, and afterwards he'd cooled off – blown her
out? – and she'd been punishing him ever since. He was bitter

about something, but it was more likely to be that the fat lady, who'd once been his friend, was now calling the tune.

'Here it is. May 16th. The article offers proof that Harry Brazen was once a woman.'

'Excellent,' Theo said. 'That's great, very good of you. Thank you. Thanks very much. That's really helpful. Thank you. I'm very grateful. Thanks.'

Lainey had to stop herself from saying that she'd hate to see him after fellatio.

The two people who did get on very well at *Brazen* were the younger boys: Scott and Dominic. It was one of those radiant friendships that could never have occurred in the wild, but flourished with unnatural logic in the greenhouse heat of the office. An unlikely pair: one serene, seductive, hip, the other eggheady, brittle and contained; none the less it worked. They giggled. Sometimes they whispered, but only when Lainey was the only other person in the office, and while that should have pissed her off, it made her feel warm and happy. She knew they weren't whispering about her, because that would have been too obvious, and there was something pleasing about anyone liking anyone in a place where the surface friendliness crackled like polyester.

Today they had a press copy of a novel written by the star of a 1970s BBC sci-fi series, who was now a cult figure, although he seemed mostly oblivious to his postmodern appeal. Dominic was reading passages to Scott, who was laughing with his head back. It was quite the most sexually exciting thing Lainey had seen in ages: their unselfconscious affection, their homo-erotic proximity, and the unguarded and involuntary spasming of their easy laughter. Their smiles were exclusive; now and then Scott touched Dominic's forearm. Slow-mo tenderness. She looked on and coveted it all, she wanted in.

'I'm suddenly ravenous,' Scott said. He turned to Lainey and smiled like the devil. 'Office girl: how about getting us some lunch?'

*

Clare had been consulting their financial adviser all morning and when she came in, sweaty and exhausted, and encountered her breeze-cooled staff with their dewy, chilled coke cans and expansive lethargy, she looked momentarily burgled.

'Anyone got anything done this morning?' she said.

'A couple of quarters,' Scott said.

'How many pages is that, now?' Clare said.

'Seven.'

'We need more,' she said, an accusation. 'Although' – her voice softened – 'half a page isn't bad for a morning.'

Clare never relaxed. She never threw herself down and said, God, I've had a shitty day, someone fix me some camomile tea and you, rub my feet, there's a lad, while I have myself half an hour of *Hello* therapy. Which was only fair, as it was an office, and she was the editor. But it was also her flat, her home, and they were also her friends, slightly, and Lainey always felt the strain of bracing herself for the moment when it all became too much, the day the buttons popped. She supposed that weight was a major factor in Clare's formality: it was important, when one was fat, to be decorous at all times. Looseness in posture would give subconscious credence to the presumption that as a fat person she was bereft of self-discipline. But she was too rigid, too careful, a Stepford fat person, and sometimes Lainey worried about her.

'Theo, could we have a word, please?' Clare said. Silently, Theo stood and followed her upstairs.

'I think we're not doing all that well,' Dominic said.

'Do you know something?' Scott asked him.

'No, do you?' Dominic said.

'No.' They laughed. 'Do you know anything, Lainey?' Scott said.

'What?'

'Doesn't matter.' He rolled his eyes, so that she could see. She narrowed her eyes at him, mock-mean. 'You do know something, don't you, Dom? You know everything. Everyone tells you everything. You pretend you're not listening, but you suck it in.

Like a sponge.' He stretched out the last word, and leaned over to intimidate Dominic. He had that Latiny elasticity of northern confidence; his body was a part of him. The way Dom moved suggested he put his on every morning, after his socks.

'I think,' Dominic said, now anxious to stop what he'd started, 'there's just a bit of a cash-flow problem at the moment. I don't know anything, of course. But they always start panicking at this time of the month, don't they? It's just their pre-publication tension.'

'So you don't think anything's happening?' Scott said.

'So you'd better get on the phone and sell space, sonny,' Dominic said to Scott, bright eyes putting an end to the conversation. Scott pivoted on one soft suede shoe, turning his back with a kind of swooping grace. Tony Manero in Little Venice. If only the advertisers could have seen as well as heard him.

A long day – she went from the office to the late shift at the Real World, and it was a really tough one. Her hands smelled of money and her head was full of unconsummated shouting at stupid customers and she just wanted to come home and close the door and lock them all out. One message flashed on the answerphone.

'I got another promotion today,' Chrissie said. 'Come out and let me buy you a drink.'

The good news was enough to finish her off, but the promise of a drink brought her back from the edge. Her body was craving alcohol, actually craving, like an addict. Her brain could remember the soothing unravel that came free with the first gulp of a large gin, her body could remember wilting like an impressionable teenager under the influence of dark, wanton pints of stout. So, leaving her wheat-free gluten-free fat-free bread-free loaf to one side, she went out again to meet her best friend.

together

John hadn't reckoned on leaving the house again that day. He'd eaten a 'take home' bag of Walkers on top of fish and chips and a doughnut. He was all carbed out. His own fault for even pretending he'd be able to come up with new material; over in the corner, the computer's cursor winked like a grinning, winking bastard. He had plans for his Woody Allen videos, and designs on a hunk of good Cheddar that was coming of age somewhere in the fridge. Ivan came home in a flurry of purpose, throwing John into slow motion.

'Credit cards, credit cards,' Ivan said.

'Green jacket?'

'Green jacket!' Ivan said, striding. 'You coming out? Chrissie just got a promotion at work and she wants me to be drunk with her.'

'Won't it be a romantic thing?'

'No, it'll be a drinky thing. 'Tsup to you.'

'Yeah, okay,' he said.

He'd already eaten so much that day that the first Guinness had to think about going down, and went on to reconsider somewhere in the middle of an ambitious swig. He put the glass down and looked pale.

'Lightweight,' Ivan said. 'This is the only Cat and Canary in West London, isn't it?' He looked at the door.

'No. There's one off Westbourne. You did say which one, didn't you?'

'It's okay, this is the one. She's just a bit late.'

'She earning more than you yet?'

'Probably. God knows. We don't talk about money.'

'But do you pay for everything?'

'No. She wouldn't let me. Well, I pay for whatever I suggest we do, and she pays for . . . if she gets tickets for something I wouldn't give her the money and vice versa. I suppose I buy more dinner. I give her presents. It's not important.'

'To you, maybe, because you've got money. I'm just wondering if I could support a girlfriend.'

'That's sexist bollocks. If I pay for Chrissie, it's because I can and I want to. If I couldn't, she would. It's about the person, John, not the accounting. So who's the girl?'

'There isn't a girl. I just like to know what goes on these days. Are you losing weight?'

'I am, yeah. I keep forgetting to eat.'

John saw Lainey walk in, looking nervous. She looked around the bar for Chrissie, and couldn't find her. Then she saw Ivan and looked relieved. Then she saw John and visibly freaked out. He was partly amused to see that reaction to him – pure horror – and partly mortified. She panicked like a metronome on presto, almost out of the door again, knowing that John had seen her and Ivan hadn't and she could still go, but then Ivan saw John staring, and, thinking it must be Chrissie, looked up and saw Lainey.

'Lainey,' he shouted. 'Over here.' She pretended to notice him for the first time and came up to them. Her fingers were locked coyly behind her back.

'Hi. Can I get either of you a drink?' she said. She looked at John – a sharp stab of the eyes – and then sweetly at Ivan.

'We're okay, thanks,' John said. 'You didn't say Lainey was coming,' he said casually to Ivan when she was over at the bar.

'Is that good or bad?'

'It's neither, you just didn't say.'

'Sorry, John,' Ivan said. 'Anyway, don't you fancy her? I think she's a good-looking girl.'

'Yeah, she is. Hey, hasn't Chrissie got a mobile?'

'Of course she has. Good idea.' Ivan took out his phone when Lainey came back with a bottle of cider, and John pretended to be riveted by the progress of the call. Ivan had a finger in his other ear and was talking the way English people did to foreigners.

'He's calling Chrissie?' Lainey said. John nodded, and she smiled, a big smile that toasted her eyes and seemed to take her by surprise, and then, looking suddenly shy, she turned away. He watched the smile gently fade into faint lines near the top of her cheekbones.

'Did I miss something?' he asked, frowning.

'Sorry,' she said. 'It just struck me as funny. It *is* funny, isn't it?'

'You mean us? That we've gone out? And they don't know it?'

'Don't they know? They don't, do they? I mean, I haven't told Chris, and apparently Ivan hasn't told her, so you . . . ?'

'No, I didn't.'

'Were you ashamed to?' There was a tang; she was attacking him with her own hurt. It felt like getting grapefruit juice in his eye. 'Sorry, don't know what I mean by that. How have you been, anyway?'

'I thought you'd tell Chrissie.'

'It didn't really come up,' she said, and sipped from her bottle. She pressed her lips together, taking off the pink lipgloss. Ivan was laughing, and then he hung up.

'She's just outside, she says. So what are we talking about?'

Chrissie bought a bottle of Taittinger at the bar and dropped one of the glasses on the floor on her way back. It didn't smash.

'The gods are being kind,' she said, bending her knees into a curtsey, but a man behind her picked it up and handed it to her. 'John. I didn't think you were coming and here you are. Key. Pour this for me, I'm really clumsy tonight.'

John poured and drank and talked and tried to catch Lainey's eye but she wasn't having it. She must have been able to feel his gaze, which came thick and fast on her partly turned face that only had time for Chrissie. Chrissie was pretending she'd had to sleep with the boss, who was a woman, and John could tell she was only saying it to put the visual notion of her as a recreational lesbian into Ivan's mind, as if it hadn't been there before.

'Do you people want to get something to eat?' Ivan said. 'What do you say, pussycat, let's go somewhere better than this. John? Lainey? Food?'

'Chrissie, I'm really a bit skint,' Lainey said quietly. 'Would you be offended if I just went?'

'Ivan's not going to let you pay, sweetheart, I just got a pay rise. Now come on, don't be silly. Where are we? What's near here?'

In the street, Chrissie walked with John, falling back to talk to Lainey when Ivan moved forward to offer suggestions about restaurants. It was cold and Lainey was feeling like a little sister: with the wrong crowd for the wrong reasons. She didn't really want to be here, she wasn't enjoying keeping up her enigmatic indifference with John, even though it seemed to be working. But Chrissie and Ivan were easy to be around and she was more afraid of going home.

They found a little Italian place. 'Now you. Don't order cheap food,' Chrissie said, as Lainey looked down the right hand column of the menu.

'I'm not all that hungry,' she said. 'Look, I'm not going to let you pay anyway.'

'No, you're going to let Ivan pay. Just eat, for God's sake. Do you ever, in fact, eat? You're looking thin, Laine.'

'It's nervous tension,' she said.

'You're not nervous now, though, are you? You're with friends,' Ivan said, and Lainey looked at him curiously. She had not, until now, been able to assign any sort of personality to Ivan, but just then she'd noticed something: he did sincere better than anyone she'd ever met, as if he'd been frozen in suspended animation for forty years and missed irony. It was an attractive trait, and she tried to reflect some of his realness, to be worthy of him.

'I get the same thing,' John said. 'Can't eat before a gig. Or I throw up. I make up for it, obviously.' She started a bit because he was speaking directly to her. It struck her as somewhat rude, his maintaining a façade of normal behaviour in front of Ivan and Chrissie when he had issues with her.

'So why do it, John?' Chrissie said. She circumcised a breadstick with her teeth.

'Because it chose me,' John said.

'We don't go for the first thing that chooses us,' she said, and the part of her that had nothing to do with John threw Ivan a beautiful look.

'Speak for yourself,' Ivan said.

'It's a shame you couldn't have been chosen by something a bit hipper,' Chrissie said. 'Comedy's dead, you know. I don't mean to be unpleasant, but it's over, isn't it? It's here yesterday, gone today stuff.'

'Actually, Chrissie, it's more successful than ever before,' John said, trying not to care as much as he did. 'There are more comedy clubs, more pub nigh–'

'Maybe there are, but that doesn't make it fashionable.'

'What does fashionable mean, then?'

'Okay, it makes it fashionable as in lots of people do it, as in the *Sun* is a fashionable newspaper, but nobody young's into it. Just middlebrow people approaching middle age who want to go out and fancy themselves shocked by some nervous overgrown student with bad dress sense, I don't mean you, John, but that's what most of them look like. I think, when it comes down to something as basic, as natural, as laughter, that when you go out and pay for it you're admitting defeat; it's like paying for sex, no, *worse* than that, it's like saying you're not personally interesting enough to even talk to your friends, so you have to pay someone else to.'

'That's not really fair. For a start, you're out now paying for people to cook for you.'

'Yeah, because I'm a shit cook. Comedy is just conversation. To go and watch it is to say you're shit at conversation.'

'A lot of people *are*.'

'Yeah, and a lot of people are stupid. That's what I'm saying. You provide a service for people you wouldn't want to spend ten minutes with. Aren't you ashamed of yourself? You stand and give light relief to dull people. You're a tart for morons.'

'Why do you go to the theatre, then. Isn't that conversation?'

'No.' She stopped and he thought he'd stopped her. 'It's a piece of fake life. There's an emotional component.'

'You could say that about prostitution, if you're going to compare –'

'Theatre is art.'

'Comedy is performance art.'

'Yes, John. And there's good art and bad art. There's Debussy and there's Celine Dion. What you're doing is –'

'Why are you giving John such a hard time, pussycat?' Ivan said.

'I'm not, am I, John?' Chrissie said sweetly.

'You are a bit,' John said. While he made the most of his comic understatement, he hoped he didn't look embarrassed. His forehead was hot and guilty, as if he'd just been caught trying to get it on with Ivan's girlfriend in front of him. Every time he saw Chrissie these days she seemed to be having something out with him. Either she was flirting or she really couldn't stand him. He wished she'd make it a bit clearer.

'Oh well, it's just what I think. I think you should try writing a screenplay or something, not standing up in front of people like an idiot.'

'Chrissie,' Ivan said sternly.

'Sorry,' Chrissie said to him. 'Sorry, John. You're not offended, are you?' She pouted and smiled at Ivan, and John saw that she really had been insulting him with no sexier ulterior, and he felt foolish, not offended. 'Now then, I expect I'm going to have gnocchi.'

While they ate – Lainey rearranged a rocket salad, Chrissie demolished her gnocchi voluptuously – the girls provided most of the conversation. They were entertaining – pretending not to like each other – but it was all set pieces, they'd practised most of it before. Lainey was doing her best to ignore John without making it too obvious – if he asked her a question she gave the answer to Ivan or Chrissie. She was rather beautiful this evening, the kiss of Chianti in the sheen on her cheeks; the warm lighting vaselined the angles of her face, her hair looked soft and slept-on dirty. He was growing increasingly desperate for her to look at him and was running out of things to ask. He'd exhausted all the small talk when they'd gone out alone.

'I know what I meant to ask you, Lainey,' Ivan said, lighting a roll-up like a movie star. 'Is Harry Brazen gay, do you know?'

'Well, this is the big question,' Lainey said energetically. There was nothing better than being the expert at the table, particularly when the table also contained Chrissie. She sipped her wine, stretching her moment of superiority. 'He's never had affairs with women, although he's had plenty of opportunities and they're always falling in love with him –'

'I thought you said he *was* a woman,' John said.

'Well, that's the other –' Lainey said.

'He's a woman?' Ivan said, animated. 'When did you say that? Was I there?'

'I don't remember you telling us that either. Now that is interesting. Now I want to see it,' Chrissie said.

Lainey, who was just remembering that the last time she'd had this conversation was alone on the tube with John, was trying hard to think of a way to move things along.

'I said it half an hour ago in the Cat, you obviously weren't listening. Maybe you were at the bar. Anyway, that's just a theory of a few fans, although there are some diehards who'd like to kill the people who cast those kinds of aspersions.'

'Do you get letters from mad people?' Ivan said.

'Do I?'

'Does *Brazen*?'

'We must – I mean, some of them must be a bit mad because
. . . well, because they're buying a fanzine about a television
programme.'

'I thought it wasn't a fanzine, it was a *real* magazine,' John
said with a grin, and Lainey turned to him warmly – she liked
being teased because it made her feel included – and then she
remembered to feel exposed and angry because she knew he
didn't like her. She looked down and rolled a little piece of bread
into a ball. John's voice lowered with her eyes. 'Anyway, Harry
Brazen has to be straight. He's too unstylish. If he was gay he'd
never put those boots with those gloves – doesn't he know
anything about accessorizing?' He stopped, and then said,
mysteriously, 'You know, perhaps he just has his affairs on the
quiet. Maybe he dates secretly.'

'Don't be ridiculous,' Chrissie said. 'We know what he does
secretly. That's how television works.'

Lainey, stirred from her antagonism by John's little ambiguity,
was thinking quickly. She wondered if he was saying it for her,
making a private joke. 'No, he could get away with it,' she said.
'Maybe he has a whole bit on the side that the rest of the cast
don't know about. It might explain why he's so smug the rest of
the time.'

'Don't you think the strain of keeping his dating secret from his
closest friends might affect his ability to save the earth?' John said,
and she let him catch her eye while she caught her breath. His
eyebrows shrugged together an eighth of an inch, questioning. She
found the subtext deliciously exciting; the privacy made her shiver.

'What's so hard about keeping a secret?' Lainey said. Her voice
was softer too now, whispery like dry ice. She tilted her chin up
slightly, showed some neck. 'Only teenage girls have to tell their
friends everything. I wouldn't have thought Harry Brazen would
be bursting to tell Kardic that he didn't get laid last night.'

'No doubt. But it might be a different story if he did get laid,'
John said.

'I can't see that happening. Like you say, he can't accessorize,'
Lainey said, playing with a fork. 'And he's not very amusing. Not

intentionally. And he acts like a dick with women: one minute cold, the next –'

'I feel quite hurt for Harry Brazen,' John said. He looked straight at her and she could feel her bra. 'Don't you like him at all?'

'Not much,' Lainey said. Her pulse quickened. 'But I get the feeling he could grow on me.'

Chrissie wanted to walk and Ivan wanted to walk her home, so they all said they'd have to do this again soon and John and Lainey set off for the tube station together.

'Are you okay getting the tube back?' Chrissie had asked her quietly before they split up. 'John's getting it too, so . . .'

'I take the tube home at night all the time, I'm fine,' Lainey had said. 'And John's getting it too, like you say. Are you letting Ivan in tonight?'

'Oh God, I don't know. I have tidied, so it's crossed my mind. But I don't know. I'll call you early tomorrow.' She squeezed Lainey's elbow and sashayed back to Ivan, who was facing away from them, smoking.

They walked in silence, not saying a word until they were actually in the tube station and Lainey had bought a ticket and John said, 'I think I was a bit of a shit when we went out.'

Lainey wasn't sure how to respond.

'Mm?' she managed.

'Yeah. I think I –'

'Look, we just didn't really hit it off. I don't know why you think that's your fault.' She was a bit pissed off that he'd made it look as if whatever he did or said set the pace for them, as if his behaviour and his opinion were the only things that mattered. She wished she could tell him this, but didn't want him to know he bothered her at all. 'If you must know, I haven't given it much thought since then.'

'I didn't expect you to. I think I just get . . . actually, you know, there isn't an excuse. I wasn't all that nice. I think it was my fault. I think I'm a very poor judge of character.'

'What does that have to do with it?'

'Well, for one thing it took me until tonight to realize exactly how gorgeous you are.'

She was taken aback, but aware that it wasn't a very straightforward compliment. There were points that she'd have liked to have raised, but she was, for the moment, disarmed by the flattery.

'Because, of course, it takes a good judge of character to work out how good-looking someone is,' she said.

'Don't take the piss, Lainey. There's more to gorgeous than the way you look. It took no time at all to see how pretty you are. I'm talking about everything else. I'm sorry I wasn't better when we went out. If you give me another chance, I probably won't make it up to you, I'll be just as crap, probably, and just as unintentionally unfunny, but I would appreciate you this time.'

'What the hell does that mean?' she said.

'Can I see you tomorrow? is what it means.'

Her mind was running through the next seven days in a thousand combinations. Her hair was blown back by the approaching train. She closed her eyes.

'This is my tube,' Lainey said. 'Are you going my way?'

2

'tell me (you're coming back)'

John was trying very hard not to be himself. But it wasn't easy. For a start, she was drooling. A glistening line snailed from the corner of her mouth. The alarm clock said 6.22. There was no way he could get out now; he was here for the duration.

As stupid things went, this had to be one of the stupidest. His best friend's girlfriend's best friend, and, for God's sake, he didn't need to get his end away that much, he'd been going without for long enough recently. Would she want to be his girlfriend now, was he in a relationship? Was that such a bad thing? What did he want? He heard himself groan and realized he needed to pee. Carefully, he rolled out of her demi-double bed. He found his T-shirt on the floor and held it in front of his tackle, then staggered around pressing wardrobe doors and walls, morning-groggy, hangover soupy, until he found the bathroom.

It was black and white like a public toilet, and the hard daylight fuzzed his naturally poor vision, giving him an overexposed, out-of-focus picture. There didn't appear to be a shower or a bath of any kind in here. He couldn't remember where he'd taken his lenses out, although he'd taken the case out with him, so they'd be easy enough to find. He looked at himself in her mirror, pushed hair forward and back, feeling the tickle of each strand falling into place again. He squeezed toothpaste along his finger and poked around his mouth, slapping it into the gums and hoping that the more it hurt the more good it would do. And then he peed: the loudest echoing, pneumatic urination of his life – he was bending his knees to try to get his dick closer to the bowl – and it seemed to last for ever. He stayed in there throughout the flush, just in case he hadn't already woken her. Every available surface was crowded with make-up or moisturizer or cleanser, and there were at least a dozen different hair-styling products that all promised some sort of defrizz action. I'm here in a girl's bathroom. I had sex last night: this is quite good but quite bad. I have to go out again now, in case I woke her and she's wondering what I'm up to. I wish I knew where I took out my lenses.

He found his lenses on a sort of community-centre black plastic chair in the corner of the bathroom and put them in. They hurt a lot and his vision was streaked and blurry, his eyes wouldn't stop watering. He dragged the back of his hand across them. The view from the window was of some tatty communal gardens; bald, dry mounds of earth, some rose bushes, dead-looking, about a hundred pigeons strutting around trays that appeared to have been left for them. It was a view of post-apocalyptic London – a city where all the flowers were dead and the pigeons ruled. He squeezed himself through the smallest crack of door he could to restrict the light he let into her room. She was still asleep, or pretending to be. It took him several seconds to get used to the smudgy dark again, although this was kinder to his eyes, which were still streaky. She had stopped drooling, which could have meant she'd heard him, but she didn't seem to be awake. She showed no sign of moving. He couldn't see his boxers anywhere. John had no choice but to get back into bed with her. There was no change in her breathing, and he contemplated, with unwilling cynicism, the kind of girl who could be unstirred by the presence of a strange man in her bed.

He lay there for a long time, thinking, the situation made weirder because he normally didn't have such good eyesight when he was naked in bed in the semi-darkness. His lenses still hadn't settled, though. He probably had them in the wrong eyes, but thought he'd leave it till he got home to switch them. Then she moved, made a noise, and he was almost sure she was awake, because it was quite a pretty noise, a slight, girlish sigh. His stomach rumbled. She made the noise again and he felt it was a cue. He kissed her where her cheekbone stood up shiny and taut.

'Good morning,' he whispered.

She stretched, and opened her eyes, which were sooty with the debris of yesterday's mascara.

'You're still here, then?' she said. He hated her a little for saying it. 'What time is it?'

'Eight. Ten past nearly.'

'Shit. I've got work this morning.'

'It's Saturday.'

'At the supermarket. I have a morning shift.' She dipped down, looking under the bed, leaving her legs in it. He wasn't sure what he should be doing. He ran his hand gently down her side, trying to do it affectionately, not lecherously, remembering her silk-slim curves. Her hipbone felt like new electrical equipment, the way it came wrapped in that soft grey almost-material. The edge of a new CD player. She made no acknowledgement of his hand, she'd found a shirt and was putting it on. 'I'm sorry, I have to get up.'

She was making it easy for him. When she was in the toilet he dressed, and she came out in a tartan dressing gown, the kind old men wore. She was pulling her hair into spikes in front of her face.

'Tell me you're not wearing my lenses,' she said.

He knew at once that he was; he squinted at her, exhausted and unfocused in front of him, and slapped himself in the head.

'You wear lenses. Jesus, I'm so stupid.' He threw off the duvet and went, naked, back into her bathroom, squeezing the hell out of his eyes, gouging with wet, fat fingers to get hold of the lenses. 'I'm sorry. I'm such a dick. Shit, where are mine?'

He couldn't see her face any more; she was standing there in front of him, blurred tartan, white blur of skin; he was projecting the expressions he imagined she'd have on to the blank. But then, he'd seen through her lenses: her eyes were nearly as bad. She was probably seeing much the same thing – lots of white skin, fuzz, the proud swing of his naked penis . . .

'I have to shower now. Um, look, this is sort of the kitchen thing through here, help yourself to anything in my fridge, if there is anything. I'm sorry to just, you know.' She walked into the kitchen. 'The, er, the shower's in here too. Try not to let that unsettle you.'

He dressed and found his own lenses – in his shoe – while she showered. He was apprehensive about going into the kitchen while she was showering there, but curious about what he'd be able to see. He reminded himself that he'd just screwed her, but that didn't really help: they had entered the formal zone. For now, every touch would feel forced and unnatural. It was a consequence of going from the mute anonymity of absolute contact to the rigorous detail of getting up. The smell of hot water reached his nostrils; he was starving and thought he might retch if he didn't eat soon, so, raising his hand to his eyeline in a gesture of chivalry, he joined her in the kitchen. There was nothing to see. Behind a perspex screen decorated with white ears of corn there was a dark green plastic shower curtain, and behind that Lainey was altering the course of the water, making splattery sounds. It wasn't a very clean kitchen – it wasn't much of a kitchen, in fact: hob, microwave, fridge, no oven, no window. She had several boxes of cereal, but they were all strange foreign varieties, with pictures of weird-looking grains. He opened her fridge. A live yoghurt (flavourless), a tub of hummus (well past the expiry date), a plastic packet of soup folded over at the top, and *nothing else*. She was a fucking lunatic. He stood up again and poured some cereal (called Kappi, but it looked like Sugar Puffs) into his hand, and went back into her living/bedroom to eat it. It tasted nothing like Sugar Puffs.

He only hoped it wasn't birdseed.

She was wearing little round glasses when she came out the shower; he could understand this – for all the skin they'd shared last night, there was something pretty disgusting about the fact that he'd had her eyes in this morning and he expected she'd be deeply disinfecting them right now. She was only wearing a towel and her skin looked opaque in the daylight, and somewhat greasy, like chicken fat. She had a few spots. With no make-up, and without her explosive hair to make her head look smaller, her eyes were too large and dark for her face. She lowered her chin shyly and he knew what he had to do.

'Hey,' he said. 'You look lovely with your hair wet.' He touched her arm as she moved to go past him and kissed her very gently, then looked into her eyes, smoothing one of her eyebrows with his thumb. She pulled the towel more tightly around her, newly coy. He moved closer, his hand between her shoulderblades, and she leaned on it while he kissed the side of her neck: her damp skin felt wonderful, tasted like peaches. His dick thought about it.

'I have to dry it,' she said, looking up at him with a fragile smile.

'Do you want me to go?'

'It would probably speed things up a bit.'

'I'll go. Can I call you?' He couldn't believe his luck; she was really throwing him out.

'If you want to.'

'I want to.'

He ran to the tube station. There was no way he was going to be able to explain himself to Ivan when he got in. It was fairly obvious where he'd been. Which meant that either they'd be double-dating or everyone was going to hate him, and whichever way he chose, it was going to be discussed into oblivion. He unlocked the door and went in to face the music. Ivan was still in bed. No, his door was open: he wasn't in bed. He hadn't come home. He'd spent the night at Chrissie's. He didn't have to know. Ivan didn't have to be told. Silly with relief, John half-skipped into the kitchen and finished the orange juice, straight from the carton without stopping. He put on the radio and found himself dancing to 'Tell Me (You're Coming Back)' by the Rolling

Stones, shouting the words tunelessly over Mick. He poured a bowl of Choco Cornflakes and started to eat them with his fingers. What he really needed right now, though, was bacon.

Ivan came in as he was laying hot rashers carefully on to soft white bread.

'I'll give you twenty quid for that sandwich,' Ivan said, and yawned.

'I slept with Lainey last night,' said John.

morning shift

It was hard to care about tofu that morning. Nobody should have to work a check-out when they've been shagged the night before. Lainey was trying to sort out her thoughts and decide what she wanted – because what she wanted was what was important here – and all the time people kept coming with seaweed and sheep's milk and multi-vitamins. She'd overcharged and undercharged all morning. If she was lucky it would all cancel out and no one would notice.

There was someone she recognized waiting to be served. It took her a moment to place him, and then she had it: he was the dark-haired boy from the party, the one who'd known Chrissie and admired the fact that she worked here. She started smiling when he reached the front of the queue and steadied his oranges on the conveyor. Peter something, she was thinking.

Peter something looked well away, so far past her that she knew he'd seen, and remembered. He handed her a twenty without moving his head an inch – so rigidly still it must have been hard for him to keep it there. Her smile turned to one of sarcastic amazement, but she didn't enjoy it. It hurt, felt like shit, and tainted and intensified the vulnerability she was already feeling about having had sex with John.

She needed a fag and a phone, and told Rosa on the next till that she had to get some air. Outside the newsagent where no one from the Real World could see her, she tore through the cellophane and lit up and dragged until she couldn't feel her head any more. In theory Lainey had given up smoking along with one-night stands and Lycra when she left college. She looked down: loose combat trousers, thank God, although two out of three wasn't good.

There wasn't going to be enough time to call Chrissie; they were allowed a fifteen-minute break, and she'd already used half of it, the rest wouldn't be enough to get through everything – including why she hadn't said anything about it before. It occurred to her that maybe John wanted to keep the secrecy thing going, although it was a bit late for that: Ivan would notice that he hadn't been home last night. Oh, fuck what John wanted and John thought: what did she want?

Well, she quite wanted Ivan, with his smooth sharp suits and straight-talking gentleness and his mysterious depths; or Dominic, and his baby-fine, squeaky-clean intelligence; she wanted Scott because she didn't want to do all the work and with Scott she wouldn't have to. And John? He had good hair. He was moody. He wanted her.

The Rules said never call – which meant that calling was, by deduction, something of a feminist crusade. A five-minute call wasn't long enough to sound desperate. She just needed to hear him speak. She called.

'Just me,' she said.

'Hey. How are you feeling?' he said.

'You're not the flu, John,' she said.

He laughed. 'Generally, though. How are you? Seeing okay without your lenses?'

'More or less.'

In the short silence, she remembered that she'd called him, and should have had something to say.

'I'm doing a gig tonight,' John said.

'Good for you,' she said, anxious that he was pre-empting her with an excuse and expecting her to want more of him. 'Where is it?'

'Camden. What time do you get off there?'

'Oh, I couldn't really, tonight. I've got some –'

'I just thought – just this minute – you might want to go for a cup of coffee when you knock off. You're sort of on my way, and we could . . . grab a quick coffee before I do my thing and you do whatever it is you're doing.'

'Go on, then.'

At six, Lainey clocked off and redid her make-up with the organic beauty samples in the aromatherapy aisle. She got to the coffee bar before he did, and woke herself up with a cup of espresso while she wondered if he was coming. She was afraid of seeing him, afraid of him looking different, because they did, after you'd slept with them. She thought he might not be as okay as she remembered. The sound system was playing Andrew Lloyd Weber songs.

He walked past the window before he saw her. He might have looked miserable and resigned, she might have imagined it.

'Hi,' he said. 'Do you want . . . ?'

She nodded. 'Cappuccino.'

'Okay.' He turned away from her. There was a sticky price label on the back of one of his jeans pockets that must have come off something else.

'Do you do the same set?' she said, as he carefully slid her cup over. 'Tonight. Will you do what Chris and I saw the other day?'

'Yeah.'

'I suppose you try out new material gradually. Just a bit at a time.'

'Yeah.'

'Have you done this place be–'

'No.' He poured two packets of sugar into his cappuccino but he didn't stir them in. He ate the chocolate-dusted foam off the top with a spoon, like an ice-cream sundae. She took her elbows off the table. 'I, er . . . had a good time yesterday – the MEAL,' his clarification coincided with the end of a song and he shouted into the quiet.

'Yeah. You get on with Chrissie?' Sounded more like an

observation, was actually more like a question: she couldn't resist. She paid attention as he answered.

'Oh yeah. Chrissie's a laugh.' Good answer. 'We should do something like that again. You think?'

'Well, I'd rather see you without Ivan and Chrissie first, I think.'

'Yeah.' They both drank some coffee. 'I'll call you, shall I? We'll fix something up.'

too early to tell

The Screwball Club in Camden was full of beautiful women. It was like a casino in a James Bond film; they lined the walls, pouting, holding drinks, laughing. John was on next and he hadn't even thought about taking a shit or vomiting. He found himself eyeing up the bag of crisps in front of some blonde's sun-kissed cleavage with an unprecedented hunger. Two minutes to stand-up and an appetite: he was hardly himself this evening.

About five minutes into his routine he spotted a friend, Ade, in the audience, and nodded to him. Ade was standing with a short good-looking man, possibly a new boyfriend, and he smirked at John and shouted, 'Get on with it! I'm getting a sore neck.'

'You know, when you say that, you sound *so* much like your sister,' John said, and people laughed. Answering heckles was usually the best thing he could do; even if his answer was rehearsed or crap, it pulled the audience on to his side – it made them aware that it was live, that they were there. Ade winked and said something into his friend's ear. The friend laughed and gripped Ade's shoulder as he answered, and John felt a chilly loneliness and wished he'd brought Lainey. He could still call her, say, Come over and stand next to me in a crowd and let me speak in your ear in public. Be with me. Or he could wait till the end of this and hope that one of the beautiful women in the audience was drunk enough to be impressed by the eight inches of microphone that gave him the edge over the other strangers in the room. There were ways of pulling within a routine: make jokes about men – how inconsiderate they were, how terrible in bed; make comparisons between the way they have sex and the way they drive, shop, iron clothes. Or find different ways to say that the sexiest actress on television is stupid and silicone-stuffed and liposucked to within an inch of her life. Those things went down well with women.

'Who are you fucking, then?' Ade asked John, after his spot. John looked startled and guilty. 'I'm right, then? I thought you looked distracted. Yes! I have the eye.'

'What are you doing here?'

'We were drinking in the pub downstairs. David lives near here – this is David, and you know more about John than you need to now – and I saw your name and said, Oh, I know him.'

'So do you fancy going back down for a pint?'

'There's three more comics to come and we had to pay to get in here – can't you get us a refund?'

'Yeah, we'll take it out of my wages,' John said, smiling.

'New girl, then?' Ade said, when they were sitting downstairs at a quiet table with three pints of lager.

'It's too early to tell,' John said, his mouth full of crisps.

'Too early to tell if you're interested or if she is?' David said.

'Both. No, I think she's . . .'

He gestured and the other men waited.

'. . . gagging for it?' Ade said. John laughed.

'Gagging for it, yes. No, I don't know. How do you tell with women?'

'You treat them like men,' Ade said. 'There's less difference than you think.'

'That's not true,' David said. 'Women play more games. They use code.'

'David zigzags,' Ade said. 'He likes oysters *and* snails.'

'Shut up, Aidan,' David said fondly. '*Have* you slept with her yet?'

'Of course he has,' Ade said. 'Didn't you see him leaning on his mike stand: that's a very post-coital stance. Post being within the last week, in John's case.'

'Stop it, Ade, you're scaring me. When did you start being good at psychology?' John said. Ade had a degree in it: a third. They'd been friends since university.

'I *am* good. It's the tutors who were small. You know, you get no extra points for writing good essays, they just wanted half a page of unoriginal writing and fifteen pages of footnotes and references,' Ade said. When he started talking about how he was cheated out of a 2:1 it was hard to stop him.

'So tell me, then, Sigmund. Sometimes I think I like her. Do I?'

'How did you feel the morning after?' David asked him.

'Oops.'

'That's fairly normal, isn't it?' David said, turning to Ade.

'Oh yeah, that's no way of telling. Bring her out with us. I'll let you know if she's right for you,' Ade said.

'As if I'm going to do that,' John said.

'Well, bring her out anyway. And Ivan. We hardly ever see him now he's got himself stuck with that tart Chrissie. You'll like Ivan,' he said to David.

'We'll do that. I should get back anyway now. I haven't slept properly in days.'

'You dog,' Ade said. 'I hope you called to thank her.'

'She called me – already,' John said, and frowned because this was a bad thing. 'I've lost her home number.' In fact, he'd thrown it away. 'Jesus. I'm going to have to get it off Chrissie. And Chrissie's going to want to talk.'

'Dum dum duuuh!' said David. 'Sorry, I don't even know Chrissie. You just made it sound as if that was a scary thing.'

'She's Chrissie's friend?' Ade said. 'How cosy.'

you get to choose

'It happened. I let him in,' Chrissie said. Their phone conversations were always briskly to the point; no need for hello or identification. For Lainey it was both awkward and savoury that she had information to trump Chrissie's now humdrum revelation. She had to pick the moment carefully; too early would be rude upfront, too late would be rude in retrospect, it would look patronizing. But too late would have to do; Chrissie could survive being patronized.

'Oh my God. Ivan got through. Did he like your flat? Could you stand having him in there?'

Chrissie didn't like letting people in. It wasn't that she lived in a mess, although she did, it was that she lived in a state of permanent and advanced privacy. Lainey knew Chrissie didn't mind having her for a few hours, but she felt in the way if she stayed all night. Chrissie would start to suffocate under her own secrecy; she stuffed things in her bedroom when people were there – underwear, laundry, food, pills, face-packs, letters, bills – but these things were a part of her, they needed to breathe too. She was always relieved when people said they had to go home. Ivan, of course, would have gone into the bedroom, and Lainey wondered where Chrissie had hidden herself . . . unless, that was, she let him see it all, the whole Chrissie experience, the bits Lainey only glimpsed through a thin sliver of hastily closed bedroom door. The idea hurt her feelings, fleetingly.

But she had a better story. For months she'd been forced to enthuse about Chrissie's back-to-back pay rises while she stacked rice cakes. Now she could strike back with a legitimate upstage; it was just a question of prudent scheduling.

'What do you mean, could I stand him?' Chrissie said.

'Oh, you know what you're like.'

'You mean . . . ? I suppose I know what you mean. But it was . . . it was as if I was normal. By the way, did you get on okay with John after we left you?'

Chrissie was interrupting her story to add suspense, not because she was interested. So it was only fair that Lainey should milk her lines too.

'Chrissie, there's something you should know,' she said, and sighed. 'Something big. God, I don't want to tell you.'

'What is it?'

'It's John.'

'What about John? Did he try it on? You didn't sleep with him, I hope?' She paused for confirmation. Lainey left an inch of silence. 'Why the fuck would you do that?'

'He just . . . We were . . . You know, actually, it was nice. He's, um, actually pretty okay at it.'

Chrissie sounded kinder, smiling as she said, 'Oh, that makes it all okay, then. Really, Laine, what the fuck? I didn't even know you liked him. You didn't say.'

'I didn't know. I didn't. Until yesterday.'

'You've hardly spoken to him. You hardly know him.'

'This is kind of awkward, Chrissie, but I do. And it's about time you knew. John and I went on a date. A week ago. I didn't tell you then because I thought you might offer me advice, and I just didn't want advice then, and John asked me not to tell you, and it seemed like a laugh, but we didn't get on at all, and I didn't want to mention it, because it didn't seem worth mentioning. Anyway, I was waiting for him to make me think it hadn't been a mistake, but nothing was happening. And then last night, we just got it together, and it was right. And I had a good time, so what's the problem?'

'I think women kid themselves that these just-for-fun fucks are a good idea, and I think they're lying. And I mean you. Because women always want there to be a context. And I mean you,' Chrissie said.

'There was a context, I told you. We'd gone out. It wasn't like a . . . What do you mean by a context?'

'Like, oh I don't know, like, wouldn't it be better if you maybe thought for a second that something was going to come out of it?'

'I do. Of course I do.' She wasn't sure she believed this, but didn't want Chrissie's context idea to get a grip. She didn't want Chrissie to know that he'd changed already. She wanted to look as if she had no regrets. 'But actually, even if nothing happens, I don't care. I had fun. You know what was good about it? *I* was *very* good. Being with him made me better. And that has to be good, doesn't it?'

Chrissie sounded okay for a bit, and then her mood blackened again. She was flipping back and forth, scary and nice, nice and scary. 'You've made things very untidy,' she said. 'Are you going to keep on with this?'

'It depends on him.'

'It doesn't fucking depend on him,' Chrissie said. 'What does he have to do with it?'

'Oh, you know, a *bit*. If he wants to see me again, then yes, I probably liked him enough.'

'If *he* wants to see *you* again? Why would he not?'

This sort of thing was fun, Chrissie being sternly flattering.

'Well, because he's seen me naked, there's a reason right there. Because, believe it or not, there are times when men have sex with a girl once and that's that.' She thought of John, monosyllabic over cappuccino, and tried to phrase it so she wouldn't look stupid, whatever happened.

'You get to choose,' Chrissie said, kinder again, voice like ointment.

'I hope so.'

'Do you want me to call him? Speak to him?'

'Please don't.'

'I can't pretend I don't know. You know I don't lie very well, I have to tell the truth – all of it.'

'I suppose you're going round to Ivan's tonight.'

'I'm seeing him.'

'Just wait, Chrissie. Don't say anything first, that's all I ask.'

'And what are you going to do?'

'I'm just going to see what happens.'

'Okay. Don't go calling him.'

'Oh, Chrissie, that's so Rules,' Lainey said. She felt hot all over. 'Of course I won't.'

munchies

When John came in he was very drunk, because Ade, being fairly fat, could hold his liquor, but being fairly fey, invited competition. Chrissie was in the lotus position on the sofa.

'John's back,' she called out to an invisible Ivan. She didn't say anything to John.

'Munchies, John?' Ivan shouted from the kitchen.

'I wish he'd drop the drug culture vocab,' Chrissie said; it could have been to herself.

Ivan came in with a plate of bruschetta. John could see freshly torn basil on it.

'Strictly speaking, this isn't munchies. As far as I know, you still can't buy this at a twenty-four hour garage,' John said. He took a piece and munched loudly. He could feel Chrissie staring at him, waiting. But the bastard in him, the part that had so recently been turned off by the rough mess of a morning girl, was feeling insolent. It felt like coming home late to an anxious bollocking from his parents, only this time he could act the way he always should have. So he shrugged and ate and let Chrissie do the emotion.

'So,' Ivan said, with laddish solidarity.

'So.' Chrissie looked up at Ivan and sucked her finger.

'Well?' John said.

'Well, John, you sod. What do you think you're doing with my best friend?' She sounded fierce, but didn't look it.

112

'I hardly think,' John said, alcohol formal, 'that this is your concern, Chrissie. We have to do this without –'

'You bastard, John. Unless you're not, in which case this is *almost* sweet. A bit too neat, but anyway. I don't think you meant it, though.'

'Meant what?'

'Whatever bullshit you came out with, when you *seduced* her. Any of it.' There was a lively smirk on Chrissie's clever mouth that wasn't entirely decent; she was having fun. John was more offended than turned on. Just.

'Chrissie. Whatever's going on between me and Lainey now is our business. We don't have to talk to you about it. So you can stop this, this, because I'm not going to play. But, if it puts your mind at all at ease, I find your little friend captivating. I think she's very attractive. And I'd like to see her again.'

The drunker he'd become that evening, the more John'd started persuading himself that he really could go for Lainey. While he'd been defending her against the innate misogyny of his gay friend, she'd grown more attractive. Now, here, with Chrissie and Ivan's para-marital vanity in his face, he wanted to claim emotions of his own to play with. He wanted Chrissie to believe he was capable of crushes on women who weren't her.

Chrissie said nothing. She'd stopped smiling.

a hostile sex

'Anything exciting happen over the wee–?' Lainey began, and stopped because Scott was shushing her.

'Theo's getting a pasting,' he whispered. Somewhere, a wall or two away, Clare was shouting. Lainey put her bag down quietly, and they listened in silence, although she couldn't hear any actual words. The shouting stopped. The sound of someone coming downstairs.

'Look. Fucking. Busy,' Scott said.

Theo was hot and bothered, but he didn't want to talk about it. The abrupt silence that met him in the office assured him he was the only one.

'I'm, um, I'm going out to get some, to get some, some, I'm going home early today,' he said.

'Is everything all right?' Scott said. Theo walked past without looking. He pulled the door hard behind him so that it thrust a breeze into the room and Lainey flinched, but he brought it to a virtual stop an inch away from impact, and left it slightly ajar.

Lainey sat down and opened the mail, beginning with the parcels, which tended to be more exciting: books and videos that distributors wanted *Brazen* to plug. There was often something that would attract Scott or Dominic. Scott had already moved into position behind her, the warmth of his body just about palpable on her shoulder.

'Trouble at mill,' he said, vowels as dense as Eccles cakes. He reached over to pick up an 8 × 10 of Gillian Anderson. 'Scully gives good monotone, but she doesn't really do anything for me.'

'What were they arguing about?' Lainey said, twisting her neck, more to feel than to see him.

'Arguing implies a two-way thing.'

'What does she think he's done?'

'They don't talk about it to us. Maybe they're having a horrid affair.'

'Torrid aff . . . oh.' She reddened because she'd tried to correct him. 'Well, it's awkward, isn't it? Is he coming back? It doesn't help that it's Clare's flat. I always feel like I'm at somebody's for tea.'

'Uncomfortable silences broken by the crunching of custard creams,' Scott said.

'Exactly.'

'Waiting for your mother to get up and say she really has to get back now.'

'Yes.'

'And you're there with your flat pop and chocolate fingers and nothing to do until it's time to go – what were you like as a little girl, little Lainey?' He was still standing behind her; she couldn't see his expression.

'Certain. I'm never sure about anything any more.'

'You know what the problem is, there?'

'Tell me.'

'Other people. Kids only think about themselves. Women are always thinking about everyone else. Solution? Forget the others. Don't listen to them, don't pay any attention. Be like a man – we're sure about everything. That's true, isn't it, Dom?'

Dom didn't lift his eyes from the computer screen. 'I couldn't really say either way,' he said.

Later, Dominic and Scott found their way into a dirty chat room for sci-fi enthusiasts on the internet, but she was too busy to join them. She was scanning pictures, which was dull and took for ever. It was a physical job, requiring little concentration – she just slapped the picture on and pressed buttons – but there was a lot of big arm movement. It looked like hard work, leaving her in the optimum position to eavesdrop on the boys.

To an extent, John had spoiled her enjoyment of them, he'd invaded her thoughts and was setting up camp there. She was in the state of suspended suspicion that came with new romance. As Dom and Scott collaborated on increasingly stupid sexual claims in their chat room ('Tell them that since you were visited by aliens you can only get aroused by anal probing with metallic instruments'), she juggled her amusement with insecurity and doubt. Men were different. Heterosexuality was just a big mad idea, doomed from the start. John hadn't called at the weekend, and now, an hour into Monday, he had not called her here, where there was no excuse.

John was a weird bastard too. He did his weird stand-up where he made out he was savage and sardonic, and then he was sweet and shy when they were alone. Or, like before, he was cold and indifferent – defensively quiet, the friendless kid in school. Perhaps the parts he showed when he was alone with her were the act. She wasn't sure why he'd wanted her; maybe because, as Chrissie said, he was attracted to Chrissie, and maybe she was a substitute of sorts. She didn't look like Chrissie, but to an unpractised eye their humour matched, they were both flaky and random. They got on; they were like each other. It could have been that John, after an evening of seeing Chrissie at her best, simply reached out for the nearest alternative. And now he'd changed his mind, he'd tired of Panda Cola: he wanted the Real Thing.

Her own motives were no more pristine. If John had a different agenda, it was probably an indication that they were a better match than she'd first guessed. After all, she had probably pursued John because Chrissie had already claimed him. Changing his mind had been the primary appeal, his apparent interest had been secondary. His character, his slow, probing stare, even his good hair – those things had hardly had a look in. They'd been part of a pleasant recollection the morning after, when he'd seen her in glasses and managed to look convincingly lustful. In fact, wasn't she just working her way up to trying to steal Ivan? She'd already admired him, blinked a few too many times when he asked her a question, and stolen a chip from his plate because 1) it was an act of blatant flirtation; 2) Chrissie's healthy appetite was beginning to look seductively hedonistic and she didn't want to look anorectic and inhibited; and 3) fat, particularly salty fat, made her lips redden and swell. Trollop. She'd been willing him to want her, arranging herself in the candlelight, giving the full big-eyed effect . . . and then she'd gone home with his best friend. God help them, she and John were made for each other.

She slapped another photograph on to the scanner and let the lid slam. Clare came into the room just in time to hear it, and looked appalled.

'You should close that scanner door slowly, really, Elaine. It might damage the screen, or weaken the hinge,' she said. 'Did . . .' She glanced around shiftily, presumably looking for Theo. 'Did Jen Mortenson fax in her piece on star cameos yet?'

Clare wasn't behaving normally. She hadn't quite managed to strike fear into Lainey with her scanner warning, and seemed genuinely surprised that Theo wasn't there. Her flesh hung looser, as if the surface tension of her skin had broken. She made her way to the kitchen and asked everyone if they wanted coffee. Usually they had Nescafé at the office, but today Clare took out a shining cafetière and spooned in some Starbucks Colombian.

'I take it Theo outlined the bare facts of our disagreement,' she said, concentrating on the coffee. For a while no one answered.

'Theo left early today,' Scott said. 'He didn't tell us where he was going. He didn't say anything, actually.'

Clare appeared to be treading the outskirts of vulnerability. Lainey slowly raised her head, trying to coax something out of her, something ordinary, something female. Women were supposed to crack in public and admit defeat, blame hormones, show some hurt. They were a hostile sex; frailty rendered them sociable. Clare narrowed her eyes and sniffed.

'Well, then. I expect we'll all have to work a bit later today,' she said brightly, and pushed down the plunger.

interference

At half past two John cracked his knuckles and dialled Lainey's number. A man answered.

'*Brazen.*'

'Ah, is Lainey there, please?' He sounded like a DJ, all lilt and warmth, and he didn't even know her surname. He'd have to remember to find out, subtly.

'I think she's around . . . Who can I say's calling?'

Oh shit, he hated that.

'Tell her it's John Truelove.' He heard a hand fold over the receiver.

'What's with the comedy name?' she said quietly, when the hand had been removed.

'It's my name. I use a different one when I'm doing stand-up because Truelove sounds too much like a comedy name. A bad one at that.'

'It's pretty.'

'Yes, and it's important for a man to have a pretty name. At school I was the envy of the football team.'

'Good weekend?'

'Yes. Well, I didn't really do anything on Sunday. I would have called you at home except I lost your number.'

He actually heard her eyes roll. 'Do you want it again?'

'Unless you prefer talking to me at work.'

'Anyway, I suppose you know I told Chrissie,' Lainey said. He wished they didn't have to mention Chrissie, but realistically there was no choice. She was what they had in common.

'She did mention it, yes.'

'You saw Chrissie this weekend?'

'Briefly, Saturday night.'

'What did she say?'

'I really can't remember. I think she sounded surprised.'

'Yeah, she was definitely surprised.'

'It's got nothing to do with Chrissie. I don't care how surprised she is.' This was a good thing to say: make her think he didn't like Chrissie. 'Anyway, I suppose you can't really talk at work. So the reason I called, I wondered if you were free this week.'

'What did you have in mind?'

'Drink? Walk along the river?'

'Yes, please.'

Sunday morning, after his Guinness binge with Ade, the battered memory of maybe shouting about how much he was into Lainey had come back to him like someone else's slide show: a series of unconnected images projected over a vague sense of torture. He couldn't remember where all the vehemence had come from, but it had happened, and he'd woken up feeling trembly, with a stale taste in his mouth. He wouldn't have called her today if it hadn't been for all the mess around them. He didn't feel ready. He didn't think he liked her enough. But there was Chrissie and Ivan – the complications – and the only decent thing to do was to take her out again and let her notice that they weren't compatible and then they could put a stop to it civilly. Doing the right thing was helping to offset the regret; made him feel noble. He might even be able to manipulate *her* into doing it for him. Still, here and there were things about her that struck him as pretty good.

He was in the middle of transferring the company's address books on to a file-making programme, and he couldn't concentrate. There was no time any more. He had two jobs (except one was his vocation, he just didn't know which) and now he had to manage a sex life at the same time. Getting what you wanted was too much like binge eating: it felt compulsive but was actually boring and, fairly quickly, it started to hurt. Which reminded him, he had a Rice Krispies square in his drawer.

'Are you doing your stand-up comedy tonight?' Samantha the temp asked him, as he struggled with the sticky wrapper.

'Wednesday,' he said.

'It's just I was thinking of dragging my friends along to see you.' She smiled. He realized she probably fancied him – the bus rule – and smiled back. She was a blonde in every conceivable way and, as such, inevitably tempting. 'Are you funny?'

'Who do you think is funny?' he said.

She chewed the end of a Bic and thought about it, listing some television comics who had left the circuit years ago: big names.

'They are funny, yes,' he said. Samantha was a poor little rich girl – she'd have been the least wealthy at her private school and felt deprived ever since. She was slumming it here, waiting for the right PR job. London was full of people like her, keeping with bad companies, treading water until they were discovered. Half the graduates he knew were temping. Samantha was never going to be discovered: she lacked the minimum qualifications – arrogance and good legs; if she hadn't networked her way in by now, she never would. She had perfect teeth and the promise of pliability, but she was a little heavy-looking – not really fat but sturdy – and the slowness in her shiny blue eyes looked potentially annoying. He thought of Lainey with her waifish prickliness, the comprehensive-school paranoia and cakey mascara. Her fat lips. 'I think you might find my stuff a bit disappointing.'

'Aren't you even going to tell me where you're on? Does it put you off having people you know there?'

He sniff-laughed, flattered by her persistence.

'You can come along if you like. The Jimmy Ha Ha off Old Street. Do you think your friends will go that far east?'

'Umm, maybe not,' she said. 'I'll do my best to talk them round.'

*

'I think I've discovered the secret of your appeal,' John said when Ivan came in, kicking off his JP Tod's and unbuttoning his dark carmine shirt.

'What appeal?'

'The girls at work who keep touching you in the West End. It's because you always have a girlfriend on the go. Women can sense it. They pick it up with their pheromones.'

'Pheromones are something you give out, you don't receive with them. So who's been touching your West End?' Ivan's voice got louder as he went into his bedroom. He came back wearing sweats.

'Blonde at work looking a bit keen,' John said.

'And?'

'I'm not *doing* anything. It's just, now I have a choice.'

'So the Lainey deal's on, is it?'

'Gaah, I'm never sure. It is with her. Maybe that's the trouble.'

Ivan sat down and reached for his tobacco. He rolled a beautiful cigarette, drawing his tongue very slowly along the edge to seal it.

'That's not the trouble. When it's the right person, the fact that she's keen isn't a problem, it's a fucking miracle.' He leaned back and inhaled, blowing out bluey insight with frustrating inner peace. 'Go with the blonde.'

'I'm not going with the blonde,' John said. 'Maybe that's just you. Are you talking about Chrissie? Is she the right person?'

Ivan pinched a piece of tobacco off his tongue. 'Chrissie's for keeps,' he said.

If John were to choose one emotion out of all the feelings he had about Ivan's seriousness with Chrissie, one emotion that was king of all the other emotions, it would be fear. He'd felt it like this when he was eight and his parents divorced: fear of being homeless. Ivan was moving on and there was no place for Ivan and John in Ivan and Chrissie's brave new future. It was the end of term and he hadn't been paying attention all year. In some ways, their affair gave him hope; the sheer romance of it all, the neatness. It let him keep believing all the stupid stuff that seemed stupider every year – things like chemistry and fate, things like love. Before Ivan found Chrissie, John believed that people in love manipulated coincidence to pretend something special was happening to them. They took dreary detail and blew it up into kismet. Really, they were just using the safety of their deadlocks to console themselves for giving up the game – even though the game was what made it all worth while. The uncertainty was the best part, and they knew it. John assumed he wanted long-term, but every time it was dangled he turned away. What made this time so frightening was that there was no reason to reject Lainey. She looked good enough, she was clever enough, she behaved as if she understood him, she wasn't even partly a nightmare. Why, then, was he holding back? It couldn't be Chrissie, because Chrissie was a mate now, an extension of Ivan that he just happened to masturbate over. So what, then – God, don't tell him he was really such a cliché – not the commitment thing?

'But for the rest of your life,' John said. 'One girl.'

'As far as I'm concerned,' Ivan said, 'Chrissie's the only girl. The rest of them are just interference.' He smoked quietly for a minute, and they both made up their own double entendres, and laughed loudly, breaking the tension of Ivan's romantic excess.

'The rest of them. Meaning there are still other women. Ivan, you're not telling me you're not still fucking other women. You stay out without Chrissie all the time. It's always work, is it?'

Ivan looked irritated. 'Yes, it's always fucking work.'

'Okay.'

'I know what you're saying,' Ivan said. 'But you're missing the point, anyway. The reason fucking around starts looking good at a time like this is that I suddenly don't need to any more. When you're with the right person, sex with anyone else means nothing. It's more of an option *because* it means nothing. You think it couldn't hurt; you think she'd understand if you did it because she knows she's the one who matters. She knows they don't matter. Or she should. But she wouldn't understand. And it could hurt.' He sighed.

'But you want to. In a year's time you'll –'

'In a year's time I'm not going to feel any different.'

Ivan's mouth twitched, down and to the left. John had managed to depress both of them.

Fate was all well and good, but the biggest factor in Chrissie's rightness and Lainey's not-quiteness was timing. Ivan was ready, John wasn't. Ivan had been around the block enough to make monogamy look like deviation, which was why he could do it. But John hadn't seen enough matching underwear or woken up in enough postcodes. What he was going through was normal. So maybe he'd look into Samantha.

two friends liking
two friends

Chrissie had made a jug of raspberry Martinis, which were so fresh that just looking at the seeds floating on the pink foam was making Lainey's mouth water. She'd also put out iced fairy cakes, Maltesers and cheesy puffs.

'How are you not as fat as a horse?' Lainey said, taking a Malteser.

'I am fat. Compared to you,' Chrissie said, taking a handful.

'Don't be stupid. You're fabulous, *and* you know it. I meant fat, like Clare's fat. If you eat —'

'I wear size fourteens.'

'You're tall. You have breasts.'

'You don't want breasts. More trouble than they're worth. Go on in, I'll bring this.'

Chrissie had the catering sophistication of a five-year-old with a taste for hard liquor, but Lainey thought the kitsch probably wasn't deliberate. Chrissie's mother had died when she was very small: Lainey guessed she was making up for birthday parties she'd never had. Chrissie put the tray between them and poured a couple of Martinis. She gave one to Lainey; the cocktail glass was incredibly light. Lainey felt the slightest pressure might crush it.

'Where do you think you're up to with John?' Chrissie said.

Lainey spilled raspberry juice on her trousers. She rubbed it in with her thumb. 'What are you calling him now?'

'I'm calling him John. I saw him a couple of days ago. And we're going out this week.'

'When? Where are you going?'

'Well, he's got gigs tonight and tomorrow. So later in the week. He was talking about the Brando season at the NFT, or the open-air cinema, so that, maybe. I'm not sure.'

'It's something of a lucky coincidence, isn't it? Two friends liking two friends.'

Lainey didn't like Chrissie's tone.

'People are friends because they have stuff in common, aren't they?'

'I'm just worried that – don't get me wrong, I'm sure he fancies you,' Chrissie began, and Lainey was irate, thinking: how did we get to having to reassure me that John fancies me? When was that in doubt? 'I just worry that it was all too easy for John. He sees this set-up, he knows you'll trust him by association with Ivan, it's like the groundwork's already done for him, isn't it? So he pushes it.'

'You think so, do you?'

'I don't know, Laine. I just want you to not confuse him with Ivan.'

'I don't want Ivan,' she said meekly, afraid she might not sound convincing.

'Christ, I know you don't want *Ivan*,' Chrissie said impatiently. 'What I mean is, you know I have this perfect relationship' – she waggled her head and did a funny voice over the word 'perfect' – 'and I just worry you'll assume John's the same person. That you can extend the Ivan rules to John. But John's just a bloke. He could be just trying it on while the conditions are good. I just want you to know that.'

'You said – before – you said I got to choose.'

'Yes, you get to choose. But make it an informed choice. It doesn't hurt to know what's going on.'

'And you'd know, I suppose.' Emptied of its contents, the glass was very fragile. Her ring tinked on it. She loosened her grip.

'I know what men are like, that's all. Men like having sex. Discount all their nobler feelings, because that's the only one you need to know about.'

'Chrissie, love, women like it too.'

'Yes, sure they do. But you know what I mean.'

'And sometimes men quite like the woman they want to have sex with.'

'Do you remember when I was doing work experience with that PR company, years ago, and I called you in the middle of the night and cried because the boss wanted to have sex with me?'

Lainey laughed. 'You *did* cry, didn't you? You woke me up and you were sobbing. Why were you crying so hard?'

'Because I was sloshed and thought I'd have to screw him. And you said he probably tried it with all the work-experience girls.'

'What did I know?'

'You were right. But I thought you were being a bitch, and I told you that I was different, and he could see it, and he was really genuine. But I still believed you, and I sent him home.'

'I was being a bitch, Chris. I'm sorry. I didn't see it then, but I see it now. He probably *did* think you were different. You are; he'd have seen that.'

'You weren't a bitch. You were right. I have no doubt he tried to fuck all the work experiences.'

'I *was* a bitch.'

'Look, forget that. You saved me from myself, Mack. Let me do it back.'

'I am glad you didn't sleep with him. He was definitely dodgy. I'm just ashamed that I was so bitchy about it –'

'You weren't. So don't be.'

'But look, this isn't the same thing. I don't need saving from myself.'

'Or from PR execs.'

'Or from comics.'

Shared history just has the edge on compatibility when it

comes to friendship. You can only agree for so long, but you can talk about people who've wronged you until the last breath leaves your body. Chrissie and Lainey still had plenty of energy left for the kids at college they'd both hated, who'd hated them both first. They liked chewing over the possibility of getting in touch with college people again. But, though they never admitted as much, they weren't really in a position to call anyone – they hadn't been liked enough. In fact, Lainey had always thought they thought *she* was okay, but she was relegated by association with Chrissie, who wasn't really. What tempted them to go back was that, now, they both had an idea of how attractive they were. They wanted another shot, armed with this knowledge. In the old days, mutual praise had sustained their closeness, but neither of them had swallowed it. It had taken the grown-up world, with its men who judged on appearances and were only after one thing, to make them feel pretty. If they'd known at sixteen what they knew now, they'd have strutted, instead of skulking with make-do self-sufficiency. They'd have been ruder. Meaner. But they probably couldn't have laughed more. Even now, trigger words took them back to that sore, hysterical paralysis. Restriction intensifies pleasure. It's harder to laugh like that when you're perfectly popular, because there's no real reason not to, no fear that you'll be heard and hated for it. It's the fear of discovery, the fear of getting it wrong, that makes the laughter so narcotic. Chrissie and Lainey had done enough to live off it for years. It was just a question of how many.

'You're right,' Lainey said, feeling a need to concede something. 'I don't know anything about John except that he's your friend – Ivan's friend. But we get on, and he's good to me. A little short but –'

'Don't use that expression ever again when you're with me,' Chrissie said, looking like electricity. 'He's good to me? What are you, a battered wife? Why the fuck would anyone spend time with anyone who isn't *good* to them? That's a fucking given.'

'You're overreacting, Chris.'

'It just makes me mad,' Chrissie said. 'How is that any kind of character appraisal? He doesn't slap me around or steal my money, so I should be grateful. I really hate women sometimes.'

'No, really? You'd never have guessed.'

'You know, if I had to worry about whether Ivan was good to me, I'd . . .' Chrissie trailed off, but not before they'd both heard her voice break. Lainey knew her friend, she'd seen her when she was vulnerable, and unsure – but not for a while. It felt wrong. Chrissie was so sure of everything, all the time, all her life; and now there was Ivan. He made Chrissie more like her; made Chrissie feel.

the chance to grow

Samantha hadn't brought her friends, or herself, which
pretty much put the kibosh on that. John was trying to muster
some disappointment, but all he could feel was relief. When a
couple of the other comics asked him if he wanted to come with
them to their private members' club, he almost refused. But there
was something about the place. Mildly infamous, but always
disappointing – no debauchery, no fist fights, just middle-aged
people sitting around on clean sofas, smoking and chatting, sotto
charlie, here and there – it still felt, more than anywhere else in
London, like success. John blamed the anticlimactic tidiness on
the drugs. Really glamorous self-destruction was still best
exemplified by drink, by marinading yourself until your face
looked like your liver. There wasn't enough of this about any
more, outside of the parks and the run of doorways and bins
around his house. In those sorts of places, where there was no
intelligence to be found with it, alcohol was just sad and dirty.
When smart people made foolish choices, it was stylish, like
models wearing gold lamé slippers, or Ivan wearing cardigans.
Real drunks were just drunks; clever drunks were making a
fashion statement. Here, among the people who made fashion,
expensive drugs were making too many of them look like
schoolboys and ponces. It was disappointing, but he was still
there. And he did all the same gear, as much as he could, if he
could afford it, or if Ivan had had a good week – he just expected

more of other people. It was a nostalgia thing, really: modernity always had a habit of looking like an upstart.

The comedians talked about women, about Edinburgh, about drugs, but mostly about films – stand-ups love films. They laughed together and it sounded like smokers' hacking, grey and sore. John caught the eye of an old man at the bar. Gay, evidently – his full head of pageboy-length white hair would have given the game away if the proposition in his watery blue gaze hadn't spoken first. John could have seen a fair bit more action if he'd been gay, Ade had said. Height wasn't such a problem and his simmering introspection was looked on affectionately, as if it were the vulnerable brooding of a teenager. He looked away, callously, turning his own predatory glare on the neat round arse of the prettiest waitress to assert his masculinity, although he flushed with guilt and scratched his ear when she came in their direction. This big, endless urge that was male heterosexuality – that was supposed to be unstoppable, unsuppressable, unreasonable – had a habit of turning bunny-soft with the slightest hint of social exposure. No more primitive or violent than any other selfishness. The penis could listen to reason. John was more than his hormones, and men who pretended they weren't were fooling themselves, or doing their best to fool everyone else.

Lainey Mackerras – Mackerras: she'd whispered it to him at work today, like blowing a kiss down the line – was affecting him. She had become a possibility. He hadn't had one of those in a long time. He could hold out for something surer, but he could be waiting for ever, and he'd have given Lainey up to keep her from getting close. Couldn't he just keep her instead? He was seeing her on Friday night. With any luck, he'd look at her and just know.

So for the rest of the evening he lost interest in the scene that used to hypnotize him. He listened to the empty warmth and leavened ranting of his peers and thought about Lainey. He watched the waitress, and although his gaze rested at the point where the short black skirt polished the long black thighs, even now he supposed he was beginning to understand how she felt as a person, and the smile he gave her was not rapacious but sympathetic. He was being offered the chance to grow. He'd start tomorrow.

'Tell me about your childhood.'

'No,' Lainey said. She was clearly in a negative mood – she had refused the offer of the open-air cinema, preferring to just walk, because she said she didn't like people who needed the sort of excuse to not talk for the first half of the date that also gave them an excuse to talk for the second half. 'I prefer making it up as I go along,' she'd said.

'Why won't you?' John said now. 'Are you afraid of giving yourself away?'

'No, I don't think you're that perceptive. I've never met a man who was.' Here he allowed himself the secret smile of the underestimated. 'I just don't think it's as important as people say. You change too much afterwards for it to matter.'

'Not true,' John said. 'You don't change, you just get hammered a bit by life.'

'And what's hammered you?'

'Well I . . .' He stopped himself. He wanted to keep it light because light was in control. The thing about women was you could spend half an hour with one and be lured into laying your soul on the line; they devoured emotions with the same offhand enthusiasm that they had for snacking on soap operas. It was too easy to come out with that sort of crap to women. You began it to get them on your side, to choreograph their sympathy, and before you knew it they were moving on, and you were thinking: no wait, we were talking about *me*, don't stop now, I have so much more to tell. 'My trouble is, I probably haven't had it hard enough.'

Lainey smiled and took a packet of Camels out of her bag. She offered him one, and he shook his head.

'You sound like you feel deprived,' she said.

'No, but pain makes you more creative, doesn't it?'

'So they say. But people who haven't had much are so sensitive to it that the slightest knock-back probably feels like a kick in the face. So they're not losing out, are they? They just have a different frame of reference.'

'You really think that everyone feels the same pain, no matter how hard their lives have been?'

'No, I don't. But I don't think that the people who feel the most pain are necessarily the people who've had the hardest lives. Some people are stronger than others.'

'You didn't smoke the first night I met you.'

'I didn't smoke that night. I'd stopped. I started again recently.'

'Why?'

'Does it bother you?'

'Would you stop if it did?'

'Would you expect me to? This is fun, isn't it?' Lainey said. 'Who's going to answer a question first?'

'Well, it's not going to be me – shit, it just was, wasn't it?' John said, and was pleased to see he'd made her smile. 'It doesn't bother me, and I wouldn't ask you to stop. I'm just wondering what would make someone start smoking again. How long had you stopped for? Not that long?'

'Two years,' she said. 'I'm not sure why I felt the need again. Stress of two jobs, maybe. Anyway, I'm not addicted, I never was.'

'I could stop anytime . . .'

'No, I could. But when something feels this good, why stop?'

He kissed her. It was not a long kiss, but he meant it. And it did taste like kissing an ashtray, but that wasn't a problem. She took a moment before she lifted her cigarette to her mouth again.

The object of the evening, John reminded himself, had been to see how he felt – no, before that, the object had been to bore her senseless so she'd never want to see him again, but there was no way he could have seen that one through, he was too interesting. So, the revised plan had been to take stock, and here he was taking advantage. He could hardly wait, he couldn't wait to take her back home. There was something about her that made all his doubts irrelevant. Even though he knew he was going to regret it, he knew there was no way he'd be able to not sleep with her tonight. She was so sexy, bad-girl sexy, with her virtuous brow and her rough and ready heroin-chic body. With Chrissie, the appeal was in her wise eyes, and lush abundance. With Lainey, it was as if everything natural in her was crying out for hard core while she looked on with her sensible English reserve, slightly appalled by it all. There was nothing more alluring than contradiction: it was the closest someone like him would ever get to two women at once.

The park was dark blue and full of lovers. He had never brought a girl here before, and he had never before felt so pleased with himself here. It was his park: he felt a proprietary self-righteousness about it, but also, usually, embarrassed to be doing the same circuit as the foreign men who cruised all the time. Not today: today he had a girl with him, and he was in the park for all the right reasons. Although he wasn't falling in love with Lainey, he was coming round to the idea of commitment. Permanent public acceptance, licence to do anything you wanted. Everything that was furtive and shameful about being a single man could be wiped out in one move. If only you didn't have to wake up with them.

He felt her start to shiver, and knew he'd have to take her somewhere warmer.

'You're cold. There's a pool bar not far from here. You fancy it?'

'Do I have to play pool?'

'No.'

'Do I have to watch you play it?'

'It's just a bar. Come on.' He was making decisions and, unusually, enjoying it. He held her hand, and saw her look at him, obviously pleased. This was too fucking easy.

'You live round here, then, you and Ivan?'

'Not too far from here. I'll show you, if you like. But let's have a drink first.'

*

With the tangerine baize reflecting in her Barbarella hair and her slim hands *presumably* aware of their tease on the cider bottle, he counted down the minutes until a legitimate pounce or a filthy suggestion wouldn't be out of place. He wanted to tell her she looked very beautiful, but he was too British. British men couldn't say things like that. First, it sounded like a line, and British men cared about originality. Apart from stupid people, who strung together clichés for conversation, the British didn't like the thought of going down someone else's route; it was tacky. And second, the other thing about being British, was the nagging suspicion that sex *was* harassment. Of all the countries in the world, only Britain had taken feminism seriously at street level. Your continentals didn't care, with their bikini-wrapped silicone on every game show and billboard, while in America, all that po-faced caution only demonstrated how liberated no one was. American sitcoms still had girls v. boys plots – battles of the sexes – plots they'd thrown away here around the time of *On the Buses*. John was left with the dilemma that the British were keeping alive: how to come on strong without seeming either trite or interested. It was what made the country great.

Ivan had told him once that the only way to seduce women was to use their methods against them. Women were trained from their teens to look fascinated by men, to nod and agree, and make their date feel clever. Ivan said that Oscar Wilde was well out – women were just as disarmed by flattery, if not more, because flattery could change a woman's character, while the most it could do to a man's was reveal it. But women were like aphids – you had to use flattery they weren't already immune to. And they weren't expecting their own flirt-by-numbers right back at them. One hour of being interested, Ivan said, is worth ten of being interesting. It was a nice idea, and John had no doubt that every word was true, but he was a comedian. He couldn't stand empty silences – they felt like dying – and he thought other people expected him to make the noise, to 'do' the conversation.

Every time Lainey turned up when she said she would, she took away more of John's insecurity, leaving complacency with the run of the place. He was never going to have a better chance to try out Ivan's advice. He could let her do the talking, and persuade her she was clever. He could bat his eyelids (bat? was that what they did?) and see what happened.

'Did you say you'd started writing for *Brazen* magazine? That sounds pretty cool.'

'I can't write at all, really,' she said. 'I just wanted an interesting office job and now they're making me live up to the lies in my application letter.'

He had not reckoned on the equally British phenomenon of tediously insecure women.

'But you must be good if they're commissioning a piece – and you used to write for something else, didn't you?'

'*Panic*,' Lainey said, as if she was having to admit to thrush in the middle of a busy doctor's surgery. 'That wasn't writing, that was *Penthouse* letters with jokes. Made-up sexual bullshit because teenagers think that sort of thing is as risqué as it gets.' She was doing everything she could to avoid his eyes, he'd really embarrassed her. 'And I wasn't good at it, I just got in first.'

'I'd love to read something of yours,' he said. He'd been planning this for a few sentences – in the light of her last description he looked like a bit of a pervert now. 'I mean, if you come up with something for *Brazen* I'd be really interested in that.'

'I wouldn't let you read anything. I'm hopeless. My writing's really dull,' she said.

Ivan's ideas might look good on paper, but they were stupid in the real world. Flattering women wasn't even possible: they just got angry and defensive – it gave them an opportunity to publicly hate themselves, and John thought they enjoyed doing that too much already.

'No, I don't believe you. You've got such a good sense of humour,' he said, without much conviction. He was giving up.

'What do you mean?' she said.

'You know you're funny. You must know that,' he said cagily, detecting a change.

'Oh, I'm not. Do you think? I mean I only ask because other people have sort of said something like that and I never know what they're talking about. But, you know, I thought you might really know about . . . being a . . .'

'Other people are right.' He liked the way his voice sounded. Certain. Matter of fact. Manly.

'Oh, pschaw,' she said, groping for a fag, but before she did she shot him the sweetest look: something like vulnerability and insatiability in the space between two blinks – two *bats* – of her eyelids.

'Mind if I have one of those?' John said, gesturing at the Camels, and Lainey fumbled with her pretty fingers and found another. She lit them both in her very capable mouth, and handed one to him.

'Did you really not like me in the beginning, or was I imagining it?' Lainey said.

'I've always liked you. I didn't always understand you,' John said. He'd been leaning on one elbow and now he flopped on to his back and stared at the ceiling.

'What is there to understand? I couldn't be easier to read.'

'I don't like reading.'

She propped herself up a bit and tried to look him in the face. 'Is that supposed to be profound or funny? Is it supposed to be an insult? What does that mean?'

'It means I don't like analysing things. I like to let things happen.' He turned his head away.

'Things don't happen without thinking. There's always analysis, whether you mean it to happen or not.' She leaned over him, but not to touch him: she was reaching for the bedside table. It was barely eight in the morning and she was trying to find her fags.

'Don't talk,' he said gently. 'It hurts my head.'

'Do you mind if I smoke? Can your head cope with that?'

'Don't get mad at me. I'm just not up to talking about my feelings in the morning.'

136

'I only wanted to know why you didn't use to like me.' She spoke flippantly, inconsequentially. John wasn't fooled for a minute.

'Sweetheart. I never didn't like you. Where is this coming from?' He was just about putting enough body into his voice to stop it sounding like a whine. He lifted his hands, as if to cover his ears, then lowered them. He brushed some hair off her forehead and rolled over to kiss the space he'd cleared. They were lying in bed together and it was Saturday morning and she wasn't supposed to be at the Real World and there was no reason for either of them to go anywhere. His curtains were tissue-paper thin; the room had been light for hours, and they'd both been awake, both pretending not to be. One of them was going to have to make a move, sooner or later.

'Chrissie said . . .' She stopped.

'Chrissie told you I didn't like you? And she'd know.'

'No, she didn't say that at all.' She smoked in silence until her cigarette burned down to the filter. 'Chrissie's very beautiful, isn't she?'

'She is, yes, although I didn't see it at first. It's not what you'd call conventional beauty. So maybe it isn't beauty at all. It could just be her.'

'How can you say it's not conventional? Long blonde hair, big eyes, long legs, big breasts, hourglass figure, fantastic skin . . .'

'It's possible to have all that and be ugly.'

'But Chrissie's not ugly. And she has all that on top of being not ugly. And you say she's not conventionally beautiful? How much more conventional can you get?'

'What do you want me to say?' He'd started laughing. 'That she's the most beautiful girl I ever met? She's a vision of loveliness. She's a stunner. A corker. Give up now, Julia Roberts, the world has Chrissie.'

'If that's what you think, why not?'

'If that's what I think? I told you what I think. I think she's very attractive, but they're the kind of looks that grow on you. Why are we talking about Chrissie?'

They didn't say anything for several minutes, and then Lainey said, 'Sometimes I hate Chrissie.' She lifted herself again to look at him. He could feel himself tipping into the dent her elbow had made. 'Are you going to tell her I said that?'

'Why would I?'

'You're all very close, aren't you?'

'Why do you hate her?'

'Oh, I don't know. I just do,' Lainey said in a little voice. 'She hates me as well. We hate each other. We wouldn't be friends if we didn't.'

'I really don't understand the female mind,' John said.

'You don't have to. It's human nature, that's all. I hate it when men assume any kind of negative behaviour is exclusively female. Lots of people hate their friends.'

'I don't think any men do.'

'You'd be surprised.'

'It sounds more like you're jealous of Chrissie.'

'No shit.'

'Well, as far as I can see,' John said, 'you don't have any reason to be.' And he kissed away the crust at the side of her mouth, and smoothed her raw-pastry skin and rested his face in her rib-defined décolleté and closed his eyes.

taking varying pressure badly

Let the world try. Let the world just have a bloody go. Lainey wasn't going to be bothered today. Whether she was in love or not, she was getting some and she was strong. She was Charlie Girl, a Charlie's Angel, a strident, verdant dilettante – she was playing at life, and she was winning. The sun was large and flaming – energy-giving. She rang the doorbell to Clare's flat and drummed her fingers on the wall while she waited for an answer. It came in the shapeless form of Theo, drawn and cadaverous. Half of his face smiled as he crushed himself between the wall and the door to let her go past.

'Morning,' she sang brightly to Clare and Scott, who were sitting together on the blue sofa. She smiled at Dominic, who was typing at the desk by the window.

'I'd like you to go to the media centre later to put some of the layout on to Syquest, if that's all right,' Clare said. She also looked bright. 'We're considering possible cover lines. I would be interested in hearing which one you think is best.' In front of them on the coffee table there were three fuzzy photocopies of George Burdis as Harry Brazen. Lainey tilted her head to read the different line pasted on each one:

The Bitter End.
Harry's Days Are Numbered . . .
They Think It's All Over.

'What are you going to do if the show is cancelled?' Lainey
said.

'To do?' Scott said. 'What did you have in mind?'

'I think she's wondering if we'll go bankrupt overnight,'
Dominic said. 'The simple answer is it should make no
difference. *Dr Who* magazine wasn't too bothered when the
Doctor got struck off. And there are more *Star Trek* magazines
than there are unexplored galaxies out there.'

'Old *Star Trek*, as much as the new stuff,' Scott said. 'Even the
new generation was cancelled – didn't stop anyone wanting to
read about it.'

'As long as evil exists, as long as the earth needs him, there'll
always be reruns,' Dom said. He and Scott shared a smile.

'I'm glad you're all so optimistic,' Clare said, and her opinion
came last because she liked to think hard before committing
herself. 'I don't think it can help, quite honestly. Perhaps it won't
affect us in the near future, but when there are no new TV
specials, or exclusives to break, people might start losing interest.
Elaine, you haven't chosen a cover line.'

'"Harry's Days Are Numbered",' Lainey said.

'That's the one I like best,' Clare said. 'These two want "They
Think It's All Over . . ."' 'These two' meant the younger men.
Theo, folded over a copy of today's *Guardian*, wasn't taking
part. More arguments, Lainey thought, more hostility. Harry
Brazen might survive his imminent ordeal, but would Theo be
around to see it? Could Clare fire him when they'd started the
magazine together?

'What about: "Is Harry Brazen Running Out Of Time?"?'
Lainey said.

'Too long,' Clare said.

'"Is Harry Brazen Out Of Time?"' Dominic said.

'Not as good. "Running Out Of Time" is a good line. We'll

use it as the standfirst, but we'll go with "Days Are Numbered" for the front. Elaine, did you manage to make any headway on your article about – what was it about?'

'It's about George Burdis's voice,' Lainey said. 'I brought it in today, if you want to take a look.'

'I'll read it in my office,' Clare said. 'I have to call a friend at Conduit Television.'

'Who's the teacher's pet today, then?' Scott said, when Clare had gone upstairs with Lainey's article and a mysterious tin that may or may not have contained chocolate biscuits.

'You resent me usurping your role?' Lainey said.

'Minx. You know what I mean. You brought in some extra homework for her, and you agreed with her about the headline.' Scott was scratching the nape of his neck, head down, looking up at her, the gorgeous bastard. He was like cigarettes – addictive, bad for her and fabulous – but she wasn't as interested any more, even if his eyes *were* dancing. She had a boyfriend. So there.

'How could I have been agreeing with her? She didn't say which one she wanted,' Lainey said, throwing herself into the flirt with the souped-up passion of someone who knows how the plot turns out. Flirting was better when you didn't need it: being able to fall back on a third party's approval rating gave you confidence.

'She put that one in the middle. She was nodding at it. She was going like this.' He rolled his eyes at the contentious photocopy of Harry Brazen's grinning face.

'It was the best line. And you're sitting in my place,' Lainey said to him.

'You gonna make me move?'

'I could ask Clare to make you,' Lainey whispered, looking towards the stairs.

'You wouldn't dare . . .'

'Try me.'

If only Theo's presence wasn't putting such a damper on things. He was frowning in her periphery, exuding despair palpable from every point in the room, regardless of where she was looking. He was using up all the available oxygen for sighing. Clare, on the other hand, was in a better mood. She'd been bouncy, not doughy, her abrasive voice playful with 'ner ner na ner ner' superiority when she mentioned her friend at Conduit. If the antagonism was crushing Theo today, it was invigorating Clare. But with either or both of them in the office at any point, Lainey had no chance to quiz the others about it.

When she tried to take their lunch orders, Dominic said he'd be out of the office for the rest of the day: he had a dental check-up. He had very British teeth – crossed all over, like the flag. Any modern dentist would throw his hands up in horror and ask why they hadn't been braced straight in childhood. But they gave him a chaotic beauty, a haphazard smile in a world of beaming cliché. Scott offered to get the sandwiches today – she could see it was because he wanted to walk out with Dom. In many ways they behaved like lovers; they asked after each other a lot, and when they spoke again after separation their faces shone, they couldn't stop themselves from smiling. Heart-warming as this repeatedly was, as they stood up to leave together, and Clare was certain not to come downstairs within an hour of lunch, Lainey realized she was about to spend some quality time alone with Theo. Already honing his moves for that year's Mr Depressed UK, Theo was likely to put a downer on her post-coital pertness.

He laid into the silence the moment the door closed.

'Yes, the end of Harry Brazen. The end of Harry Brazen. Do you think it's going to happen?' His false enthusiasm gathered wonky momentum, like an egg rolling down a hill. 'What I'd like to happen is for the writers to think it's the end, and make an episode that tries to tie some ends and answer some questions, and then for them to unexpectedly get another, a new series. That would be the best of, best of both worlds.'

'It would be ideal, yes,' Lainey said.

'Have you become more of a, more of a fan since working with us?'

'I think I'm becoming obsessed with it,' Lainey said. 'I feel like I did when I was doing *Women in Love* for A level. I just couldn't stop thinking about it, almost to the point where I half-believed I was Ursula. Now, often when I wake up I'm thinking: but why did the white-haired man let him live? Or, you know, stuff like that.'

'Ah, the white-haired man – we get the most mail about that episode, you know. I . . .' He had been looking at her, now he leaned back, putting the computer screen and a shaft of dazzling, dust-filled sunlight between them. His chair spluttered in that indignant way wood has of taking varying pressure badly. 'I suppose you've noticed Clare and I aren't getting along all that well.'

There it was – lulled into small talk about Harry Brazen and he was going to stick her with the big stuff. It was all the more unsettling because she could no longer see his face. How long did it take Scott to go and fetch a few poxy sandwiches?

'You're not?' she said.

'You haven't noticed, then?'

'There's maybe some tension, maybe. I suppose that sort of thing comes and goes when people work closely.'

'We used to be good friends.' She guessed he'd forgotten he'd already told her this. 'Best friends, probably. We should never have decided that there had to be one editor, one voice, one person making the decisions. Of course, she's completely power mad now. Literally mad. She's a megalomaniac in a tent dress. You know she'll start, start, start *screaming* about something and the rest of us are trying to calm her down, or at least I am, and she'll just go crazy and come out with something really hurtful. Really . . . Without thinking.' Lainey didn't say anything. The more she contributed, the more likely he was to remember having this conversation. If it was left as a one-way rant, he might almost forget what he'd said; he'd have just been thinking aloud, no more. 'It was fun when we started. You know, we'd just branched out alone, taken risks. We said we were going to be different. Not some bloody . . . dictatorship. I tell you, Dr Dirk

Breck has nothing on her. At least he has a reason to be mad all the time.'

'You know Dr Dirk Breck blames Brazen for killing his wife, but was there actually that episode ever, or do they just refer to it?' Lainey said, grasping at the change of subject with grim determination.

'They did it as a flashback in *Realm of the Vortex*,' Theo said, on sci-fi autopilot. He was still angry, but the interval had given him space to remember himself. He leaned forward again to look at her, and she pretended not to know he was doing it, and hoped she wasn't blushing or twitching under the scrutiny. Theo was a bit of a weird and creepy fuck, sometimes. He didn't talk again until Scott came back with lunch, and even then he moved a little way from them. Scott started to make her laugh with his impressions of Dom – what with that and the relief of not having to be alone with Theo's bad temper any more, she was a bit heady, trying not to snort, not to laugh too loudly, not to spit bits of food everywhere. She realized why Scott was so irresistible. He took her back to being at school again – when she laughed with him it was that forbidden laughter – only this time she was hanging out in the cool crowd with the best-looking boy.

They were still eating when Clare made an unprecedented lunchtime appearance. She stood in front of them, eclipsing most of the sunlight, so the rest of it framed her, plating the edges of her frumpwear with a dazzling aura.

'I have some rather good news for everyone,' she said. 'Harry Brazen has been reprieved.'

coordination

'Peter Sellers?'

'Yes.'

'And John Lennon.'

'Yes. Peter Sellers and John Lennon.'

'You can't tell the difference?'

'Yes, I can tell the difference,' Lainey said. 'But sometimes I get them confused.'

'Don't be ridiculous,' John said, dropping a slippery mushroom on to his chest. He picked it up with his finger and thumb and ate it. 'One's Inspector Clouseau, the other's one of the Beatles.'

'You don't say,' Lainey said, wrinkling her nose. 'Look, it's like this. Both of them defined the British character in the sixties.'

'Well, not just them. What about Michael –'

'Wait a minute. They did, did define the mood of the sixties. That's the first thing. They were both heavily influenced by Spike Milligan – you know, that sort of surreal minutiae – the trivia of the ordinary. That celebration of archaic English unimportance – *self*-importance. Enjoying quaint language like "Steady on, old chap". It's all over Lennon's lyrics, and those God-awful books he did. And Peter Sellers –'

'Goons, yeeeaaah,' John said. 'But everyone was doing that in the sixties. You're confused because Sellers did that *Hard Day's Night* take-off. That's what it is.'

'That's not fucking what it is. I haven't finished. They both looked the same.'

'They didn't look anything like each other.'

'They could be brothers.' She kept talking while he looked overtly sceptical. 'Both of them were survived by not very interesting little men who spent the next ten years or more dining out on, and doing talk shows about, when they knew them. With John Lennon it's Victor Spinetti, with Peter Sellers, it's Graham Stark.'

'You're completely mad. Do you know that?' John said. He watched her picking water chestnuts out of the fried vegetables with chopsticks. He was pretty impressed by her coordination. She went on.

'Sellers was in *How I Learned to Stop Worrying and Love* . . .'

John finished off the title faster than her. 'Yes, yes. Lennon was in *How I Won the War*! Hm?' She leaned over him to spear a piece of chicken, and pulled a what-do-you-think-about-that-then face.

'So they appeared in films with similar titles. I suppose if you think about it, *Help!* is just another word for *Return of the Pink Panther*,' John said.

'Both of them died in 1980.'

'My God!'

'See!' Lainey said.

'Maybe this goes further than we know. Maybe they were both on an FBI hit-list. You don't think they were actually the same person?'

'If you're going to take the piss.'

Truth be told, he was trying just a bit too hard to find her adorably eccentric. Truth be told, she was trying too hard to *be* adorably eccentric. In fact, her Sellers–Lennon hypothesis was quite persuasive. But the problem wasn't with the material, it was their delivery that was flawed. They weren't happy most of the time they were with each other. Not unhappy either, just not happy. There was a piece of him holding back. But he did his best to pick holes in her argument, because he knew from experience

– or maybe Ivan had told him years ago – that girls didn't really like being taken seriously. They weren't sure what to do with significance. He looked for more things to find fault with.

Lainey took the last spring roll and sat up a bit; she was getting a crick in her neck from leaning against John's shoulder. They were sort of at right angles to each other on the floor, supported by the sofa, with the takeaway more or less between them. There was too much food – she'd thought it important to make him believe she ate. It was one of those things that men thought told them a lot about women. They never watched how much you ate, just how much you ordered. She ordered a lot.

'Okay, the best sitcom. In your opinion,' Lainey said.

'Best or favourite?'

'Whatever.' Her mouth was full.

'Technically, the best is *Cheers*,' John said. 'Perfect minimalist single set. Bias on male characters, which is unusual for a sitcom, but always works better than an equal ratio or a predominantly girlcom. *Larry Sanders* and *Seinfeld*: all more men than women.'

'*Home Improvement* – there's another,' Lainey said.

'Yes, funny. *Cheers* also had the perfect unresolved fuck – in fact they carried it off *twice*. And none of the characters is thoroughly likeable. That's what makes it good.'

'My favourite's *Laverne & Shirley*,' Lainey said. 'I like it when they sing.'

'Can any spawn of that atrocious Fonz shit really be anything other than . . . shit?'

'Don't you think the Fonz is cool?'

'Oh, don't come that cheesy retro-bullshit with me. You know you don't really believe it.'

Lainey liked it when John was strict and critical about these things. Earlier, when they were on films, she hadn't admitted that *Dirty Dancing* was her favourite, because she wanted to pitch it at exactly the right level. *Dirty Dancing* was, in fact, not an uncool choice at all, but she thought John probably wasn't cool enough to see that. Arguing about it might have brought his limitations out into the open between them, and she was happier when she couldn't see them. So *Dirty Dancing* was out, *Laverne & Shirley* in, reflecting the relative weight of their respective genres. But she liked John's narky taste-Nazi persona, because it let her believe – maybe pretend – that he was smarter than her. Good enough for her, in other words. It also meant that he'd stopped being precious around her, and men didn't get to that stage with girls they just wanted to shag.

She dropped her chopsticks into one of the tin trays and wiped a little kung po sauce from John's cheek with her thumb, and then sucked her thumb, without making a big deal of it. But the gesture made him look at her, and he lifted his fingertips to her face, and brushed his thumb across her lips.

'Oh, have I go–' she began.

'Shhh,' John said. His face was so close, too close to see all of him, his shiny black eyelashes drawing her deeper into darkest eyes, the sliver of space between them throbbing with almost, and he delayed kissing her until she could hardly stand to wait any longer. He steadied his shoulder, pressing against the sofa, but pushed it backwards so that they toppled flat on to the carpet. Both of them tried to shift food containers out the way unobtrusively, to keep the spontaneity of their passion as hot as the kung po. Lainey arched her back and picked a couple of spare rib bones from under her.

'Ivan's not going to walk in, is he?'

'Unlikely,' John said, breathing. 'He's drinking with his –' Lainey kissed him. 'Work colleague people.' He unzipped her cardigan, following his fingers with his mouth. 'So he won't be back until much later.'

'How often does he do that?'

'Few times a week, maybe,' John said, scooping the small of her back with his hand, pulling her body up to his. She locked on to him, squeezing her thighs up around his hips.

'That must piss Chrissie off,' Lainey tried to pull off her jeans as John dry-fucked his pelvis against hers. The sound of their clothes friction was sexy and immediate; his shirt being dragged off was the noise of fresh linen sheets ruffling.

'You'd know that better than me. They –' She did something good, although she wasn't quite sure what. He tumbled more heavily on to her, then rolled them both over so that she was on top of him. 'God. Um . . . mmmf . . . They have their own lives, it's no big deal.'

Desire drenched her like a chilli flush, pushing open her veins. 'Yeah, I su–' The pressure of his thumb on her knicker-line; she stopped talking.

All this created something of an awkward pause. Still only eight o'clock. They couldn't go to bed now, and he was hoping she wasn't going to stay.

'Thank you,' Lainey said shyly, and looked a shade more beautiful than she usually did. He was embarrassed by her thanks, not sure what to say, reluctant to be trivial because he was also ridiculously pleased that she'd said it. 'I loved that.' For the first couple of syllables, his heart beat scarily. He kissed her. They were surrounded by impromptu-intercourse shrapnel, the scattered, spilled remains of the takeaway, and clothes. He certainly wanted to have some more sex, but what with the vigour of that episode, on top of a full stomach, he thought he couldn't possibly be up to it for a while. His lips buzzed from the orgasm and the MSG. He slumped against her and sucked her earlobe gently, thinking he couldn't eat another thing – although, of course, in an hour's time he'd probably be really ready to do it all again. He sighed, reproving his weak internal stand-up, and struggled not to fall asleep right where he was.

'It'd be just like me to actually pass out now when Ivan's about to come in,' John said. 'We should move.'

'Do you have nights?'

'Uh?'

'I mean, is Ivan out because it's your night in with the flat?'

'Oh, right. No, we don't do anything like that. We've never

actually . . . that's never really been an issue.' He stopped short of running through their dating patterns. 'Of course, you and Chrissie don't have that problem at all.'

'Well, we don't have *that* problem. We don't interfere with each other when the date is still happening. It's afterwards that we start making things difficult for each other.'

'I know I asked you this before,' John said, 'but why do you both live alone? Last time I asked, you didn't answer properly, I think, or I can't remember what you said. It's a bit unusual, isn't it? Most people live with people.'

'I can't explain it. It seemed like a good idea at the time. Like a big symbol-of-independence move. And now I seem to be out of the flat-sharing-with-other-girlfriends loop. Anyway, I'm also pretty happy where I am. Not doing the usual arguing and stuff. None of the irritation or accountability. And, like, other people I know have really high powered jobs by now, so they'd be wanting to live in places with high rents. And talking about their high powered jobs. Neither of which I can keep up with.'

'What about Chrissie? Couldn't you rent a room at her place?'

'It was never on offer. Well, she only has the one bedroom. I know we could still do it, but, to be honest, neither Chrissie nor I could stand it. I'd be adding strychnine to the sugar within a week. And eating it myself.'

John laughed. 'You're always pretending you don't get on. You told me you hate her half the time. But you're closer than any other girls I know. You've got this weird co-dependent thing. You refer to each other all the time, you know? She does, you do.'

'We don't pretend we don't get on. We really don't. Most of the time, though, we do. Chrissie's, you know, the way she is, and I'm, like, the way I, whatever, and it just works. We don't sit and fight all the time when we're on our own, but we don't put it on for people either. And when it works, it's just better than with anyone else. Girl friendships are essential, you know, and this one's just, essentialer. Both meanings of essential – we've stripped away the pointless stuff that most people keep. Lying and politeness, that sort of thing.'

'And Chrissie's cool.'

'Yeah, Chrissie's cool.' Lainey turned her whole head towards him; since they were spooning, this was probably uncomfortable. He wondered if he'd said something stupid and tried to qualify it.

'Like Ivan's cool. I can see why they're together.'

'You two never argue or hate each other?'

'Ivan and me? We never argue about ourselves. Just football, or groups and stuff. Nothing very deep.'

'We're not deep.'

'Yeah, you're deepish. Both of you. That's probably why you're friends. You're at the same end of the pool.' He wanted to know if they'd ever had sex, but he thought he'd leave it for now. Work through the possibilities in his spare time before she confirmed it one way or another. 'You've sort of aligned your weirdness.'

'Well, yeah. I think, basically, we like the way we are with each other. That doesn't mean we don't get pissed off some of the time. But it's like family. Falling out doesn't leave any marks.'

house-on-fire stuff

Lainey sat cross-legged in a free *Brazen* T-shirt, watching a free video – *The Real X Files: True-life Stories the CIA Don't Want You to Know.* ('Of course you can take it – if you really want to,' Dom had told her. 'You could review it for us, actually.' 'What, really? You trust me?' she'd said. 'Of course. We have high hopes,' Dom said, and although he was being loosely ironic and mannered, she took it at face value because she wanted to. He turned back to his work, letting the smile fade slowly. Men got handsomer when they gave compliments.)

'This is shit,' Chrissie said. She was on the floor, leaning against the bed, eating the blueberries she'd brought. 'You have to have some of these, they're *so* good.' It was perhaps the third time this evening she'd said it. Lainey, who resented the inference that Chrissie was introducing her to something new and exotic – Battersea's own Walter Raleigh – when in fact she was doing nothing of the sort, was abstaining.

'The thing about working at the Real World,' Lainey said, 'is you become almost as fanatical as the customers after a while. I just can't eat non-organic produce any more. I start to get panicky and think I can taste the pesticides.'

'You're right, of course. I should start buying organic – but I always find the taste of beetles even more intrusive than the pesticides. Maybe it's just me.'

'That's a myth.'

'You told me it. You said, when you'd just started working there, that there were spiders in all the strawberries and worms in the apples.'

'One spider. One pack of strawberries. And it was dead. And I lied about the worms. I was being funny.'

'Well, it gave me the willies,' Chrissie said. 'I like my fruit to look like fruit. Not like the bits the man from Del Monte said no to.'

A girls' night. How much fun did that sound? It had sounded like a lot of fun all the way through the planning stages, and felt like fun when Lainey was going round the supermarket after closing, picking up what was reaching the nadir of its saleability, and even felt like fun when the doorbell rang and her friend was standing there in the doorway, tall and stunning, with Mardi Gras and blueberries and cardamom ice cream. They poured a couple of glasses of Mardi Gras and put in the video, and then got down to it and compared salaries (Chrissie won) against creative fulfilment (Lainey won, but cheated) – the usual rigmarole.

Lainey started to tell her about the great sex she'd been having with John, and Chrissie seemed curious but was also blocking it.

'I think,' Lainey had said, 'that I've mastered the blow job.'

'Oh my God, shut *up*!' Chrissie squeaked.

'Okay, sorry.' Lainey laughed.

'Why, how are you doing it?' Chrissie said. 'No. Really. Shut up.'

'Okay.'

'Is there some kind of – is there something I really should know?' Chrissie said. 'Ivan's really, you know, big, and I don't really . . .' She breathed in through her teeth and covered her face with her hands. 'I'm not saying this.'

'You don't have to put the balls in too,' Lainey deadpanned, and they laughed hard. But the laughter was strange, coming in the middle of not really getting on, and as it faded she tried to hold on to it. Afterwards the silence between them was conspicuous, like an empty space where there used to be big furniture. Lainey wondered whether she wasn't just forcing the sex talk on to Chrissie to score points, because it was something she really knew she could do. They were incapable of saying anything to each other that was not, in some way, combative. It all had to prove something, say something. It was a small blessing they didn't have penises – all the better to tug out from boxers and measure against each other. This pantomime ugly-sisters routine again – even John had picked up on it. Was it really stupid, them still hanging out after all this time? Once, Lainey thought, once, it had been different. Better.

Lainey and Chrissie had met at sixth-form college and clicked in the cafeteria when they'd both picked someone else's fight.

'Have one!' a skinny red-haired boy was saying to one of the serving staff. He was waving a hand of over-long fingers above a plate of undercooked chips. She was shaking her head and looking past him.

'I'll have one,' said Chrissie, behind him in the queue, waiting to pay. She took a chip from his plate and bit, grimaced, then recovered slowly. She replaced the uneaten chip-half on the boy's plate, defiantly, like an upturned glass in a schnapps-drinking contest.

'Hard in the middle,' she pronounced evenly. 'And cold.'

Lainey, in front of the boy and choosing sugar, prodded one of his chips.

'You can tell they're frozen in the middle,' she said.

'They've gone cold with all this messing about with them,' the canteen woman said. The three dissenters laughed with ironic bitterness, like communists, and the boy put his hands on his hips.

'I just want my money back,' he said, reasonably.

'No one else has complained,' she said.

'Your chips are still frozen, lady,' Chrissie said.

'You can't expect people to eat frozen food that's still cold,' Lainey said. 'It's illegal.'

They sat down together at a table, where the redhead put his coins in a tray-fronted leather purse, and the two girls quickly realized that he wouldn't do for them. They did not reach the same conclusion about each other. Chrissie had been to school with most of the people around them, but she was odd – she ate alone most of the time. And Lainey was the new girl; her school had a sixth form, but didn't teach the A levels she wanted, so she'd come here to study sociology and law. Chrissie's strangeness at this school was like old-money, long established, while Lainey's was nouveau: none the less, they were the strangest people around that day, and they found each other.

House-on-fire stuff. Chrissie told Lainey how attractive she was, how clever and funny, how different to everyone else in the place – she didn't say it all outright. Sometimes it was implied in her insults of everyone else, which automatically excluded, and in self-congratulation, which naturally included Lainey. In return, Lainey listened to her. She liked, too, that Chrissie didn't gossip. At first she'd thought it was just because Chrissie was aware that, as a new girl, Lainey wouldn't know who she was talking about, but a year later Chrissie still wasn't talking. At least not about other people. But, although this resistance to really fun chat could sometimes make her seem dull and stuffy, it also gave her integrity. She was clean, like a 1940s British film star. And, apart from all this, she was good-looking and bright and funny, and that sort of thing was always nice to be around. Lainey made other friends in the college, more than Chrissie, who'd known most of them since she was five, but those two were different, they were bezzies, the best in the place. They had this loyalty that made other girls envious, if they noticed, and sparked rumours of a friendship that went beyond shopping for bras and swapping Biros.

Chrissie and Lainey knew this, felt this, never discussed it. It was the one thing that divided them – each of them was afraid

the other might think she was a lesbian. It didn't help that
Chrissie never had any flings, so Lainey flung herself into the
hetero-scene with gay abandon, although she would have done
that anyway. She liked men, and sex, and holding hands at the
movies.

At some point things had gone wrong. It felt recent. It had
always felt recent. They had one opinion between the pair
of them — perhaps Lainey had just got sick of Chrissie always
voicing it. But the only other option was to stop. They couldn't
stop.

'Is this ice cream organic?'

'It's cardamom.'

'Do you know what they do to cows?'

'Milk them?'

'They feed them shit. They inject them with hormones and
steroids and antibiotics.'

'Lainey, if I cared about cows I'd probably eat fewer
McDonalds.'

'As if you eat McDonalds. Anyway, it's not the cows I care
about. It's the fact that all the hormones and antibiotics go into
the milk.' Oh, she was being obnoxious, and she meant it. The
only reason Lainey ate organic was that it was free or cheap. It
did give her a frisson of relief when she read the scare stories in
the newspapers and thought of her pristine fridge with its pious
choice of politically superior produce, but the fact was, if she got
a proper job she'd be back at Tesco before you could say
'genetically modified', and if it was a good job she'd be eating
Indian takeaways with a vengeance. Tonight she wanted to
annoy Chrissie and unsettle her, to be the one with something
to tell. Chrissie, however, had the infuriating habit of looking
so uninterested that it hurt whenever Lainey said something
new.

'What doesn't kill you makes you stronger,' Chrissie said,
licking the snowy peak on her long-stemmed spoon.

'What makes you think it isn't killing you?' Lainey said.

'Is this a diet thing?' Chrissie said. Lainey sighed waspishly and reached for the bag of tortilla chips. 'And what if John wanted to surprise you with dinner at Pont de la Tour? Would you look down the menu and turn your nose up at anything that hadn't eaten sensibly before it was killed?'

Chrissie didn't say this to advance the argument but to compare John with Ivan scathingly. She was listing the ways that Ivan was a more exciting boyfriend to score points. Lainey considered lying, answering as if it were purely hypothetical, and then just as she opened her mouth she hit on the best reply of all. Chrissie was expecting Lainey to fight back so that she could crush her further.

'John would never do that,' she said quietly. Make the bitch feel guilty.

They put on the video Chrissie had brought, a romantic comedy with one of the *Friends* in it, and didn't speak much for the next couple of hours.

'How's Ivan?'

'Oh, you know. Ivanish.'

Lainey wanted to talk about John. She knew that once they were into that, although Chrissie would probably be rude about John, she'd say nice things about her. The only time Chrissie was mean was when they were being petty and competitive, like before, and Lainey was trying to be as big a know-all as Chrissie. Maybe the erosion of their friendship could be traced back to university, when Lainey had learned a thing or two, and Chrissie had hated not being the one who'd told her.

'Do you see a lot of John these days, or don't you go round there so much?' Lainey said.

'I haven't seen John for a couple of weeks. He's been out when I've gone round, doing gigs.'

'Yes, his comedy's really beginning to happen for him,' said Lainey.

'Do you see him perform much?'

'Never. Not since with you.'

'Why not? Does he not like it, or do you not like it?'

'I've never been able to work that out. I don't know. We just don't do that. I don't know. This is weird shit, isn't it? All of us, doing this. Together.'

'This double-dating? Except we're not.'

'No,' said Lainey. 'We're not. Why are we not? Are we stopping them from doing it or are they playing into our hands?'

'I think the thing is, no one double-dates between puberty and pregnancy,' Chrissie said. 'And at the long end of the scale they call it dinner parties, not double-dating. Shall we have a dinner party? Force them to do chat while we give each other secret looks and them marks out of ten? Ivan's a good cook.'

'He would be.'

'So then?'

'No, Chris, we're not having a dinner party with them. It would be hell.'

'But fun hell, not bad hell. Anyway, boys respect you more if you put them through hell from time to time. They like a change of pace.'

'Why do you always have to sound like a warped Doris Day?' Lainey said. 'I thought we weren't trying to manipulate men any more.'

'No? We're still trying to marry them, though.'

'How hard are you trying? Are you really thinking about it?' She sharpened and sat forward. 'Are you getting close to it?'

Astonishingly, Chrissie blanched. Lainey pretended she hadn't seen, and didn't say anything else. Smaller again; the Ivan effect. Chrissie breathed through her mouth, as if she were slightly short of breath.

'He is,' Chrissie said.

'Bloody hell, Chris, you're frightened. You pretend you want to get married and it's not true at all, is it? You're not really ready. Neither of us are.'

'Neither of us *is*,' Chrissie said feebly. 'No, I'm ready. And he really is. That's what worries me. What if I'm not enough for him, what if he gets bored with me? And yet – he's ready.'

'Of course you're enough for him. Why are you saying that?'

Just like family, the ones who pissed you off the most could still turn your stomach with worry about them. When Chrissie looked like this, Lainey forgot to fight with her.

'I just can't believe he's always going to be the way he is with me now. Sooner or later he's going to want more.'

walking on lettuce leaves

'In the unlikely event that you'd forgotten,' Lainey had said, the night before, 'I don't have breasts. What you see now is bra. This is all going to go when I take the bra off.'

'What?'

'I'm just preparing you. Because tonight, as you see, I have knockers. But I won't in a minute.'

He was kissing the depression at the base of her throat, his chin nudging the springy softness of the top of her breasts; she was lying on her bed, wearing non-matching underwear, just over half of which was a push-up bra.

'Don't talk,' he said, unhooking the bra. 'Stop being neurotic.' His kiss stubbed her small, perfect breasts, and she melted and sighed and softly tugged the hair at his temple.

'Sometimes I wonder,' she said dreamily. 'The breast thing. What's in it for you?' She pushed her palm down along his stomach, into his boxers, rolling them off with the back of her hand, the fingertips of the other hand tracing the curve of his shoulder, his spine, and he relaxed on to her. The hard, high bone of her pelvis pressed into his thigh. He liked that she made him feel heavy. It was kind of butch.

'You have – incredible – breasts,' he said.

'Oh, it's not that. Although thank you. No, I mean the whole men-wanting-to-touch-breasts situation. What's in it for you all? They're just fat. Well, not so very much in my case, but you know. They feel like any other part of me.' She brought her hand back up to squeeze her chest, as though it were Play-doh. 'Not that exciting, is it?'

He lifted his head to look at her. She was pouting and smiling, and breaking the mood. But he laughed.

'What's in it for—?'

'For men, yes. What? What's the big deal about the whole breast thing? As far as I can see you don't get anything out of it.'

'It doesn't do anything for you, then?'

'For *me*? Oh, *God* yeah, but –'

'I wouldn't lose sleep wondering about it, if I were you.'

Today, slowly roasting in the steady heat, John stretched out and closed his eyes and remembered the outline of her light, exquisite body, and wished he wasn't such a self-sabotaging deviant.

In the evenings, no problem at all: she was great. The night before, her hair had seized the light as she lowered her body over the length of his, letting the tips of her nipples stroke his chest, his stomach, his penis, her hair, charged like nylon, sweeping heavily behind. When she kissed the insides of his thighs, dragging flattened full lips along hot skin, he wanted to make her promises; he wanted her to ask him to. But several shared nights and all the positions he knew later, he was still not warming to Lainey's glutinous white waking appearance, with the cluster of spots and conspicuous bleached facial hair; the slothful reluctance to get up when he did, the unsteady smile that cracked open her face. When they had sex in the morning he closed his eyes and pretended she wasn't there, and wished he wasn't.

He smiled at a three-year-old kid with a duck on a string who'd suddenly blocked his sunlight, and cleared his throat, bringing himself back into focus, while the image of last night's sex faded. Just a perfect day. The park in summer was a very different animal. He no longer needed the excuse of exercise to be there. It was about community. It was about London feeling very pleased with itself. You provincials think you're so great with your fields and birds, but look at us: green; water; birds. More of them than you can shake a stick at. Ha! And we still have all the good delis.

The three-year-old with a duck on a string fell over. She looked around to see if anyone had noticed, deciding whether it was in her interest to cry. John braced himself, held his breath, felt urges in his arms to help her, felt his knees twitch. The child's mother laughed, so she laughed too. John smiled again, relieved. The mother was young and beautiful, and when she kissed her daughter's knee she looked like an angel.

I could do fatherhood. I'm nice. I cried at *Schindler's List*. I did a benefit gig for (the exposure) the *homeless*.

Too often, with Lainey, he found himself frowning, and he had to remember to relax at regular intervals so this wouldn't happen. She made him feel like a bad man; when he was with her he felt guilty for not liking her more and not screwing her less. She was making him hate himself. All this hate could hardly be good for a relationship. It was time to put a stop to it. He lay back on the grass with his hands behind his head, and listened to the whirl of the park around him. The three-year-old with a duck on a string was laughing somewhere not far behind. Keep laughing, little girl, John thought. May you grow up to be as gorgeous as your mother, and never have your heart bothered by a man who isn't good enough.

When he got home he called Lainey and got her machine. Shopping or a shift at the supermarket, he wasn't sure. He was going to leave a message breaking their date that evening, but realized she might not get it in time. Keen as he was to find an easy way out, he couldn't leave a girl waiting for him in some dive in Kentish Town. A little, whippet-thin girl with hair like burnt-sugar strands. John changed into more comfortable shoes and went to buy some groceries.

There was a large painting of a rainbow over the shop's sign, and sandwich boards outside tempted customers with an organic wine-tasting and free introductory aura-reading. He saw her back: she was standing at the check-out wearing a little blue apron, tied tightly, and he watched her for a while. She was fast, compared to the other check-out people she was slicker, and he couldn't be sure, but it looked like more shoppers smiled at her as they signed cheques or took their credit-card receipts. He slipped past with his head down and went for a look around, to see if there was anything he could buy.

This shop was taking the piss. Alfalfa sprouts, which he only knew from the joke in *Annie Hall*, which he really only knew because it was quoted in *St Elmo's Fire*; tofu any way you liked it; books on healing and crystals and Deepak Chopra. More types of bean than he could ever have imagined, and lead-heavy-loaves of something that didn't even have the face to call itself bread. If he had to eat this food for a month, his paunch wouldn't be a problem. Only the meat counter, staffed by middle-aged men with spotless white aprons who were about as normal-looking as men who cut up animals could be, had anything tempting. He was surprised to see it at all; he'd assumed the flaky New Age types didn't do flesh-eating. This counter, however, attempted to lighten the mood by making a joke of its prices. Lamb at £18 a pound. Chicken breasts at £6 each. There was no way you could feel guilty about murdering an animal that had the audacity to be so costly. John moved on. The kettle chips that set him back about a pound in Sainsbury's were half as much again here, he realized, putting a couple of packets back on the shelf. Finally, he plumped for apples – he had a strange, ticklish urge to watch her weigh something – and rainforest chocolate. He took them to her check-out.

She spotted him in the queue and looked surprised, then smiled naughtily. There were two people before him, and she treated them both to a little banter as he edged closer. When he reached the front she did not acknowledge him.

'These are Braeburn?' she said, taking a look in his carefully folded brown bag.

'Apples,' John said.

'Apples,' she said, as if corrected, tapping the PLU code in. 'This is very good chocolate. Very virtuous.'

'You mean it helps me lose weight?'

'No, it helps starving children. Indirectly.' He watched her press the staff-discount button in the corner of the till. 'Three ninety.'

'For apples and chocolate?'

'The chocolate's two fifty,' she said. 'Think of the starving children. As you eat it.'

'When do you knock off?'

'Wait till there's a lull. I've got fifteen minutes.'

They leaned on the wall in the alley next to the supermarket, smoking. It felt like school, right down to the urgency imposed by the briefness of her break period.

'Why did you come here?' she said.

'I wanted to see you at work, and . . .' He stopped. He had been about to tell her that he couldn't see her tonight, but then, as if it were a premonition, he imagined the evening as it would be without her – Ade dropping names, Fucked-up Bob dropping acid – and he had a sudden and selfish change of heart. He wanted to walk in there with his pretty girlfriend. More to the point, he wanted to walk out of there with his pretty girlfriend. He could always finish with her some other time. 'Look, are you sure you still want to meet some of my friends tonight. You don't have to. They're not exactly . . .'

'I'm looking forward to it,' she said sweetly. 'Is that why you came? To warn me that your friends aren't exactly?'

He nodded. 'Shall I meet you somewhere else first?'

'No, I might be late. I have to wash my hair.'

'You've got really pretty hair.' He felt clumsy giving her a compliment in broad daylight, scared of giving himself away, even though he meant it. 'It always looks good.'

She laughed. 'But I still have to wash it. Is it going to be too late if I turn up at nineish?' The alley was so cool it felt damp. She was looking up at him and the question lingered on her lips like an invitation. The curves of her mouth made conventional voluptuousness look too obvious, obsolete. He couldn't stop himself from kissing her. It was like giving up Crunchies: the more he held back, the more he wanted her. She broke away first. 'I have to get back now.' She held his hand as she led the way back to the street; they were walking on soft lettuce leaves.

'You check out very well,' he said, squinting when they were back in the sun. Right now, in the daylight, she was glowing.

'I know.' She walked back inside without turning to look at him again, and raised her arm, more a how sign than a wave, and the door swung shut behind her. John looked inside his paper bag and broke off a line of rainforest chocolate.

a steady breeze

Lainey knew at once they were John's friends, even though John wasn't with them. They looked like him; they had his lofty shiftlessness, and wore similar clothes. She couldn't approach them without him, and was relieved when he emerged from the crush at the bar with four pints of lager. He saw her and mouthed something she didn't understand, setting the lager down in front of his group. He wiped his hands on his jeans. She was anxious, and worried that he was going to sit down with them and not come to fetch her. But it was okay, he was making his way over, smiling too regularly for comfort. He offered to get her a drink, but she didn't want to be left having to decide whether to wait for him or go up to his friends, so she pressed up to the bar with him, while he bought her a bottle of cider. She always drank cider with John. She drank lager with everyone else, but pints were a bit too much like trying. The bottle was halfway between butch and femme, and slightly suggestive of oral sex. She drank with her top lip inside.

He introduced Ade and Bob and Martin, and she squeezed into the last space of the bench seat, next to Bob. Being the only girl was not, to Lainey, a problem – it left her options open. When there were other girls she was expected to bond with them immediately and form a sub-group, which was nice enough but made her feel she was missing out on the best conversation. The problem was being next to Bob, because Bob had an aversion to group conversation, using it only as a springboard for one-on-one dialogue. When she was trying to break into the main discussion, Bob would turn quietly to her and ask her the sort of questions that she didn't want everyone to hear the answers to, because the answers were stupid. It was impossible to humour Bob without sounding as much of a moron as he was. If Bob had been interesting she wouldn't have minded the attention, but he was the worst kind of loser: an optimist, and the worst kind of optimist: an ex-smackhead. Bob spoke like the Oprah Winfrey show – a loop of positivity and self-knowledge. He was thankful for everything, although, as far as she could see, thanks weren't necessary. He was full of hope, full of determination, full of shit. Lainey looked from his down-turned unfocused eyes to the point just over his shoulder where John was ignoring her, and listened to Bob's life. It didn't always make sense.

'So I just have to you know thank God all the time because I was losing it man I'd lost it and if it wasn't for my mates they think the sun shines out of my arse they really do I'd still be there on the streets injecting like you know my arms are really messed up but I'm telling you I've got my mates and they've stood by me they've all really stood by me and I know that I just have to take it one day at a time but I've been off the heavy shit for two weeks now and I haven't even had anything at all today not even a little spliff to help me cope because I'm telling you I've made it through man I'm out of it actually to celebrate this bloke I know in Brixton's given me some good shit not like smack or that because you've got to let go and still live you know what I mean I could go on like I have been just feeling the same all day every day but I'm telling you that kind of thing makes you mad and I'm over the worst of it now I'm never going back down that road like you see I didn't value myself I thought I wasn't worth shit and now I've realized how important it is to have self-respect and it's all because of my mates I'm telling you if you don't have mates like these you're lost they've saved my life man I owe them my life.'

Finally John caught her eye.

'Bob. Shut the fuck up,' he said, shaking his head. 'Leave her alone.' And to Lainey, 'Come here, swap places with me.' He steadied her with his arms on top of hers as they squeezed around the table. 'You have to *not listen* to Bob,' John said. He lowered his chin handsomely, checking she was okay, and raised one eyebrow – the nearest John got to winking.

'No, we're just talking, man,' Bob said. 'This is one lovely girl you have.'

'I hate Bob,' John said in a low voice. 'I don't know who calls him, but it isn't me. Just ignore him. I do.'

Soon, though, John was deep in conversation with Bob – or at least was listening to Bob, even though he scowled and tried to look as if he wasn't. Of his other friends Lainey liked Ade, who treated her to such an efficient combination of interest and charm that she decided he probably fancied her (either that or he was gay), but she didn't really like Martin because he was on the annoying side of pointless and talked very quietly, and she had to make him repeat things she didn't even want to hear in order to give a reply he wasn't going to listen to.

By half ten more of John's friends had come in. The stiff borders between different groups of people had softened, and the place had the feel of a party; conversation with anyone seemed permissible. On her way back from rebrushing her hair, Lainey started talking to a lively Irish girl, who said she knew John through her boyfriend.

'John's always seemed very nice,' the girl said. 'He does stand-up, doesn't he? Have you ever seen it?'

'Only before I started seeing him. I thought he was all right.'

'I haven't seen him do it. He's always very funny down the pub, though.'

'Chuh! I hadn't noticed,' Lainey joked, because she had reached the stage of domestication where she knew she ought to start insulting him. She looked at John now, and as if in slow motion he turned to see her, questioning, slightly cross-looking. Silent empathy briefly drew them closer, but she couldn't work him out yet. He hadn't been the model boyfriend tonight. He had rescued her from Bob, but he had sat her next to Bob. They'd hardly spoken all evening, but his gaze held her now with something like possession, which was nine-tenths of his allure: now and again he just looked as if he needed her there.

'How did you meet?' the Irish girl asked Lainey.

'Through a friend.'

'His flatmate, I suppose, none of this lot.'

'Actually, yes! His flatmate goes out with a friend of mine. Chrissie?'

'He's a slick one, all right. Ivan, isn't it? She's not expecting it to last, I hope?'

'Well, like, kind of.'

'Sorry, I shouldn't have said that. It's just, you know, his reputation and all. Never shown up here with the same girl twice.'

'People can change.'

'I think he already has: he used to come out more than he does now. I suppose it'll be that friend of yours being a bad influence on him.'

'Or a good one.'

The girl laughed. 'Oh, you're right, a good influence. Only don't go being such a good influence on our John. We all like to see him here.'

Lainey hated the presumed sensitivity of women. They always knew what they were saying, and as a woman you were expected to understand every word, and then some. That was the foundation of feminine intuition: they'd just been trained to concentrate. So Lainey had to spot the uncalled-for barb in the Irish girl's last comment, and now she had to move on, because she didn't know what to say, how to get back to the comfy neutrality of being strangers. She just smiled and pointed at her bottle of cider over on the table and went to get it.

Bob was peeling the label off Lainey's cider, which made

her feel slightly sick: he had black fingernails and might have touched the bottle's mouth. She leaned over the table to take it, and John hooked his finger in her collar and pulled her face close to his.

'You okay?'

'I'm a little tired,' she said.

'Do you want to go?'

'No stay, stay to the end, I'm fine,' she said.

'Everybody likes you,' John said.

'Sure they do,' she said sarcastically, stupidly flattered. 'That girl says that Ivan never comes in with the same woman twice. Is that true?'

'Oh, Ivan used to go through girlfriends. Before Chrissie.'

'So he's stopped all that, now?'

'Well, who can say? I think he has good reason to.' John was just drunk and enthusiastic enough to bother her. 'He seems happy,' he said, spotting the mistake. She took her cider and stood up again, heading for Ade, who was standing by the bar with a couple.

'Lainey,' Ade said, as if she were an old friend. 'Have you met Nav and Melissa? Lainey came with John. I don't know how he managed it either. Must have drugged her.'

'You're lovely,' she said to him, because the cider was going to her head. 'I like this pub a lot, too. Is this your local . . .' She stopped talking because her voice wasn't working any more. She could see Ade's lips moving but she couldn't hear his answer, because the strangest thing was happening to her brain. It was as if there was a cylinder in the middle of it – about the size of a loo roll's inner tube – through which a steady breeze was blowing, upwards, and she suddenly couldn't see any more and her heart was surely beating really too fast, too fast to work, and she thought she was going to die. All the time this whooshing feeling, upwards, rushing. Lainey gripped the bar.

'What's wrong?' Ade said. 'Are you okay?'

'I think my drink's been spiked.'

His arm was around her, he was feeling her wrist.

170

'Your pulse is racing,' he said. 'Do you want to get some air?'

'Oh my God Jesus Christ, what's happening,' she said. 'I'm going to die, aren't I? I'm going to fucking die.'

'Come on, just come outside with me,' Ade said. 'You'll be fine. I've got you.'

They sat on the kerb outside and Ade said calm things while she trembled. He took her face between his hands and looked her in the eye.

'What have you had to drink?' he said.

'Just a couple of ciders. Oh God, I left one in front of Bob. Do you think he'd –'

'Calm down, take it easy,' Ade said. 'No one here would do that. Least of all Bob – he's such a smackhead that if he had anything you couldn't make him share it. Your pulse has slowed down now. Are you taking any medicine, anything that could have reacted with the alcohol? Have you eaten today?'

'I've swallowed something, I can tell,' Lainey said. 'I don't feel normal. I'm really really buzzy.'

John had joined them and he sat on Lainey's other side. She could feel them whispering over her head.

'What do you think's the matter?' John said to her.

'I think someone's put something in my drink,' Lainey said, but now she wasn't so sure. She couldn't tell if the buzziness came from hyperventilating, and if the wide-awakeness came from being frightened. She couldn't really remember what she'd been feeling before.

'How do you feel?' he asked her.

'I felt like there was air, like, whooshing up through my brain, like, really fast . . . air. My head sort of detached, couldn't hear properly.'

'That doesn't sound like any drug I've ever taken,' he muttered.

'Well, everybody reacts differently,' Ade said.

'Have you ever felt anything like that?' John said to Ade, driving his point home with what felt like excessive force from

171

where Lainey was sitting. He stood up and started walking around them both, being annoyingly restive. 'You're tired, you haven't eaten much. You're just having a bit of a fit, that's all it is. Do you want me to take you home?'

'No, I don't,' Lainey said. 'I'll get a cab.'

'I don't think you should be alone right now,' Ade said. 'John, go with her.'

'I'm going to,' John said, sounding pissed off. 'Come on.'

'I'm getting a cab. You can go back in and finish your drink,' she said, and started to walk off. The two men hovered with her while she paced backwards and forwards over the same three feet of road, holding her face. A cab turned up and she called it over and got in.

'Are you sure you don't want me to come?' John said.

'I don't want you to come,' she said. She was so angry with him for not coming that she almost didn't want him to come. He was actually going to let her go home alone in a taxi to die alone of a suspected drug-spiking. Her mind was still squeaky clean, white, wildly alert, but she was becoming less and less sure about whether it had anything to do with a drug.

'Look, what is this mystery drug you think you've taken?' John kept asking her, keeping the cab door open. 'There's nothing like that. You're just imagining it.'

'So you've got nothing to worry about,' she spat. 'Just go the fuck back in there and let me go home.' She pulled the taxi door hard and he had to move to let her close it. Which he did. The last face she saw was Ade's, frowning with concern while he made a call-me mime, which was a nice thought but she didn't know his number. John had his back to the cab as it drove her away.

Chrissie wanted to come round, and Lainey wanted her to but she kept saying no. On her friend's instruction, she had spent the last ten minutes of their phone conversation looking in a hand mirror to see if her pupils were dilated.

'How do you feel now?' Chrissie said.

'Really awake,' Lainey said, 'but it might just be the anxiety. God, what have I done? Am I going mad?'

'Let me come round.'

'It's Saturday night, it'll take you years to get a cab out here, and you don't need to. I'm not going to die.'

'I can't believe this. They know some weird people, those two. I'm so fucking mad at John.'

Lainey momentarily resented Chrissie appropriating responsibility for John's behaviour, but she needed her friend now.

'*I'm* fucking mad at John,' she said, trying subtly to upstage her. 'He just kept telling me it was all imaginary. Oh, what if it was? I don't know what I feel any more. I can't remember what normal feels like.'

'Well, that sounds like you've taken something.'

'My pupils are massive. There's hardly any eye around them. What do I sound like?'

'You're a bit . . . awake-sounding, I suppose. That's maybe all. But if it was, say, speed, that's all you would be. Do you think it's speed?'

'I don't know. They never did any of that when I was at university.'

'You may not have,' Chrissie said, 'but I hardly think there was none of it about. How's your pulse?'

'Normal maybe. God, I wish I knew. At the time it was so frightening, I was so sure I was going to die. I mean, where did that come from, I can't have imagined that.'

They talked for another two hours, maybe more. Chrissie made her laugh, and never stopped sounding calm and soothing, but a couple of yawns made it into her voice, and Lainey agreed she'd try and go to bed.

'I'm just scared of that thing like in *Backbeat*, where I'll be staring at the ceiling all night.'

'Just close your eyes and try to relax. Don't try to sleep. Just feel how comfortable you are and relax.'

They hung up. Lainey took another look at her pupils, which, even in the strongest light – admittedly it was not very strong – were large round black holes. She got into bed and tried to monitor various parts of her body. The clock said 2.40. She switched off the lamp. She was out like a light.

redial, engaged, redial, engaged

'I tried to ring you last night,' John said. 'But your phone was off the hook.'

'I was talking to Chrissie,' Lainey said. She was still angry with him, her voice was controlled and icy.

'Did you manage to get any sleep at all?'

'No, I didn't.'

'That might just have been because you were worried.'

'Jesus, John, will you stop trying to find ways to prove I imagined the whole thing? Can you not just leave it?'

'No. I can't. Because I was worried about you. And I don't want to think any of my friends would do something like that. I *don't* think any of them did.'

'They're such great friends too. Bob in particular is a real gem.'

'You know I hate Bob. But he says he didn't do it.'

'Did you enjoy the rest of the evening, then? Taking the piss out of me, telling everyone I imagined it?'

'Oh, come on, Laine.'

In fact, Lainey would have been more than a little thrilled by John's performance after her dramatic exit. He swept about the place asking questions like a detective, he grabbed Bob's shoulder roughly, dragging him round to face him, and asked him over and over if he knew anything about Lainey's behaviour, and

175

nearly punched him, just for the hell of it. He sat alone with his head in his hands for a minute or two. He tried to ring her on the pub phone until about eleven, and then caught a cab home (even though he had a travelcard) and called her number non-stop for hours. Redial, engaged, redial, engaged – he asked BT if there was a fault on her line and they told him the line was in use. He punched the wall and spilled some beer. Then, while Lainey was dreaming about riding ponies with her childhood best friend, he lay in bed and tried to recall everything that had happened, and felt alternately slightly sick with worry and really mad at her.

He was drinking milky tea at the kitchen table when Ivan came in in his dressing gown.

'Who were you calling last night?'

'Lainey decided someone at the pub had spiked her drink and that she was tripping. So she starts panicking and fucks off back home, practically blaming me all the time. I thought you went over to Chrissie's last night.'

'Yeah, I didn't stay. So was she?'

'Was she spiked? I don't think so. No one knows anything about it. She said she had a bog roll in her head or something. Some air thing. It doesn't sound like anything, does it?'

'You think she just imagined it?'

'I think so.'

'Isn't that even more disturbing?'

'You think I'm going out with a psycho?' John smiled, and his face almost objected to the idea, it felt unnatural. He got up to pour Ivan some tea. 'I've been trying to put a stop to it.'

'Have you? Why?'

'Chemistry. I don't think we have any.'

'There's no such thing as chemistry,' Ivan said. He added three sugars to his tea, and agitated them below the surface. 'It's an exact science, but it isn't chemistry. It all comes down to finding someone who's exactly the same standard as us – when the account is perfectly balanced, that's what people call chemistry. But, really, they've just checked off their looks against their intelligence against their money, with no remainders.'

'That's not true. You can have a girl who's got everything going for her, and there's just something about you together that doesn't really work.'

'One of you is out of the other's league, and the strain shows.'

'Come off it. There's more to it than comparing salary and I Q. There is something else.'

'So go out with a thick girl. Or an ugly girl. You're just as likely to find your "chemistry" with them, surely, if it's this mystical logic-conquering force.'

'So you're saying either I'm too good for Lainey or she's too good for me and that's why I'm not sure about her. But if I meet someone who's my exact equal in all the important fields, then I'll think I'm in love. Although there's no such thing, it's all accounting.'

'There is such a thing, *and* it's all accounting. Yes, that's more or less right. But you don't have to match in all the fields. You just have to balance out altogether. That's why ugly rock stars go out with beautiful models.'

'Who's out of whose league, then? Me or Lainey?'

Ivan sipped his tea and grimaced. He added another teaspoon of sugar. 'Why did you spend over an hour last night calling her?'

'I didn't want her death on my hands.'

'You were worried about her.'

John laughed. 'So what's your point? Are you saying I've turned the corner? I'm falling in love with her?'

'No.' Ivan scratched his ear and lifted his chin to smile assuredly. 'That's what you're saying.'

just the fizzy stuff

A week after the unprecedented passion of his walk-out,
Theo missed five days in a row before it occurred to Lainey
that he might never come back. Nobody mentioned him at all,
which proved that they all knew more than Lainey, and she
wasn't sure which of them would be the best to ask about him.
She went for Dominic, because he was the first person she
happened to be alone with, and because she believed him to be
too pure to lie.

'Has Theo left for ever?'

Dominic looked startled, his eyes flicked like those of the
animals that aren't lions that feature in wildlife programmes the
week they're doing lions. She found herself enjoying unsettling
him. His edgy vulnerability was pretty appealing; it made her
want to reach for him.

'I'm probably not the best person to ask about that,' he said.

'Well, has he phoned in?'

'To, to the office?'

'Why, has he called you somewhere else?'

'No,' Dominic said. 'He hasn't called me anywhere at all.'

Lainey fast-unrolled some sellotape so that it shrieked. 'Do you
know where my scissors are?'

'No, I don't know anything,' Dominic said, and started typing
fast, head down and almost kissing the keyboard.

Scott came into the office at midday, wearing good sunglasses (she could tell from ten feet that they weren't cheap – he wore them too well), a snug black T-shirt that hugged his demure but defined six-pack, and low-slung trousers with a tiny indigo-and-black check. Here, Lainey thought when she'd managed to wipe the wanton from her mind, was sanity. It went hand in hand with good dress sense. The maddest people on the streets always wore the brightest clothes.

'Pellegrino?' she asked him, opening the fridge.

'We got any Limpia?' Scott said, removing his glasses in a smooth, cuffing motion.

'No, just the fizzy stuff.' She waited with the door open, hoping she looked like a game-show hostess. He stepped over to her and stooped to look in the fridge. She didn't move an inch out of his way.

'I really wanted something still . . .' he said.

'Mm, it wouldn't do to have something too exciting this early in the day. Tap?'

'Have to be tap,' he said, and filled a glass himself. 'Clare been down much today?'

'She's out again this morning, speaking to the publishers,' Lainey said.

'Shall we go upstairs and look through her stuff?'

'No, we won't! How could you even suggest that?' Lainey left her mouth open.

'Don't gape, young lady, I was joking.'

'Were you really? Yeah? I'd believe anything of you – except for everything you say.'

'Why can't I charm you?' Scott said thoughtfully, as if he were really considering it. 'You're the one person I can't charm.'

Embarrassed by her inability to meet his sex appeal without grinning like an idiot, Lainey tried to think of an answer that didn't sound stupid. She retreated into the office space. 'She locks the door, anyway.'

'Oho!' Scott said. 'You've tried it already, then!'

'I *heard* her,' Lainey squeaked. 'I *heard* it locking.'

'You expect me to believe that?'

She threw her hand down, a gesture of dismissal, defeat. 'I have work to do and you're a distraction.'

'Flatterer.'

She had hoped he would follow her and keep it up, but Scott went and sat with Dominic so that they could whisper together. She called Chrissie.

'How's work?'

'How's things with John?' Chrissie said.

'Oh, him. Should I call and apologize?'

'What for?'

'Because I obviously imagined all that, you know, that thing with Bob, because I fell asleep. And I insulted his friends . . . I don't feel like I can face him again. I feel like he knows.'

'But he wasn't good about it, and he didn't know whether you were dying or not,' Chrissie said. 'Why should you apologize to him?'

'That's true,' she said. 'But I think I'm beginning to really . . .'

'Really like John.' Chrissie couldn't keep the derision out of her voice.

'Maybe.'

Lainey couldn't really talk at work, but at the same time she wanted Scott to hear her discussing her boyfriend, just to tweak a bit of reaction out of him. She realized that she was scarily close to really getting somewhere with John now, so close that she was stretching out to find anything that would keep her from it – like flirtation with the lavishly engaging dandy at work. In the beginning, her thing with John had been tarnished by its proximity to the Chrissie/Ivan coalition, had felt uncomfortably like imitation. But she knew that, since then, they'd changed. Their affair had grown a personality of its own.

'If it were me,' Chrissie said finally, 'I don't think I'd find it easy to forgive him.'

'For what?' Lainey said. 'What did he actually do?'

'He was unsympathetic.'

'And I was unhinged.'

'Fine, do what you always do. Blame yourself. Be needy. I

forgot how much you like to be treated badly. You know, whatever turns you on, Laine. I have to go.'

Chrissie always made it very easy to do the opposite of whatever she said. Her advice might have been sound, but her intentions were transparently merciless. She always had an agenda; she wanted to prove one of her prejudices, not help. Still feeling the burn of her friend's temper, Lainey would have called John that minute, had she not been at work. Talking about men in front of Scott was one thing, talking to them might have put him off. She enjoyed having Scott around, because he always behaved as if he desired her, he kept her warm through John's cold spells. Chrissie was wrong about her wanting to be treated badly. What she didn't do was go wherever it was easy, because life was tougher than that and it was pointless pretending otherwise. There'd been a soft, greasy boy at college who said he loved her, bought her flowers – Ian Cheal: he would have made for an easy life. According to Chrissie's law she should just have stayed with Ian. But in the real world people didn't do what you wanted just because you wanted them. Just as Ian couldn't have been cool and charming, John couldn't be attentive and thoughtful all the time. It was a trade-off: she happened to value personal appeal above willingness to please. Despite her friend's insinuation, this was the opposite of masochism – it was making a choice that suited her. It was very *Cosmo*; she had nothing to reproach herself for. And even if she had, Chrissie was managing to do it splendidly without her help.

Clare was surprisingly unsweaty in the heat. She panted like a horse when she got to the top of her stairs, but that was as far as the similarity went. Unless you counted her mad eyes, white-rimmed and squinting, like a champion showjumper dead against the last hurdle.

'Can I get you something to drink, Clare?' Lainey said. Sucking up to a woman was always permissible: solidarity, not sycophancy.

'Just some still water, please, Elaine.'

'We've only got fizzy left,' Lainey said.

'Anything, then,' Clare said, and rolled herself out of the sofa. 'Elaine, it looks as if the next issue is going to be delayed, temporarily, because of difficulties with our backers. So there isn't going to be much for you to do over the next couple of weeks. Thank you for everything you've done on this edition, it's appreciated. Shall I give you a call when things start moving again?'

'Oh. Okay,' she said brightly. 'It's going to be, what, a couple of weeks, you say?'

'I can't really be sure how long these things take,' Clare said. 'Thank you.' She took the water and sipped as if it were medicinal.

'I still have some scanning to do,' Lainey said feebly.

'Yes, you'll probably finish that by this afternoon, I expect. Don't worry if you don't, though.'

'And I've helped Theo with subbing before . . . I could probably . . .'

'It's a fine suggestion, but we have a regular freelance sub in to check things over,' Clare said. 'Thanks for all your help over the last few, er . . . Well, thank you, anyway.'

Lainey, screwing the cap on to the Pellegrino with increasingly weak fingers, was feeling faint. Her eyes slipped out of focus, and something more or less the size and shape of the inner tube of a loo roll seemed to lodge in the centre of her skull and start to channel air, a tiny reprise of her performance the other night. She held on to the work surface while she rode it out, remembering how to breathe again. This was fucking capital. Not only had she probably just been made redundant, but she now knew for sure that she'd really accused all of John's friends for nothing. This was how her body liked to panic.

a really good bit of wall

'I saw my GP. He says the proper Latin medical term for it is a panic attack. He says they're fairly common for people my age.'

'Mmm?' John said, and it came out a little nastily. He'd meant to put some nastiness in there, but deliberate, considered nastiness, nastiness for a point, was a hard thing to gauge. As with false flattery, easy to go too far. 'So how often do you expect to be having these panic attacks?'

'I don't *expect* to be having another one at all. Are we okay? Do you forgive me?' She said it in a mock-pathetic little voice that John chose to find amusing, as long as she didn't make a habit of it. He was glad his friends hadn't hurt her.

'I'm doing a sort of friendly gig tonight –'

'As opposed to a hostile one?'

'It's like someone's party. Do you fancy coming along? You don't have to see my set or anything, I mean, you could come later if you wanted. There's going to be a free bar for a while, I think.'

'I'd love to see you tonight.' He liked it when she said things like that, which was how he could tell he was halfway serious about her. Normally, he'd read it as an indication that a girl was very keen, and given the sort of monsters he usually attracted, that would mean it was time for him to start looking for exits. But with Lainey these slight, simple nudges towards togetherness were curiously touching, and nothing to be scared of. 'But I'm doing a girl thing with Chris. It's kind of an attempt to prove we're not outgrowing each other.'

'What's to prove? I can't believe you were ever any closer than you are now.' He felt hurt at being awarded second place. She'd known Chrissie for ever, did they have to bond tonight?

She sounded tired, but stubborn: 'Well, you're right. It's really little more than some weak, selfish attempt to hold on to our youth. If we keep the routine going, then *we're* not changing. Not that changing would necessarily be a bad thing.'

'So cancel it and come out with me.'

'I can't. Cancelling her for a better offer is such a strong card that I have to save it for something important. If I did it all the time it would be pointless.'

'How about you forget the tactics and just do what you want?'

'The tactics get me what I want. That's the idea, anyway.'

'I wouldn't be a woman for the world,' John said. 'I'd lose track all the time.'

'Oh, it's just me, it's just me,' she said carelessly, sighing into the phone. He thought of her tossing her toaster-element hair as she spoke, maybe taking off a few clothes and running her hands over her breasts as her lithe, light body glowed with a fresh sparkle of perspiration. 'Sorry I can't make it.'

'Yeah. So am I.'

'Do you know what the trouble is?' John said to Ivan, when his eyesight was getting blurry – a sure sign that the brief spell of blinding clarity from the smidge of coke earlier in the evening had long since worn into a fog of drunkenness. His cleverness was dying; it was time to switch to affection and candour that he could regret in the morning. 'Do you know why I've been so indecisive about her?'

'No,' Ivan said.

'I don't think she thinks I'm any good. And it bothers me. Really bothers me. When I'm with her I'm constantly wanting to say to her: so what, do you think I'm funny, then? Because she never seems to want to see my set. And she never fucking laughs. I mean, she does, but not like uncontrollable, uninhibited head-back ha ha haaaa . . .'

'This is a sex thing. You're really trying to find out if you're the best she's had. You're afraid she's faking orgasms. You want her to lose control laughing because you want to see her like that to know if the other thing – the bit-of-the-other thing – is real. Male sexual insecurity: the root of all the world's problems.'

John took a few moments to consider. 'No. No!' he said, the drugs in his bloodstream making him right. 'The sex is great. This isn't the sex. This is about comedy, mate. If she doesn't think I'm the funniest bastard in the world, what's the fucking point?'

'It's the way her shoulders shake, and what they're shaking for.'

'Exactly.'

'Elvis Costello, "I Want You". It's about sexual insecurity.'

'You're one-track, that's your fucking problem.'

'Sh, look at that.' Ivan was pointing to a girl just behind John. She had black corkscrew curls and big tits and wore a white dress. She was dancing up against the wall – *not* dancing, really, this was the way women masturbated in porn films. She was raking her curls and stroking her thighs, head back, eyes flickering half-shut, hips grinding, pelvis curling. She appeared to be taking it up the arse from the wall.

'Is she on something?' John said.

'Either that or she's found a really good bit of wall.'

'What makes a girl do that? Is she really that aroused just dancing, or is it all advertising?'

'See what I mean? Men have no idea about what turns women on. Or at least they've got no confidence in it. We've seen too much top shelf to have any idea about what's real now.'

'That's because they're not real half the time. Lainey has this thing about Chrissie, for a start. You know, it's all about scoring points when she's with her. They're faking with each other, what chance have we got? But' – John relocated his thread – 'this isn't about sex. I just want to know she thinks I'm good. You know, it's the most important thing in my life, and if she thinks I might as well not bother, then either I might as well not, or I'm wasting time with the wrong girl, or . . . What does it mean?'

'Excuse me, love,' Ivan said. The dancing girl opened her eyes, looked soft and post-coital. 'Do you think I could stand where you're standing?'

'What?' Her eyes narrowed, she frowned.

'It's all right, ignore him,' John said. 'Do you see what I mean? She has to be behind me for the things that matter or I can't –'

'Oh John, shut up about Lainey. You're boring. She's boring. Shall we pick those women up?' Ivan pointed out a pair of maybe sisters who'd been looking at them for some time.

'Are you serious?' Ivan was already walking in their direction, while John was trying to focus on their faces.

'We really liked your act,' the taller sister said. 'Really funnee.'

'Yeah, we was creasing ourselves,' said the shorter one.

Good reviews from stupid people were not unlike bad sex. While conducive to loathing and self-doubt, they still felt good.

'We like your shirt, too,' said Tall to Ivan, who looked down, as if he'd forgotten what he was wearing. The girls were desperate to be chatted up, giving everything they could. The raw material was presentable enough, but there was nothing behind it. The vacant look of stupidity at rest could dull the shapeliest smile; it paralysed thick girls' faces, taking over like a screen saver when they stopped speaking.

'Where are you girls from?' Ivan said. John wondered how far he was willing to take it.

'We're living in Balham right now,' Tall said.

'Together?' John said. 'Are you sisters?' They giggled – the sharpness of their laughter making a shrill contrast to their wit.

'Everyone says that, din't they?' the bigger girl said, and the small one nodded.

'Everyone says that,' she agreed.

'We're not, though.'

'You're just friends? Do you work together?' Ivan said.

'Yes, we're beauty consultants,' said the tall girl. She was the talker. 'No, don't look like that. People think it's just selling lipstick but there's really loads of science to it nowadays. We've had to do, like, loads of chemistry and biology courses? You know, when we tell people we're beauty consultants they think we just put make-up on and do our hair all day, but, you know, we do have a brain, you know.'

'Yes, we do *have* a brain,' repeated the little one, and turned away to giggle, revealing a profile that was wasted on her.

'Between you,' Ivan said under his breath, and John snorted – an ugly, snotty sound, which he pretended was a sneeze. He thought he might be allergic to coke, or wine. Both of them made his mucus react badly.

'Where'd you get your shirt, then?' asked the shorter girl. It sounded aggressive, but probably wasn't.

'Boateng,' Ivan said. He looked somehow bilious, as if he'd reminded himself who he was, and it made him ashamed.

'I don't know that one,' Short said. 'Is there one on Oxford Street, or is it something really posh?'

'It's not far from Oxford Street,' Ivan said. 'It's quite posh. Do you have someone to buy for?'

'My boyfriend,' confessed the smaller girl, then looked to her friend as if she expected to be told off. 'But he wouldn't wear something like that. I don't mean that nasty, I just mean he isn't brave enough to wear them colours.' Ivan nodded. None of them spoke for a few beats. '*I* like colour,' she said into the widening space between them.

It was Ivan who decided not to pursue the non-sisters. John wasn't sure why: the tired, sad look was impenetrable, he could only imagine it was guilt of some sort that drove his tall friend to tell tall stories and move away. Maybe it was John being there, as a direct link to Chrissie, making him have second thoughts. Those nights when he wasn't with Chrissie and he didn't come home and he said he'd crashed at a friend's – maybe he took scenes like this to a conclusion. But not this time, and John was relieved. Chatting girls up was always a nice thing to do, but those girls had been very easy – who could tell how far it might have gone if Ivan hadn't given up? Sustained monogamy was leading John to a new appreciation for the infinite variety of women, but had also introduced him to a whole new version of insecurity. Lainey, for all his uncertainty, knew him. His dark side was safely untapped, of course – whose wasn't? It was the surface flaws, the obvious inadequacies, that she was familiar with, and which had not yet deterred her. He'd been surprised to find that the more she saw of him, the more reluctant he was to start all over again, explaining himself to somebody new – there was just too much of him, too much secrecy that he'd hardly known existed before. In a way he belonged to her now, like a blackmail victim.

And he'd changed; she'd changed him. These things were hard to prove, but the facts spoke for themselves: he was never nervous going on stage now – recently, when he'd fluffed, it had been down to boredom, a result of his mind wandering, not backfiring. He didn't vomit any more, the loose stools before a poor performance were a thing of the past. And he'd stopped overeating. Down to her? Or to having someone? John hadn't had a real affair since university. A few one-nighters, a lot of rejections, a few lessons in etiquette that had come to nothing. Lainey was the first to make a dent in a long time. At university he had fallen in love twice, and it was impossible to tell whether that was just a symptom of youth, or unfortunate scheduling.

First up, Lisa, the bad girl. Lisa was unfaithful to him more than once, but he would have forgiven her. He wanted to, but he wanted to make her sorry first. During the we-need-to-talk, John was fierce and resolute, but she didn't let him get any further. She started shouting at him, walked out, walked back in to shout some more, and he weakened and started apologizing. He could hear himself, and hated himself, but he couldn't stop it. His voice failed; it could have been a bit of phlegm at the worst time, even he couldn't be sure, and he wanted to catch the tremor back, stamp it to death. But what happened was that Lisa did it for him. When she left him, her eyes were cruel and magnificent.

He spent a few months hating her. He'd never stopped hating her, of course, but for a few months, that was all he did. Then . . .

Desi, the good girl. Desi was scrubbed and boyish and entirely without artifice. She used to sleep late in his single bed; he'd be trying to get up and out for a lecture, running around grabbing clothes, and she'd turn over softly, maybe open one eye and say, 'Oh, you're not going to move me? Can't I just stay here when you go?' And he wouldn't go. Desi broke it off, too, the bitch. She just said one night, fucking *before* they had sex, 'John, I don't know how to put this. It just doesn't feel like . . . like *it*, does it? We don't have the thing.' He made her explain and the more she said, the more it sounded like a fuck-you. She kept asking impossible questions and then just leaving him on his own with them. What are we going to do about it? You think the same, don't you? You had to have known I felt like this, didn't you? But then she was still on for it, she was still prepared to have sex after blowing him out. He was disgusted with her for being so cheap. Mad at her for not loving him. He felt used and desperate, and after she'd gone he didn't leave the house for days or get dressed in the mornings. She came round a few times to ask him if he was okay, and he acted like a child. So she stopped coming.

Since Desi, nobody had really bothered him. Rejection, if it came early in the game, didn't hurt, just smarted, like biting your tongue. He couldn't imagine Lainey hurting him because she hadn't yet, and he couldn't project emotionally. It didn't look likely; she was more into him than he was into her. At least, she *had* been.

a little push

Chrissie was swirling a Martini with her finger. She looked bored. Lainey *was* bored, but at least, she felt, she was making an effort. They were at the most single-minded of all the singles bars in London, except, because this one was in a fancy department store, it was the only acceptable singles bar. Romantic love was going through a rough patch: to be authentic, it still relied on coincidence, on the illusion of magic at work in the universe. But due to all the expectations everyone had, love that came effortlessly was getting harder to come by: it needed a little push. Except little pushes felt clumsy – love was either arranged or it happened, and anything in the middle was too much. Singles bars were as contrived as it got: a smoky haze of desperation blown out of nonchalant cigarettes, hope yellowed by nicotine. Hungry people trying to look well-fed. This setting – a natural extension of shopping – offered just enough of a front to make it palatable. If coincidence was going to be manufactured, presentation was everything. Chrissie and Lainey came here on girls' nights because they could usually be guaranteed some unwelcome attention. They weren't disappointed – within minutes, two men bought them a glass of champagne each – but they *were* disappointed, because Chrissie didn't seem prepared, or perhaps able, to do the thing she did, and the men said they were going on to a nightclub and they went alone.

The barmen slid change on silver platters across the bar, all the way round, and the bar's fairground glitter twinkled back at them in the windows, and outside, through the glass, London was dark and lonely.

'Fancy a bit of comfort at the Maroush?' Chrissie said. 'I'm suddenly starving.'

A silent cab ride to the Edgware Road. Their eyes met twice in the dark patch of the driver's head in the dividing screen. Nights in the city were circumscribed by windows the way the day never was. Lainey was aware of the safety of the glass boxes, but also the fragility. She felt as if she were between two microscope slides, being examined. They were both more animated now, more awake; twenty minutes before, they'd been ready to quit. A change of scenery was all it had taken to bring them back. Lainey was sad that nights out with Chrissie weren't good any more. They were too close to be interested in each other. When they were static, like tonight, being with Chrissie was worse than being alone, because she had to try but got nothing out of it. Their friendship was a refrigeration of laboured nostalgia, getting staler by the second. Lainey thought they might never be better again.

'This is it, ladies,' the driver said.

They perched on high stools and Chrissie sipped thick, syrupy coffee and ate heavy baclava like there was no tomorrow. Lainey had mango juice. She often used her lack of appetite as a weapon against Chrissie, to make her feel a little self-disgust.

'How did we get here?' Chrissie said. Lainey thought she was talking about the flatness of their friendship, but she wanted to pretend she didn't know what Chrissie meant, so she just nodded. It was a good job she hadn't committed herself to an answer, because Chrissie was talking about something else. 'How the hell did we end up with the same men?'

'They're not so alike,' Lainey said.

'No, I know. But you know what I mean. It's like we've turned up at a party in the same dress.'

'Not quite the same.'

'Okay, it's like the same dress but mine is green and yours is black. Or it's the same material but mine's short and yours is long. Why are we doing it? It can't be healthy.'

'Do you think one of us should stop?'

'No.' Chrissie chopped a pistachio pastry into small pieces with her coffee spoon. 'But I was first.'

'Naturally,' Lainey said impatiently. 'Tell you what, if we go out anywhere together, I'll make a point of telling everyone we meet that your relationship came first. Or should we just put an ad in the paper?'

'No. That would just bring attention to it,' Chrissie said. She asked the man behind the bar for another coffee.

High stools made Lainey feel young and tiny, not being able to touch the floor with her feet. 'Does this really bother you?' she said. 'I thought you were just making conversation. It's not so weird, is it? Even if couples don't know each other's friends beforehand, they always end up doing, so what's the difference?'

Chrissie didn't answer right away, but she smiled shyly – the look she usually used when she was talking about Ivan, but this time it was for Lainey. 'I just don't want you to say things about me to John. There are things you think about me that I don't want Ivan to think.'

'Don't be silly,' Lainey said softly. Chrissie shrugged and looked away. Lainey waited for her to say something, until it became clear that she wasn't going to. 'I haven't said anything that you wouldn't want Ivan to know.' Chrissie's mouth twitched. She still said nothing. 'Look, what do you think he's going to find out? What haven't you told him?'

'It's not a question of me not telling him anything. Different people have different sides with different people, that's all.'

'So what are you faking with him?'

'What am I faking with you?' Chrissie said, mostly under her breath.

'I have known you longer,' Lainey said, trying to keep it light. 'I think I can tell what you're about.'

'Yeah, well. Just . . .'

'I wouldn't tell John anything that would make Ivan . . . There's nothing *to* tell.' She gave up. Chrissie was being childish and ridiculous. 'Do you and Ivan mention me and John when you're together?'

'Yes, a bit.'

'What do you say?' Lainey said, waiving her right to attack.

'Not much.' Chrissie yawned. 'What's John up to, then? Things like that.'

'Who says that?'

'I do, of course.'

'And what does Ivan say?'

'You see, this is what I'm getting at. No one should have access to a second opinion about a relationship that's actually not far from the truth. It's like a textbook with answers at the back. When things are too easy it does nobody any good. It's deceptively easy, too. And impossible not to cheat. Can you imagine if we keep trying to know what's going on? It's like we're all reading each other's diaries.'

'Or we're all Betazoids.'

'*Brazen?*' This time her yawn threatened to eat her head whole.

'*Star Trek.* Betazoids are empathic. They feel other people's emotions. They still have normal relationships – even good ones, and their deep understanding of each other seems to intensify their feelings. Doesn't seem to make it any easier, though.'

They were being given the eye by a couple of men at the window. Lainey had just got wordier to indicate that they didn't want to be interrupted. There were times when fending off a pick-up felt like fun, and times when it felt more like danger, it depended on many things. The hour, the postcode, the way you were sitting, the men doing the eye-giving. The other reason she was being a deliberate sci-fi bore was because she liked Chrissie to think her job was a doss, that she didn't really work, she watched television. The irony being that, by the looks of things, she really *didn't* work any more. Whether Clare had fired her or not, either way she was drifting, and freedom was the only currency Lainey could compete in. Doing without felt okay when you reminded yourself that at least you weren't part of the system. The *system*. It just meant having a job, a little money, some idea of how the next few months were going to turn out. Out of the system meant no job, no money, no responsibility, no certainty. It meant being a kid for longer, at the whim of circumstance and other people, rather than making your own choices. Spontaneity. Indifference. The adolescent indulgences denied to everyone who'd made it. Winners had deadlines and mortgages and promises to keep. Small comfort to the losers without, but just enough to incite a shiver of envy in all the right places.

Chrissie wasn't listening. She talked over the end of Lainey's analysis of Troi's relationship with Worf.

'I'd like to go on holiday. How about you? And John. And Ivan. How about all of us together? Go the whole hog! Wouldn't that be creepy? I'm desperate to get away.'

'I can't afford to go on holiday. I doubt if John could.' She saw where this was leading: Chrissie was asserting *her* freedom.

'It wouldn't have to be something expensive,' Chrissie said. 'A little cottage somewhere.'

'Whatever. Maybe. What's the CD?' Chrissie was chain-yawning – it was unbelievably annoying – and she'd started to look through her bag, the way she did when she had run out of things to say. She turned the pages of her diary, which all had writing on. Lainey didn't have a diary; she wrote everything on pieces of paper and lost the pieces of paper.

'It's Bob Dylan. It's Ivan's; he wanted me to listen to it alone.'

'Why alone?'

'There are some Bob Dylan songs you have to hear alone,' Chrissie said. 'No don't do that!' Lainey had taken out the booklet and was folding it back on itself. She looked up to see Chrissie looking genuinely worried.

'What?'

'You're going to crease it?'

'It's only a . . .' Chrissie took back the booklet and Lainey watched her insert it into the plastic frame with ridiculously visible care. 'Why are you scared of him?'

'Scared of Ivan?' Chrissie looked at her, possibly for the first time that night. Her eyes were round, amazed. 'How could I be scared of him?'

'You're always nervous about his stuff. You go all sort of stupid and frightened when you talk about him. Always asking his opinion and making sure everything's okay for him. If this was me, if I was behaving like this over a man, you'd be telling me off.'

'I would never –'

'You would! You're always, like, don't be grateful if they're being nice to you, you're the one who decides everything, not them, don't let them get away with anything. But you! You worry that you're not enough for him, you tell me he wants more than you, and when you mention his name you're all subservient and mustn't-upset-Ivan. You *are* afraid of him, and I have no idea why.'

'Scared of Ivan,' Chrissie repeated softly, as if she hadn't heard Lainey since then. 'I'm scared *for* him.'

you don't seem to be
yourself tonight

John jumped when the doorbell rang. He was drinking vodka alone, with a joint, because he was feeling sorry for himself, because Ivan had gone off with work people who just happened to have been at the party, and he'd been gently excluded, and he'd decided it was because they were going to go on to somewhere very hip to take very expensive drugs, and he was jealous. When he jumped he spilled vodka over his hand, and sucked it off as he went to the door, as if it were a bleeding cut.

It was Chrissie.

'Chris,' John said, frowning with confusion. 'Ivan's not back yet. He's networking.' Her cool grey eyes dimmed, and the envy jabbed like a spike in John's head. She really loved him.

'Can I come in and wait for him?'

'I don't know when he'll be . . . Of course you can. Sorry.' He stood back and let her come by him. She smelled of cigarettes and coffee and red roses. 'What are you doing here so late? Are you okay?'

'I've been out with Lainey and I didn't want to go back home tonight.'

'Is she all right?'

'She's fine. She's good.'

'Do you want a drink?'

'I'll have some of that.'

He fumbled with CDs, everything he had was too noisy. He put on Bacharach, which seemed a bit obvious. Her knees were together, but her thighs didn't touch, and she wasn't wearing tights. She was sitting on the sofa, and he sat next to her, to show her how much he wasn't thinking about sex with her. They both put their feet up on the coffee table, and he let his joint burn away in the ashtray.

'What do you mean, networking?'

'He met a director he knew at the party, and they went on somewhere. They were talking about a project.'

'What was he called?'

'Steve, I think.'

'What did he look like? Never mind. You don't think he'll be back at all, do you?' She said it as if she expected to catch him out.

'I really don't know.'

Chrissie drained her glass and held it up to him.

'More, please.'

He was so tired. He yawned through everything he said, and had to keep apologizing and saying it wasn't her, but Chrissie didn't offer to go, or ask if she was keeping him up. She just kept on talking, and when she didn't, she let the silences stretch out just long enough for him to almost fall asleep, and then she'd say something else and he'd realize he'd actually been half-dreaming, the pre-sleep madness where possibilities feel like they're really happening, and dream characters start speaking everything you hear. She was talking about a film that she'd seen and he hadn't, and she was being pretty boring – it wasn't just that he couldn't keep awake anyway. She was still being her, so she still had that oddness, that Chrissie-take on things, but he was too used to it to be too charmed tonight, and she was still being boring. He smothered a yawn as long as he could, then gave in, and let his mouth hang wide open so long he thought he might have forgotten how to breathe with it shut.

'Where'd you go with Lainey?' he said.

'All our usual places. Fun fun fun.'

She didn't say it sarcastically, but she meant it to be. He was offended – she had no right to insult his girlfriend. He turned away from her smile. She understood. 'I don't mean it like that,' she said. 'I was the boring one, not her. I'm just in a crap mood today.' She leaned closer. 'Put the television on, give me something to do when you fall asleep again.'

'Sorry,' he said.

'No, don't be. It's not your fault.'

'I'm not tired any more anyway.' He made a real attempt to be awake, which brought on a big yawn, but that helped. 'No, that was it. Awake!' Another yawn. 'Honestly.'

'Oh, go to bed, John, I'll just sit here.'

'I'm awake.'

She leaned over him for the remote control, staying for a while half-lying on him, as if she didn't have the energy to swing back up again. Then she leaned back, sank lower, and switched the television on. Ad for a chat line. Ad for an insurance company. Another chat line. Then a film, from maybe the second or third part, with Robert Vaughn. Chrissie was dipping her fingers in the vodka and sucking them: he wondered if she was trying to turn him on, but it just looked pretty silly, mutton dressed as Lolita. She was too sharp to come the coquette.

'Lainey asked me earlier why I was scared of Ivan,' she said.

'I didn't know you were.'

'Exactly. She's insane, isn't she? How could anybody be scared of Ivan?'

'Because he's unknowable.'

'You don't think you know him? Even now?'

'Of course I know him. You just asked me how anyone could be scared of him and I told you. Ivan's generally pretty unknowable. A lot of my friends say he's a tosser, but it's because they can't work him out.'

'Who says he's a tosser?'

'No one you know.'

'I bet you're lying,' she said. 'I bet I do know them.' She

crossed her legs and they made a shushing sound as they slid against each other. She said slowly, steadily, 'Do you ever think we've got things the wrong way around?'

He had a feeling he knew what she meant, but he was going to pretend he didn't. He took the remote control from her and started flicking. *News 24* on the BBC, *Open University*, more ads on Channel 4. He went with the ads. Another chat line – stills of rough-looking blondes with dated class-specific haircuts, a tinny rave soundtrack. Chrissie leaned on him and presented her glass for a refill.

'John. John, look at me,' she said, and giggled softly. He could tell that it wasn't real. 'This vodka's really going to my head. Do you think Lainey's scared of you?'

'No,' he said, a perfunctory laugh dismissing it.

'No, maybe not. She just looks scared all the time. Probably something to do with her size.'

'That'll be it,' John said. His suspicion had woken him fully, now. He wanted to know what Chrissie's game was, and why she was pretending to be drunker than she was, and a pain in the arse. 'Are you feeling all right, Chris?' He didn't really care, of course; he'd remembered something Ivan had told him about women. That they were never really feeling all right, that they always concealed some kind of tragedy, or thought they did, and they were waiting for someone to see it in them. And they were waiting so hard that the slightest prompt was enough to look like the deepest sensitivity. 'You don't seem to be yourself tonight.'

'Not myself?' she said. 'Why would you say that? Do I look –'

'No, my mistake,' he said. 'It's me, I think.' What the fuck did Ivan know, anyway?

'Well no, you're right, really. I *am* feeling weird. Subdued. I think. It's Iv–' she stopped, as if she'd decided she couldn't trust him, or herself, or had just weighed up the possibilities and reached the end already.

'You want to talk about it?'

'I don't, no.'

'You don't know?'

She almost laughed, put her head on his shoulder. 'You idiot. So how's the comedy thing? How was tonight?'

'Tell me what's wrong.' He was cooking now. He could have talked about himself but he'd gone straight back to her and her feelings. Strangely, this felt like a test. What with Chrissie not doing his head in tonight, and the possibility that he could somehow manipulate her looking real, he was experiencing a sort of weird clarity and power. He wanted to do it properly.

'I don't like Lainey any more, and Lainey doesn't like me. In fact, she started it, and the reason I don't like her is that she doesn't like me.'

'Did she steal your Barbie?'

'Yes, I know it sounds stupid, but it's a big thing. She's, in fact, my only friend, really, and I'm not sure what you do without a girlfriend.'

'Well, you're speaking to the expert, but maybe not the right person. You know I'm only going to say nice things about her. If only because you might just be trying to catch me out and report everything I say back to her. And even if that isn't your game, then you're bound to make up with her and do exactly that if I say anything – anything – about her now.'

'You've got things to say?'

'No.' He grinned and poured himself another drink. 'See how easy this is. Why've you fallen out with her?'

'We haven't fallen out. We just don't like each other. I bet she's told you that.'

'. . . No.' He'd hesitated on purpose, to make it clear he was being discreet.

'Thought so. Can I lie down?'

She turned her body ninety degrees and put her head in his lap. It was at this point that he began to seriously worry about the behaviour of his prick, but it seemed safe enough. Somehow, he was immune to Chrissie tonight.

'Why do you have to be friends if you don't like each other?'

'Well, I told you. In my case it's because I don't have any other friends . . .'

'And in hers?'

'There's one thing you should know about Lainey, John. She doesn't like anything to stop existing. She wants to be all times all the time. She wants to be omni . . . omni-timey. She doesn't like having a past that isn't still around now.'

'And in English?'

Chrissie closed her eyes. 'Just don't expect to be extinct when you're her ex, that's all. She's like the FBI, she doesn't close any files. Aren't you dying to kiss me?'

'I have to say the thought hadn't occurred to me.'

'Well, not today, maybe.'

He looked down at the blonde on his lap, with her hair over his knees, her eyelids criss-crossed with dark silvery-indigo creases of eyeshadow, and her lips slightly pushed into a deliberately inviting, deliberately mocking pout.

'What do you want from me, Chris?' He was relaxed and amiable, like a favourite uncle.

'Just to kill the "what if".'

'It's there for a reason.'

'It doesn't have to be.' They stayed as they were for some seconds. Then she picked herself up slowly, folded her hair into a pleat and leaned back on it. She looked like a child searching for a reprimand or a pardon. 'I see,' she said. 'Fair enough.'

He felt she deserved an apology of some kind. He couldn't tell how much of it was a joke, and how much she meant it. 'Your timing's off,' he said. 'Believe me, if you only knew how much I –'

'You think I didn't know? You think I'd just roll the dice and take a chance unless I'd seen something? What am I, stupid? Come off it, John, I made a mistake. I thought you were a bit less scrupulous than you evidently are. Although I'm not sure who you're bothered about – him or her.'

'I'm not sure either.'

They sat in silence for the next few minutes, by which time John was almost nervous. The feeling was exacerbated when Chrissie decided to snigger to herself. He didn't ask her to share.

'I just wanted to know what you were like at kissing.'

'No, sorry, that's not enough,' John said. 'If I'm going to throw myself into the whole guilt thing I need more than that.'

'Why would you feel guilty kissing me?'

'Wouldn't you?'

'Not in the slightest.'

He turned his head – she closed her eyes slowly and waited, and he pulled his head back an inch to look at her. Mad, this whole thing. What the fuck was she on tonight? He kissed her. Mouth closed, softly, lip to lip. As he started to draw away she applied pressure, holding his bottom lip with her lips, making him stay. He spoke into her mouth. 'Chrissie, you can stop this now. I told you it's a stupid idea.'

'As I recall,' she said, still kissing him, 'you said it wasn't enough.' Her hand was on the waistband of his trousers and she let one button go. He grabbed the hand and pulled it away, feeling himself redden, suddenly really flustered by her.

'Fucking hell, Chrissie, don't be stupid.'

'I see, you're playing the victim. Okay, if that's how you want me . . .'

Her hand was back in his waistband, she traced a finger along his frighteningly not hard enough stomach, and he thought suddenly of Ivan's washboard and withdrew into the sofa cushion. She followed him back; she had undone the next couple of buttons and her thumb was tracing his prick through his pants. The erection came almost instantly, so hard it was almost against his stomach. He shut his eyes, decided and undecided fifty times. Fuck it, why not, was where he left it, as he leaned over her and let his hand slide down her back, pulling her close.

But then something happened. In fact, nothing happened. Chrissie had made her way inside his boxers, but she was making no progress. She'd been running her fingers slowly over the shaft of his cock for a good time, without increasing pace or pressure, and his penis was beginning to tire of it. Slow, soft manipulation, the sort of contact it might receive, say, in the early afternoon when he was reading a paper and paying it very little attention.

He wasn't sure what he should do, and she seemed intent on persisting with the manoeuvre. He tried to turn his attention to her, but Chrissie seemed to be following her own agenda, and wasn't ready to accept anything else. And suddenly he became desperately aware that the erection was going as quickly as it had started and there was nothing he could do about it, except feel it fall and wait until she noticed. It took about a minute. Then she sat back, cleared her throat, didn't look at him for a while.

'Chrissie –' he began. She stood up hard, like she had pins and needles.

'I'm going home.'

'At this time? Do you want to call for a cab?' As much as he wanted her out of there, he didn't want to find out she'd been murdered in the street, and have to explain the last he'd seen of her to Ivan.

'I've got my phone. I'll be fine.'

'Chrissie, you're being silly. We nearly, and we didn't. That says something for us.'

'It says something for you, anyway. Look, don't make a big deal out of this, I just think there's no point me staying anyway.' She looked at the door, then at her fingers. He could feel that she could see him in her peripheral vision. 'I have a lot of bad ideas, you know; this has just been one of them. Well, I'm going. Tell Ivan something. Or don't.' Frowning, she left him alone.

3

drink some tea with me

John's park. Almost enough to give her a frisson. Almost adultery – going to his place behind his back, consorting with his turf and landmarks without him. The possibility of being caught, of running into him. Almost like stalking him, too. Weird. Five days now, since . . . He'd brought her here several times, it was definitely his, definitely him, that was why she was here. To be close.

Lainey breathed in: the freshest air, so fresh it felt heavy, full of oxygen, and the taste of wet green leaves. Nothing like town air, which was light, but suffocating, like fibre glass. Could she feel the difference in her head, or was she imagining it, like the spiked drink that hadn't been? Grey squirrels watched, but didn't see her as a threat; the grass was soft and alive beneath her. She thought she saw John but it wasn't him.

At the big pond she stopped and followed a wave all the way across with her eyes. Something about water soothed the soul; for the first time in a long time she was wide awake, glad to be alive. She sat down on a bench and tried to hold the feeling. She watched the swans. ('Fat bastards,' John had said, when they'd walked through a crowd of them. Or was it a flock? Definitely a crowd. Swans had too much leg to be a flock.) She felt like she didn't much like anyone in the world right now. She was looking into computer courses at the Marylebone Library. She blamed other people for her having reached this level of desperation. *Brazen* had not called. Nor had John.

In front of her, an old man stopped and looked down. He lifted his head to grimace at a child crying loudly near him, then looked again at his feet. He was wearing grey trousers, a grey jacket – different greys – and brown shoes. His right leg twitched. Then he walked again, his hands in his pockets pulling up his trousers, so Lainey could see four or five inches of dirty white sports socks. After every few paces, he shook his right leg to one side, as if dancing the conga. His shoes hurt; the socks were bruised with old polish. Lainey felt achingly sorry for old men. The purpose of old women was clearer, somehow; there was a place for them. There were all these weak little men wandering around, alone, without a very good reason to go on. They had to know it. With little idea of her own future and no particular job, Lainey thought she had grounds enough for semi-detached empathy; her eyes moistened with the force of her compassion, an intense film of clarity thickened over her lenses. She looked again across the big pond and let her problems drift and dilute, revigorated by the brief liaison with unselfishness.

It took some seconds before she realized that the figure approaching was Ivan. She thought it was John at first, not because he looked anything like John, but because she knew she knew him, and she was here, and her brain couldn't expect anyone else quickly enough. Ivan was smiling and waving, but she still tried to devise a means of escape.

'I thought it was you, Lainey,' he said, when he was still almost too far away, and because she didn't reply straight away he repeated it as he got nearer.

'Hi. How are you?' she said, hearing her voice come out a false, whiny sing-song. The thing about Ivan was he was always relaxed and easy – it brought out her own natural artifice. 'I was watching the ducks.'

'Yeah? I've been running,' he said. 'Trying to 86 the old beer gut in time for my holidays.' He tugged at his worked-out stomach, presenting a couple of inches of skin and T-shirt as evidence. She tucked her legs up on to the bench, nearly into the lotus position, and twisted her hair nervously. She wanted to say something casual and jokey about him not needing to lose weight, but she knew it wouldn't come out the way she meant it to.

'When are you going?'

'A week on Friday. Didn't Chrissie . . . ?'

'Yes, she did, I just have a bad memory.' And nothing to say to fill an awkward silence. 'That'll be nice.'

'John'll have the place to himself for a bit. Always does us good to be apart for a while. We're like an old married –' He stopped himself. 'Sorry. I probably shouldn't talk about –'

'Oh, don't be mad. Of course you can talk about him. I ended it, didn't I?'

'Yes, you did. Why did you?'

'Oh, it was . . .' She looked the other way, squinted into the low sun.

'You're right, it's none of my business. But listen, you know, we should get together some time soon, me, you, Chris, even without John if you like.'

'Yes. Totally we should,' she said.

'Well, anyway, I'd better . . .' Ivan said.

'Yep.' They nodded in time.

He looked at his watch, smiled, and started to jog away. She didn't watch him go. But she heard him approach again, several seconds later. This time he was standing with his back against the light, and she had to shade her eyes to look at him.

'Do you want to be on your own or something?' he said.

'Not at all.'

'So come and drink some tea with me now,' he said. 'We'll do that.'

The tea room was dazzlingly sunny and strangely cool, even though it was pretty hot outside and the doors were open. The waiter was good-looking, and young: the public-school vacation-job type. He tried to inject personality into his order-taking, the way she'd once tried to be an interesting check-out girl. It worked a little.

'So why *did* you give John the elbow?' Ivan said cheerfully.

'I thought you said it was none of your business.'

'It wasn't out there. Out there I was just your friend's boyfriend. Or your ex-boyfriend's friend. Not any more. We're drinking tea together. We're serious friends now.'

She laughed. 'I see. Okay, if you really have to know –'

'I don't have to.' She was disappointed by his interruption. He had lured her into confiding, with humour and the honey warmth of closeness, and now he was being coolly polite again. She had to raise the value of her stock by pretending there was something worth knowing.

'Would you hold it against me if I didn't tell you? As a serious friend?'

Ivan sighed. 'You know, the man's depressed. Really down about it. And I have to live with him. Not that I'm going to tell him what you tell me now, but it's always good to know more than everyone else. Still, if you don't want to talk about it . . .'

'He's depressed?'

'Suicidal.'

'Piss off.'

'He is, in fact, listless and grumpy. Lacklustre. He's not happy, let me put it that way.'

'It wasn't just that I finished with him, it was that he let me.'

Ivan waited for the waiter to put down the teapot.

'Thanks.' He smiled at Lainey as if they were communicating secretly. 'I may sound like a neophyte, but don't you have to commit yourself to finishing with someone before they can let you?'

'Do you, bugger. You say it first to scare people. You want them to stop you. You want them to reassure you. You don't want them to –'

'But you know – surely you know – that John doesn't go through this thought process. He hasn't read the same magazines.

If you said something, John didn't look at it as the start of a discussion. He would have seen it as the final word.'

'I see your point, but no, that's not good enough. He didn't say the right things.'

'What did he say?'

you've lost me

John blinked and said, 'Oh, right.'

'Well, what do you think?' Lainey said.

'It doesn't really matter what I think, does it?' John said, at this point thoughtfully. 'These things have to be sort of joint, don't they? It doesn't really work if . . . You know, if even only one person thinks the other one's an arsehole, the whole thing kind of breaks down there.'

'So what are you saying, are you saying you don't think we should stop seeing each other?'

'No, I'm not saying that. I'm saying it wouldn't matter if I didn't. Anyway, no, fair enough.'

There was a long silence. John sipped his beer and wished she'd just go.

'Well?' she said.

'Well?' he said, quite cruelly, and regretted it.

'Right, then,' Lainey said. 'I'll go, then.'

He shrugged.

'Are you okay about this?'

'Yes,' he said, trying to sound as if he was trying not to sound pissed off.

'I'll go, then.' She waited, looking at him. He didn't know what she was looking for. He hoped she didn't find it. 'Don't you want to say anything?'

'Were you expecting me to?' he said. As soon as he'd said this he wished he'd left it, but he wanted to know more.

'Not *expecting*, John, that's the fucking point.'

'Well,' he said, 'you've lost me. But as I said, I don't suppose it matters.' He knew there was something he should be getting by now, and he wasn't getting it. But he wasn't going to give her the satisfaction of a show of emotion, because she wanted one so much. Lainey was being so obviously manipulative that he sure as shit wasn't going to indulge her. She was behaving like a typical girl, and although he didn't understand it, he recognized it. Besides, he didn't even *feel* all that emotional, and he definitely wasn't going to start faking it. All he felt was embarrassment and confusion and small-scale irritation.

'I don't *expect* you to say anything else, because I don't know what you think. Maybe you don't think anything. But I was *hoping* you'd have something else to say. I'm not so old-fashioned that I have to be in love with the man I'm screwing, but it would bloody maybe help if I thought he could be . . . in love with me. At some point in the future.'

'You want me to tell you I'm in love with you. You want me to say things?'

'Look, it's not you. I need someone who makes it a bit more obvious. You don't worship the ground I walk on, you don't treat me like shit, and frankly either of those would probably do, but this, this middle thing just isn't enough.'

'You'd prefer it if I treated you like shit,' he said. The absurdity restored a little of his self-confidence. This was his territory, and he eased into it. He sat up a little straighter, feeling less stupid. 'They always told us this at boy college, and I never believed them. Would you like me to hit you or just stand you up occasionally?'

'That's not what I meant.'

'I could tell you you've got a fat arse, if that'd help . . .' He waited for her to stop being serious; she didn't. 'It isn't fat at all,' he said, quietly, even desperately. 'Crap joke. Look, I'm never going to be the kind of . . . *extreme* . . . whatever it is you want. You're right. It's just not me.' While he thought there was still a chance of saving things he was trying to save them, but his motives were muddy. 'I thought we were having a good time. Obviously it was just me.'

'It wasn't just you.' She almost smiled at him, but that didn't last long. 'The more I think about everything . . . Look, here's the thing: the further this goes, the more I need to know that . . . that it's *really me* you want. And not, you know, not someone else.'

'Meaning? Jesus, if there was someone else I'd be with someone else.'

'Not if she was going out with your friend, you wouldn't.'

'Oh Christ, not Chrissie again. I don't. Want. Chrissie.' He felt himself get hot and tried to keep his face blank. Telling her about that little episode with the hand-job wasn't going to help anything. Anyway, he was too ashamed of what had happened. And he was never going to come out of it looking as guiltless as he really was. Not with the way she assumed stuff.

'*Okay,*' she said softly.

'This is pointless,' John said. Because if she wasn't going to go, he wanted to. Now. 'You've said everything. There's nothing to talk about.'

'You haven't told me what *you* want.'

'Like it's up to me? Like, you want to stop seeing me, but I get the final say. It's just a bit too reasonable. And if I do, then I'd have to assume that you don't really *have* any particular preference, and it's all down to how I feel. In which case, what does that make you?'

'That's a horrible thing to say and I don't even know what it means. What *does* it make me?'

'Easy,' he said, and watched her expression change. 'And difficult.'

something had to be decided

'Well, of course he said that,' Ivan said, adding lots of sugar. She believed he put in the last spoonful because he knew she was watching him; an act of bravado. 'What else would he say to that? You didn't expect him to beg you to stay, surely?'

'It might have been nice.'

'Lainey, the male ego. Male ego, this is Lainey. Apparently, you two haven't met before.' Lainey had edited out the Chrissie angle when she told him what had happened, but she was interested in knowing what Ivan thought, and maybe even learning what Ivan knew.

'Tell me, then.'

'I just did.'

'It's all a pride thing, is it?'

'Why did you say it to him in the first place. Not a pride thing?'

She was struck by how much he reminded her of Chrissie. Was it because they spent so much time together, or were they in fact real-life split-aparts, actual soulmates? 'Isn't everything a pride thing? So yes. But not the way you think. We'd reached a point where I just decided something had to be decided.'

'How did you reach that point?'

*

'I thought you were out tonight,' Chrissie said. 'With him.'

'Him cancelled,' Lainey said. 'Last-minute gig came up.'

'Oh, that's not good,' Chrissie said. 'Not good at all.'

'I don't mind,' Lainey said.

'Doesn't matter. Doesn't matter whether you mind or not. What matters is that he thinks he can do that to you.'

'Love means never having to say you're sorry,' Lainey said. She yawned to show her indifference.

'You sound unhappy,' Chrissie said. 'Are you?'

'Not as far as I know. Are you?'

'You forget I know you. Better than anyone. You don't have to put on a brave face. Are things not going well?'

Lainey crumpled under the heavy compassion. She was glad Chrissie couldn't see her face. She changed ears. 'Well, you know how depressed I've been over the job not happening. And, you know, you find yourself alone when you didn't expect to be alone and everything just seems quieter. Bigger.'

'I've seen your flat. You could use the space.' Chrissie laughed. She didn't laugh at her own jokes unless they were insults.

'Yeah. I'm just having a miserable night, that's all.'

'Do you want to come round? I'm in all night.'

Lainey thought Chrissie was only offering, so she said no. After hanging up, she made herself some hot carob drink and wished she had a bath tub. She dialled the first ten digits of John's number and let her finger rest lightly on the last one, let her nail tip into the number's shallow impression. He was out anyway, she could press it, but she just hung up again and drank her carob, and watched *Blind Date*. This is wrong, she thought. He is a bit of a shit, blowing me out like this.

Later there was an award ceremony, her and Chrissie's favourite type of programme. So when the ad break started she gave Chrissie another call. The line was engaged. She watched the next part, and even wrote a couple of notes, to remind her of points to bring up. During a boring man's speech, she tried again. Chrissie picked up.

'Did you see that dress?' Lainey said. No more information required.

'*Oh* yes,' Chrissie said.

'And no bra,' Lainey said.

'Career move,' Chrissie said.

'Do you think men like it when they career move like that?'

'They like anything that reminds them they're there.'

'As if they'd forget. I once asked John what the big deal with tits was.'

'What did he say?'

'I can't remember. Something not quite good enough.'

Chrissie yawned again. 'Haven't you finished with John yet?' she said breezily, before the yawn was over.

'No – was I going to?' Lainey said. She knew Chrissie was joking, but she was surprised by the question, maybe offended.

'Oh, I don't know. I always think you're about to. He's hardly good enough for you, is he?'

'They never are,' Lainey said, keeping it light. 'Why are you asking me this?'

'What? No reason,' Chrissie said.

'Do you know something I don't? Did Ivan say something?'

'No,' Chrissie said. 'It's just you've never been *that* mad about him. I always thought he was sort of . . . a hobby.'

Lainey laughed. 'Well, he is. But he's a hobby who's beginning to say all the right things. A hobby who also happens to be a really good shag.'

'I thought he said things that weren't quite good enough.'

'No, I was just saying that.'

'You think he's serious? About you?'

'Yeah.'

'Okay.'

There was a pause. 'Well, don't you? Do you have reason not to?'

'God, it's like I said,' said Chrissie. 'This thing about dating friends is we always think there's a right to full disclosure of information. Which can only cause trouble.'

217

'*Is* there inside information?' Lainey said, smiling.

'No. Forget I said anything.' Chrissie was smiling back, talking in a tsk voice. 'I was just letting my mouth go on without me, and not listening.'

'But it was a weird thing to say. Why are you asking me if I've dumped him – is there a reason? You went round to see Ivan the other night when you left me. Did Ivan tell you something that I should know about him?'

'Ivan wasn't –' Chrissie said and stopped abruptly. Then began again. More quietly. 'Wasn't even there. So I went home.'

'Oh God, did *John* say something about me?'

'No. Of *course* he didn't.'

'So what, then? John didn't say I was stupid or ugly or something? Is there someone else – is it you? Does he still want you, is that it?'

'No. He really doesn't. There's nothing.' She said it perfectly. Flawless delivery. Absolute conviction in a lower register.

Except it was the first time in the conversation that Chrissie hadn't been flippant.

And there was something else in her voice, suddenly. Like guilt or something. And Lainey wasn't sure if she could believe her or what, but she started paying attention to her.

'If you're insecure about it,' Chrissie said, 'it means you don't know what he feels about you and you're not sure about him. That's not the best position to be in.'

'Are you in love? Is he?' Chrissie said.

'I think you should really try and work out what John's playing at. Whether he makes you feel the way he should make you feel. And if you really don't know, maybe the answer's no, and maybe the best thing would be to think again. Or have a break, at least,' Chrissie said.

'I'm just worried about you,' Chrissie said.

As the light faded, Lainey stared into space, and saw everything clearly: that this was all wrong. That she and John had just taken up the slack when Chrissie and Ivan created it, almost without thinking. They were wasting time with each

218

other, while they waited for something else – either for a completely different person to turn up, or for a not-that-different person to turn around and change her mind about which flatmate she wanted most. She decided to tell John he didn't want her enough, and see what he said.

And John blinked, and said, 'Oh, right.' And Lainey said, 'Well, what do you think?' And John said, 'It doesn't really matter what I think, does it?'

Ivan said, 'I'm sorry but that's all bollocks, really, isn't it?'

'Which part don't you believe?' She had kept back the part about Chrissie saying John didn't want her. Just as she'd kept back the part about John blushing the colour of his bollocks when he'd told her he didn't want Chrissie and she'd felt so sick she hadn't said anything else, in case he'd said more. First of all, she was afraid of putting the idea in Ivan's mind. And second, she couldn't have made Ivan understand the nuances. So much of it had been damn nuances that the further away she got, the harder it was to remember if there'd been anything there at all. Anyway, this wasn't about Chrissie. It was about John not wanting her enough. Chrissie didn't need to feature in the equation. Not here.

'I believe it all, sadly,' Ivan said. 'It's completely believable, but it's completely bollocks, too. You decided it should be meaningful – you and Chrissie did – and you decided if it wasn't meaningful it had to be – by a pretty profound process of elimination – meaning*less*. And that was the end of that.'

'Yes, I did. And he didn't stop me.'

'Girls are nuts,' Ivan said. 'You'd have liked this play at the Barbican I saw the other day with what's-his-name? The man who plays a writer at a party in that small film that got good . . . oh what's his damn . . . he was also in the series on BBC2, the one set in London in the eighties . . .'

Ivan had changed the subject. For the first few moments, Lainey reacted with comic disbelief, as if he were being outrageous, because she thought he was finding a particularly funny way to say something profound about her, and then she realized he'd really just changed the subject, and he hadn't been trying to make things better at all. He'd just wanted to know and, now that he knew, he was moving on. She'd mistaken his quick, comforting insight for giving a shit. She was reminded of Chrissie telling her off for being self-obsessed and smiled, because, deep down, she liked it when Chrissie was right. It meant she could relax.

'We'd better get the bill,' Lainey said.

'You know what,' Ivan said suddenly, really lightly, 'when you can't see all of something, you can make the mistake of thinking it's the same all over.'

'I haven't a clue what you're talking about.'

'I mean, you think everyone else knows what's going on, or everyone else is doing things right, but they're not. At least, not necessarily the way you think is right. Or even the way they think is right. It doesn't mean it doesn't work. Anyway, it doesn't matter.'

'You can't stop there. I *think* you're trying to tell me that Chrissie and you have bad patches just like any other couple, and everything's not really so sugary. Well actually, that kind of bitterness I could live with. It's the complete absence of the fairy tale, from the word go, that I can't get my head around, not the chance of an unhappy ending.'

'That's rather sweet,' Ivan said. 'Yes, that's what I meant, but I don't think you fully get the situation. I'm not trying to tell you we . . . I'm trying to tell you . . . Oh bugger it – you know you have the wrong idea completely about me and Chris. We're not the fairy tale.'

'Close enough,' Lainey said, trying not to sound surly.

Ivan shrugged, frowned sweetly, and drank what must have been cold tea.

'You know I'm gay, though.'

'Fuck, no, what? Oh, are you taking the piss?'

'Nope.'

'John would have –'

'John doesn't know.'

'Well, Chrissie would have.'

'Apparently she hasn't.'

'Are you saying Chrissie knows you're gay – are you honestly saying you're gay?'

'A *little* quieter, I think,' Ivan said, playing with the sugar spoon.

'Oh God, I'm sorry. Well?'

'Chrissie knows.'

'So if I asked her, she'd be cool about it.'

'Don't ask her. Please. Don't speak to Chris about this.' His brown eyes were relaxed, but earnest.

'But she does know?'

'Actually, we've never discussed it. Not directly. But I believe she knows. I wouldn't waste her time. I wouldn't mess her about. I love her too much. There's a difference, though, between knowing and discussing something. And an even bigger difference between her knowing, and her knowing *you* know. I don't think she'd like that.'

'Ivan, you can't just come out with something like this. Are you saying you and Chris don't have sex?'

'Well, what an impertinent question,' Ivan said. Lainey looked for a hint of humour to let her off the hook and found it. 'Not that it's any of your business, but we do, thank you very much, enjoy sexual intercourse together not altogether infrequently.'

She took her hands off the white tablecloth, in case she stained it with the deep blush that was flooding her body.

'Jesus, I'm sorry, how disgusting of me.'

He tipped his head to one side, reasonably. 'A little natural prurience. Only to be expected.'

'But if you sleep with her, then you're' – she lowered her voice to a whisper – 'bi.'

'I know that the reclassification is offered with the kindest intentions, but I'm in fact not' – he lowered his face and whispered the next word – 'bi.'

'Fuck me, Ivan.'

'That wouldn't change my mind, either. But thank you.'

221

She took a break from gaping to give him a wide, beautiful smile. Then she laughed. 'Ivan, will you stop being so fucking glib! You know what a fucking bomb this is. I don't understand!'

He softened. 'Sometimes fate can be cruel. And when you meet the right person, the one who means everything and makes everything mean something, sometimes they can be all wrong for you.'

'What I don't get, though, and you're putting it so nicely I almost do, but I know when I walk away I won't –'

'It's not just that,' Ivan went on, dropping his comic formality, meeting her eye for the first time. 'We want to have kids and we would have great kids. I don't want to break my mother's heart. There's a thousand reasons why, and hardly any why not. I couldn't live with a man – I know, I know I am, but I mean I couldn't *live* with a man. I expect too much from men, and it's never worked, and then there's Chrissie: she meets all expectations. I love her.'

'I'm not questioning your morality. Not entirely. But I want to know why you're telling me. Why me and not John? You can't tell me John doesn't know.'

'Really, he doesn't. Look, when I first lived with John we were at university, and I wasn't gay then. I mean, obviously I was and obviously I thought about boys and shit, but I thought about Courtney Love and Sandra Bullock too. And I always got on with women and it was easy going out with them, and they liked me.' He looked deeply embarrassed, but kept his smirk. 'I always had that womanizer reputation, and you know bad reputations are their own good publicity. I never kept affairs with girls going because I didn't ever connect. But it was easy to be straight at university because that was where all the action was and because I wasn't *sure* then, and you know, I'm a man, I'm going to take all the sex that's offered.'

'Even if it's the wrong sex.'

'It's strange. It's not that I'm not physically attracted to women. Because I am. And it's not that I don't like them. It's like

– the emotional sexual element isn't there. I can't really explain it.'

'Is it like a chemistry thing?'

'You and John love that idea, don't you? No, it's not really chemistry. More like English lit.'

'Oh wait, is it like, um – like when I have sex with a really big man I feel really protected and safe, and when I have sex with a wiry feminine man I feel insecure. Or something. Something like that?'

'Well. Maybe. Yeah – *something* like that.'

'So if you're not bi, what's it all about? Lie back and think of boy bands?'

Ivan smiled, but he looked hurt. 'Something like *that*, yes.'

'And with Chrissie –'

'I'm in love with Chrissie.'

'But when you –' she laughed this in, because she didn't have the vocabulary – 'when you – *went* gay . . . John's your best friend. And he's not, sort of, uncool or anything.'

'It's actually hard telling someone who knows you better than anyone that he doesn't really know you at all. I didn't want him to change with me. We're close. Why risk fucking it up?'

'Ivan, there's no way you don't think I'm going to talk to Chrissie about this. Is that the point? Do you want me to?'

Ivan took a deep breath and smoothed the tablecloth with his large hands. He fixed Lainey with a look of such devastating vulnerability that she wanted to take his head to her bosom. Her heart was thumping like she'd had the scare of her life, and she couldn't believe they were in the same place, having just had tea in a quiet little tea room in the park, with little old ladies and plates of scones in most directions. Her whole body was tense with unexpressed shock; she needed to do some shouting.

'I'm telling you,' Ivan said, 'because you looked as if you needed to hear a good secret. I can see how much you want to talk to John, or at least talk about him, and it's not really my business to advise you, but I think Chrissie behaved fairly badly letting you get in that state of mind about him. I think it's even reasonable to say she encouraged it. I know you're going to want to talk to Chrissie about this, but in the end, you're just not going to be able to, because you won't know where to start, and your conscience won't let you, because even if you wanted to hurt her, which you don't, you're too thrown by the intimacy of my confession, and my soft, trusting nature, to ever betray me. I've impressed you, the way few people have ever impressed you or with my startling sincerity, and although you're utterly gobsmacked now, somehow you'll manage to keep it as secret as your own blackest secrets, and may even come to enjoy, like a gift from a' – he cleared his throat – 'fairy godmother, this unspeakable bond we now share. It will, in fact, cut through all the usual jealousy girls feel of their best friends' boyfriends. So I'm not afraid of you.'

'Fuck me, Ivan, you're such a dark horse.'

'Yes, but I'm worth the effort. Bill, please.'

Hindsight can be as big a mind-fuck as any hallucinogen. How large and important the drabbest memories become, how reinterpretation rocks reality. Lainey was really never going to keep this one to herself. Ivan was gay? Ivan?

Was gay?

She caught a bus home, exhausted by the emotion, and from time to time laughed. She didn't see the shops she always looked at, or read the *Standard* she'd bought. She started remembering conversations and looking for giveaways. He was always very well dressed – was that a politically incorrect thing to think? She was more than a little shuddery at the thought of the one-up she now had over Chrissie, but grounded by the fact that she couldn't use it. Ivan had overestimated her by assuming that she'd never want to hurt Chrissie: sometimes she did. Sometimes there was nothing she wanted more, just a tiny amount, just enough. Perhaps she wasn't quite as machiavellian as she painted herself – perhaps she was, deep down, just worried about Chrissie. Sure, Ivan was sure that Chrissie knew, but did she really know? All this talk about babies – would a friend really let a best girlfriend commit herself to a hypocritical relationship, based on the falsest foundations, in which no authentic happiness could realistically develop? Or would a real friend sit her best girlfriend down, and in a low, steady voice say, Your boyfriend's gay, he's gay, *that's* how great your so-called perfect bloody so-called super-clicky relationship is: *your* boyfriend is gay. Oh, *calm down*.

Of course, this really put things into perspective. Chrissie telling her that John was a waste of time, in much the same way that Chrissie used to tell her the boys she dated at sixth-form college weren't good enough for her. At the time it felt flattering, and because she wanted the flattery it felt true. It was only after she'd let Chrissie persuade her that the boyfriends were unworthy dicks that Lainey sat back and felt crap, promising herself never to let Chrissie talk her out of anyone again. Until the next time. She couldn't believe she'd just let it happen again now, at their age. Chrissie with her talk of how Lainey shouldn't let John take her for granted, how she had to set the tempo, not let John amble through at his own pace. Chrissie with her intangible insinuation that John still preferred her. These insights from someone who couldn't even get a straight man.

Calm. Down.

Her stop. She got off at the lights, needing the extra distance because her body was crying out to do some pacing. God, Chrissie and her fucking perfect life, and it was all a lie. Lainey couldn't decide which was better – Chrissie knowing her life was a sham and passing it off all the time as something it wasn't, with all the accompanying guilt and fear of being found out putting her off her swagger . . . or Chrissie as a clueless dupe, who'd one day get the shock of her life.

And Chrissie didn't deserve this. Lainey wasn't sure where it was coming from, this vicious release. She was scum. But for tonight, she was happy scum.

feeling his age

After Lainey had told him to fuck off, in her own way, John had spent a day or so each on embarrassment, annoyance and, yesterday, relief. But today was reserved for depression, and feeling his age. Silver-grey hairs all over his fucking head, a frog's belly under his chin. He looked like shit, that was why. That was why she'd changed her mind, and all the 'you don't express your emotions, you don't treat me like shit' shit was just another fuck-off that he should have heard before, like 'it's not you it's me' or 'I like you too much as a friend'. Women liked rejecting men so much that they strung it out as far as they could. 'It's over. Now go away' just wouldn't be fun.

Ivan just sat there reading a paper and said, Call her. But he couldn't call her. He didn't even want to, because when he thought about her he didn't feel any sense of loss, just self-hatred, and resentment. Multiply the two, and you got depression, and feeling your age.

And only a few days before he could almost have had them both – her and Chrissie. He scratched his palm with the stubble on his face. Sometimes being old enough to have hard hair growing out of his cheeks was still something of a pleasure. He wondered how he'd gone from possibly two to certainly neither, and, not for the first time, tried to work out whether he'd done something wrong. Lainey had to know about what Chrissie had done. He just couldn't believe she wouldn't have brought it up –

maybe it was because she wanted *him* to, because she wanted him to feel the blow when he hurt her. The resonance. If that was what she'd wanted, maybe he should have said something, hurt her. He was over-thinking this. Maybe he'd give her a call.

He didn't, of course; couldn't. He'd been drinking with his workmates most days these days, and enjoyed in a sore, wallowing way the slick anonymity of a crowd. Conversation stripped down to clichés and lies; the safety in talking shit. In the late evenings, when workmates pushed off home to steady girls, he met up with other comedians and drank until he puked a lot. Late-night drinking with stand-ups was slightly different: just as morose and competitive, but more assertively inclusive than with other men. All men drank a lot, but with his comedian friends, it was more selfish, more of an attempted obliteration than the standard pack-mentality drinking, which suited John. At home he smoked a lot of blow and listened to the greyest CDs he had, only these days they were in colour. A lot of the time he wanted to tell Ivan about when Chrissie had stuck her hand down his trousers, just to see Ivan's face, to watch the pain pull it down into the pit of his stomach. He wanted to matter to someone, to fuck someone else up, just to see if he had any effect on the world any more. And for someone else in the world to feel as shit as he did, because then they couldn't all laugh at him. It would be easy. A few words, that was all. Ivan would believe him.

He wanted to be a bastard to someone because the things Lainey had said about him not treating her like shit had stayed with him and were bothering him. She'd made him a pushover and he wanted to kick back, to prove he wasn't as bland as she thought. The embarrassment pissed him off. He made a career – well, he didn't, but he tried to – out of being shameless, standing up talking about the things other people didn't say to each other. Now he was being softly deadened by embarrassment, which showed up in his body as post-viral fatigue. He felt stripped of his strength, small and dark, like cold winter days. He drew hard on a joint and held his breath for a long, long time. The sky

227

through the window was the blue of oceans, and he had nowhere to go tonight.

He heard a key turn in the door: Ivan, in from jogging. Ivan didn't say anything, didn't hang around to be seen, he just went for a shower. John listened to the muted roar of the water and felt sticky. He didn't know where to put himself. He was unusually conscious of Ivan's naked body in the next room, and alive to the fat folds of his own. He sensed that Ivan was avoiding him, thinking what a wreck he was, just slightly scornful, in that serene, unrufflable way. Before all this, they'd been level-pegging, more or less. In fact, what Ivan didn't know was how far the scales had really been tipped in John's favour. What hurt most was everyone thinking he was a loser, because if they only knew everything that had happened they'd think again. His indifference pose would be credible.

Ivan came out of the shower and combed back his hair (slight widow's peaking going on there, he was definitely going to lose it), and said, 'Oh, guess who was in the park?'

'Who?'

'Ahhh.' He leaned back into the armchair, and rolled his thumbs. He was being amusing and John didn't feel up to it. He was ashamed of his testiness, but couldn't master it. He was slightly worried about losing control. Blurting. He felt like a small boy with a penknife.

'So who was it?'

'Lainey was in the park. We had a chat.'

'You talk about me?'

'Yep. But not exclusively. And I didn't give anything away, I promise.'

'Maybe you should have. Unplanned, you know, it could have looked good, it might have made a difference.'

'I didn't know you wanted me to make a difference. I don't know what you think about her. If you do. But anyway, presumably you want me to tell you how she feels about you.'

'Yeah, whatever.'

This would have been a good point to bring it up. To just drop

228

into the conversation the fact that Ivan's girlfriend paid him the odd visit as well, and, by the way, she's not all that good at it, actually, is she? Because the look on Ivan's face – so frigging relaxed – wasn't one he would normally have been able to take. How paradoxical – if he hadn't had the ammunition, he'd have done his best to rattle Ivan's smug kindness. But he had. And, of course, just knowing was enough, it was plenty, it took the edge off his hunger. John's problem was he wasn't the bastard he wanted to be. Not even close.

'Well,' said Ivan. 'She misses you.'

back

It felt weird to be going to work again. Proper work.
Back up the street she thought she'd left for good, past the
greengrocers who stood outside with their fruit, and the toy-shop
that sold imitation Teletubbies, and the little church, and the
school yard where the boys played football in the middle and the
girls stood in little groups all the way round the edges . . . and
she was hopeful. Why wouldn't she be? Clare had asked her
round. Something was happening. She knew it could be nothing,
and warned herself to be steady. But she was hopeful, all the
same.

If the gods were smiling, Scott would be there today. Some
days he wasn't; those days were the hardest. Maybe Theo had
come back! Maybe that was why things were back to normal,
why she'd got the call asking her to come in. Lainey mentally
pan-and-scanned the room and imagined Dom in the corner,
and, for whatever reason, the thought of him made her feel really
happy. He was always the same, always sweet. But 3-D sweet,
sweet with an edge. Much nicer than John, better than him.
John. Gosh. She hadn't thought about him at all today. It was
nearly midday. Something of a record. They'd spoken for the last
time less than two weeks ago: she was ahead of schedule.

She rang the doorbell, and waited quite a long time. It crossed
her mind that she might have dreamed Clare's phone call. And
then Clare herself opened the door, and tried to smile. It was a

dismal failure – a mutation of the clichéd smile that doesn't reach the eyes; this one barely reached the mouth. It was a strange inward, upward pulling of cheek muscles, and it would have made Lainey laugh if it hadn't looked so genuine.

'Hi, Clare,' she said. 'How's it going?'

'Thank you for coming round at such short notice, Lainey,' Clare said. 'You want to . . .' and she turned her back, and led the way into the office.

No one was there. No Scott, no Theo, no Dominic. Clare stopped and stood in the middle of the room as if she were posing for a photograph. It was messier than normal, swept with abrupt withdrawal like the *Mary Celeste*.

'Nobody else in?' Lainey said, aiming for breezy, but it came out like the last gasp of a dying man.

'Coffee?' Clare said, and started to fill the cafetière.

What with Clare being Clare, it just wasn't possible to ask questions, because Clare didn't like to be rushed. She stopped telling stories if you asked her the wrong question at the wrong time, or stepped out briefly on a tangent. She liked to control the dramatic tension and was certainly letting it build now. This was how it felt to be the first guest at a party you didn't even want to go to. Clare wasn't offering any explanations. The smell of fresh coffee helped to fill the space.

'I made,' Clare said, 'a decision. Yesterday. I've got the material, I can roughly work everything I need, and I still . . .' She paused, looking at the ceiling, scratched the soft white flesh on the underside of one under-dressed arm, then went on briskly, 'I still know enough people who can help me get the magazine out. So I thought, you know, why not, I will make the last issue. Let's make it the last, but let's give it a proper send-off.'

She was posh today, the hard faux-London glaze had gone from her voice. In its place, a glimpse into a little private-school girl who'd tried to set up the school paper or save the school rabbit, or maybe written a letter to President Nixon. That type of little girl, the type with projects instead of friends. She was hurt, and hurt made people regress.

'I don't follow you, Clare. *Brazen's* shutting down? Since when?'

Clare showed no sign of having heard. She was gazing out of the window, looking – surely she wasn't – a bit shiny-eyed.

'Oh, you didn't know?' Clare said; the off-hand yawny mumble wasn't fooling anyone. No matter where she was or who she was with or how things were, Clare couldn't help faking it. 'It's over. We sp– Theo is setting up a new *When Voyager?* magazine. I don't know what he's calling it – *Brazen* over my dead body.' Lainey could tell that this was supposed to sound something like a joke. Not funny, but flippant. Careless.

'And so, what, why are you finishing, though? Even if there isn't room for two of them, you're the ones with the following, the fan base. Wasn't Dominic going to start up a web page, too? Nobody's going to –'

'The boys went with him.'

Lainey felt awful. Boys. Which was what they were. The boys went. Like her sons had left her, and gone to live with their father.

'They've gone to work with Theo?'

'I thought,' Clare said, 'I assumed, I suppose, that he'd asked you, too. I thought you knew all this.'

No, that didn't work. If she had, she wouldn't have asked her round today. Unless she wanted to know what was going on over there. Where were they? Then the implications of Clare's purported assumption made sense all at once, and she felt like she'd been slapped hard in the face. They hadn't asked her. She'd thought Theo liked her best of all. He hadn't asked her to come and join his new magazine. All thoughts of Clare's feelings were trampled by her own self-pity. She wanted to make calls, ask questions, get herself in there: she was desperate to get out of here, now.

She was wasting time. For God's sake, what was she doing with this bloody *woman*, when the winning team was playing somewhere else?

'Cream? Milk?' Clare said.

'No. Thanks.' She took the coffee. 'So. Um. You want to put out the last issue. That's really sad, Clare. I can't believe it's happened. It's so unexpected.'

'Well, surprising, maybe, the way they did it. But I should have expected something like . . . It was on the cards for some time. Anyway, I am, yes, going to go ahead as planned with this month's *Brazen*, and the reason I asked you round is because I need some help putting the articles in, transcribing, and so on. The kind of things you'd started to do before . . . before. I'll pay you, of course.'

Lainey didn't know what to say. It hardly seemed fair to accept money from Clare for a job she'd been quite happy to do for free in the past, especially now. Besides, the money wasn't relevant. She didn't want to be here. The flat was enormous with none of the men there, just the low radioactive sussuration of abandonment. What were they going to talk about together? What she had to do was get up and leave now. Say no. But she was afraid to.

'Where do we start?' Lainey said.

where's his six-pack?

Ade couldn't drive to save his life. He undertook all the
time, and you could feel the lane changes – he steered the car like
a dodgem, really turning the wheel. The constant, uncontrollable
phantom braking was making John's legs ache, but he was
getting to Brighton for free, so he couldn't really complain.

'To tell you the truth,' Ade said, 'she was always a bit
unstable. She did do that mad thing when I met her.'

John laughed. 'Yeah, she did the mad thing when you met her.'

'You'll get some tonight. You're with me.'

'Ade, I'm not looking.' Then, as if he'd only just noticed the
absurdity of Ade's prediction, but also because he needed the
compliment of repetition: 'I won't get some.'

'Don't knock the rebound. Some of the best shags I've ever had
have come immediately after the end of a thing.'

'Yours or theirs?'

'Oh, I don't remember. Both?'

'I'm not trying, anyway.'

'Yes, well, we'll see. What about Ivan and that slut, they still
together?'

Not telling the world about Chrissie's surprise overture had
proved harder than John could have imagined. It was, he
supposed, tied in to the fact that he'd longed for her so badly all
the time before, and when you got what you wanted the urge to
brag was fairly close to insuperable. Ivan talked about her in

234

exactly the same way he always had, but these days with oblivious resonance; it was all ironic now. John didn't even need to tell him the score as much as – just once, even – offer a short cynical 'Ha!' It would have been enough, but it would also have been too much. He nearly managed to convince himself that telling Ivan might even be seen as the honourable thing to do – responsible best-mate behaviour – but he was bright enough to know that not only was this self-righteous impulse not altogether credible, it didn't take the aftermath into account, and he was fucked if he was going to be there for that. Sense won out, every time, but living with this scary sort of intelligence wasn't as much fun as it should have been.

'Yeah, still together,' John said.

'Sorry, I think you always had a bit of a crush, didn't you?' Ade said, zipping past the left shank of a juggernaut so fast that the Fiesta shook. 'Although I was never sure which of them you had it on.'

John didn't fight back. He just smiled and kept his eyes on the road.

Ade had friends in Brighton that he was always meaning to see more of, and when John had talked about the gig he'd been offered, Ade had said they should make a night of it, because they could do with getting out of London. There was something about the capital that made it just a bit more than a city – like all big places, it had the added bonus of being an ordeal, too. Getting away from London always lightened your spirits. It was recklessly enjoyable, like an adulterous grope with a thick tart you had no intention of leaving your real girl for: the joy of the temporary. Besides, John liked non-London audiences more. They were more predictable – he could look out and know what to expect from their clothes, and go for material that was more likely to suit them. At home, any crowd could give any response, there was no way to prepare for it. Here, he was in with a fighting chance whichever way things were going. Outside London the audiences were prepared to try a little harder with him, even if they were trying to hate him and fuck him up.

235

Attention of any kind was, in retrospect, always better than indifference. Far more fun to look back at the day you were destroyed than the day you did something completely forgettable. For the crowd, too: audiences remembered the comics they'd reduced to jelly: they liked making a difference.

They wound down the windows as they pulled into the town centre and Ade whacked up the stereo (Blur: *13*). For Ade the evident pleasure of being looked at in a loud car, and for John the relief of being off the motorway, developed into a deeper mutual indulgence, looking at semi-naked young people. It was hot, and the local kids were seizing their chance to advertise. Ade drove round the one-way system a couple of times more than he needed to before they left the car in Hove and walked back into Brighton.

Girls in tight dresses with knock-off sunglasses: a few of John's favourite things, although he hadn't known it until then. There was possibly nothing as pretty as girls by the sea: they were all head-turning; destructively gorgeous. The barest, straightest, shiniest legs, long brown arms – he loved their arms. Sunglasses exoticized plain faces, reducing them to sweet simple smiles: every girl in Brighton was smiling. He couldn't stop staring.

The big pebbles made it hard to walk on the beach and they stopped at one of the beach bars for a couple of lagers.

'Why don't we live here?' John said. He squinted out at the sea, which was glittering.

'I know what you mean. I know it's a cliché but you really can breathe . . .'

'Look at them. I know they're not your thing, but bloody look at them. You don't get women like this in London.'

'You don't get women like this here either. They're all on holiday, probably. They're not women either, since you mention it. These are little girls, you dirty bastard. I'd be surprised if any of them's old enough to drink here.'

'Yeah, like no one gay ever wanted anyone under age.'

'It's different for boys. We may not mature faster, but we want sex sooner.'

'Anyway, they're women. There: she's at least twenty.'

'Leave it, John. They wouldn't look at you. They're holding out for Dawsons, and I'm a lot Creekier than you are.'

'Piss off.'

A week earlier, at a bus stop on Oxford Street, John had waited for the number 7 with three little schoolgirls: two black, one white, all of them fly – whatever that meant – but they were. They were pulling apart the classic Yves Saint Laurent jeans ad, the one with a naked Saint Laurent sitting in a half-lotus with his Jesus hair and thick black bins.

'Oh my God, that is the most disgusting thing I've ever seen in my life!' one of them was saying.

'Yeah, he's, like, so stringy and skinny, innit?' said the white one.

'Yeah, but he's got, like, no muscle definition,' said the third. 'Look at his spare tyres, he's just, like, saggy, yeah? Ugh, it's rank. Why'd they have such a foul model? Where's his six-pack?'

'He's skinny but he's, like, fat,' concluded the first.

John, contemplating his navel more literally than normally, had flinched at their candour. He'd spent the last ten days sustaining his return to being single with regular pastries. Today, knowing better than anyone else in town what lay underneath his black T-shirt, he was not about to admit that Ade was right, but gloomily tried to arrange himself so that his paunch looked less like a lifestyle choice, and reluctantly tore his gaze from a pair of girls whose thighs were so uneventful that they almost certainly hadn't even heard of O levels, let alone taken any.

John and Ade moved along the beach all afternoon, at one point crossing the road to a more traditional pub when the sun faded and a breeze started to rattle the plastic bunting around them. By this time John was more pissed than he'd intended to be, and knew he wouldn't sober up much before the gig. This wasn't all that bad a thing; he'd done plenty of sets when he was too pissed to know what he was really saying, and sometimes they worked and sometimes they didn't. At about six, Ade's friend Warwick turned up. John had been expecting him to be gay, and he wasn't, but then Ade was non-scene. John had never, in fact, met a gay man who wasn't. Warwick had gone to school with Ade and the conversations they had were exclusively nostalgic, with a palpable sense of strain attached: they were just a bit anxious to not run out of things to remember. Most of the stories were about puking and giving each other wedgies and they were funny enough for John not to mind having no part in them. They ordered chips and sandwiches in the pub, but John couldn't taste them. He'd drunk so much that his mouth was numb.

Predictably, he brought some of it up before, and shortly after, the gig, but it wasn't a nervous thing, it was an alcohol thing. His routine had probably gone okay. The audience'd been rowdy, and seemed amused enough, but it was always hard to differentiate success from pub-bore delusion. Afterwards he'd started talking to some girls, the loudest of whom spat on his face from time to time but it didn't matter. She was tall and pretty. The girls mentioned the name of a club and asked Ade and John along, and Ade, who'd said he wanted to dance his arse off tonight, was all for it. That was how they ended up at Beach Blanket Bingo, which, even though the dance floor only had three walls, was hotter than a jogger's arse cleft. Three different people tried to sell them Es – Ade raised his eyebrows, John shook his head. He wasn't in the mood to be out of it and he didn't trust drugs unless he knew the bloke who knew the bloke who sold them. He was so pissed that he didn't feel tired when he danced; it was as if his legs were happening to someone else. The music was hard eighties gender-bender disco: 'You Spin Me Round', 'You Think You're A Man', 'Searching'.

'Is this a gay place?' John asked the loudest girl. Her name was Eleanor.

'Could be,' Eleanor shouted, spitting on him again just a little. Her voice was crisp and sexy. 'Don't think so, though. I think it's just eighties night.' Her two friends danced even more quietly than she did, making little circles with their hips, keeping their arms low. He wasn't sure why they'd all tagged along with him and Ade – the possibility that they were impressed by his potential fame didn't seem likely, but you never knew with local girls. Maybe he was the closest they got to fame.

He lost sight of Ade and felt suddenly self-conscious, dancing with three younger women, so he went to the bar for them and looked for somewhere to sit for a while. There were wooden benches outside the club that looked like they'd been carved from the whole trunks of old trees. The four of them sat in a line.

'Do you do this most nights?' John asked one of the quiet ones, just to spread his bets. Eleanor was a bit intimidating. He wasn't put off, but he didn't really fancy his chances.

'No,' she said, so scornfully that he suspected this had already been explained. 'We're at UCL. We're just down for the weekend.'

'You live in London?'

'Well, we find we get into lectures quicker that way,' Eleanor said, and looked meaningfully at her friends. He looked down to acknowledge her point, and smiled, rubbing the label of his beer. She was good-looking; not a natural blonde, her eyebrows were too dark. By now most of the make-up had been sweated off her face and she looked post-coital. The bruisey bags under her eyes made her gaze intense. He had a feeling that he was in love with her already. He was dying to touch her.

Her friends wanted to go. Eleanor said she'd be okay, they could leave her.

'I'll be there in an hour or so,' she said, as they dawdled reluctantly. They walked backwards a few steps, giving her a look. 'I *will* be. I just want to feel the air get colder before I leave it behind. I'm too awake right now.'

'Where are you staying?' he asked her when they'd gone.

'We've got a hotel, it's not far. You'll walk me back?'

'Sure.'

'I'm not, you know, making a play for you. I just don't want to go back yet,' she said.

'Sure,' he said. 'I didn't think anything else.'

She smiled, and bit her lip.

'Just as well,' she said. He was almost sure she was flirting with him.

'I'm glad I don't frighten you.'

'What a weird thing to say. You didn't until you said that.'

'Well, I don't mean . . . you know, strange town, strange man. It's nice to know I don't look like a murderer. Sometimes I think maybe I do.'

'You're traceable. My friends saw you do stand-up in a pub. You're unlikely to do anything too psychotic.'

'But even so. If I did look like a murderer, you wouldn't have let them leave you.'

'This is a really unusual line. I wonder if you've had any success with it.'

'Eleanor, I'm not trying to get you into bed. I would. Believe me, I would. But I've just broken up with someone and the idea of . . . is just really a bit ambitious at the moment. And you're a bit out of my league. Just the fact that you're not telling me to fuck off and stop following you is kind of an ego boost.'

Why did he do this? The thing about men not talking about their feelings was one of those bollocks things everyone knew wasn't true but they still said it. Put him next to a girl with dark eyes and a straight stare and within minutes he'd be losing the fight against telling her everything that had ever made him cry and everything he wanted to do before he died. The drink didn't help, but it wasn't the drink talking. He was dying to tell Eleanor about Chrissie and Lainey, but he fancied her so much that he knew he had to be strong. One question from her would be enough, and although he longed to hear it, the rest of him was hoping she wouldn't ask – just for his own dignity, which was fatally susceptible to sympathy.

'Who broke up with who?' she said.

'She did.'

Eleanor shivered and slipped her arms into the cardigan that had been tied around her waist.

'To tell you the truth, I don't really want to hear it,' she said. 'I'd much rather you sat and said funny things and tried to pick me up. It may be selfish, but I don't think it's going to help you me sitting and nodding about someone I've never met. If you'd finished with her, I might have been interested, because what a man finds wrong with a girl is always a good indicator of what's wrong with a man. But if she'd had enough of you, I'd rather not know.'

'You're really clever,' John said. He was drunk and stupid enough for his genuine admiration to shine through. 'Is there any way I can see you again? Some time in London?' He didn't look at her while he waited, he didn't dare. After a moment he couldn't even stand waiting any more, because he was acutely reluctant to embarrass her; he liked her too much. Instead of pressing for a reply, he said, 'Bloody hell, "The Chauffeur". It's the best thing Duran Duran ever did: you'll dance with me to this, yeah?' Now he met her eyes, and she frowned so prettily that he was even more grateful for her smile.

The place was still packed: they touched fingertips so they wouldn't lose each other. Ade came over. His eyes were a bit stary, and John guessed he must have bought an E after they'd split up. His face was all one colour, spotted with sweat like condensation, and he looked over his shoulder a couple of times, but his paranoia was softened by a smile.

'Sorry to disturb you, kids. Nearly got into a bit of a scrape, I think. Spilled some primate's pint.'

'Is he still in here?'

'Yeah. It's okay now. But maybe we should move on. Well, I'm going to, and I thought you'd probably –'

'He's over there.' The high, hard, near voice of a man looking for a fight. More fucking Londoners.

'Let's just get out,' John said. He looked again at Ade and recognized what he'd thought was cheap E as adrenalin. Ade was bricking himself and John wondered what had happened. There were three of them and they were heading over. One of them pushed Ade's shoulder, hard. His body flipped back easily.

'We think you should pay for our next round.'

Ade couldn't move away without coming into the man's space. The *man*. They weren't even men, they were kids, no older than eighteen, but big. John didn't say anything, waiting for them to lose interest and back off, but the boys were pissed and bored and they wanted some. The same one pushed Ade again.

'Why don't you just fuck off?' Eleanor said.

'Why don't you shut up, you cunt?' one of the boys said. Gallantry would have been the sexiest move, but John was already heading in the other direction, pulling her after him by her wrist. He was pushing people out the way, heading towards outside, getting tetchy looks from the kids he was squeezing through. He looked for Eleanor – although he had hold of her hand she wasn't next to him, there were people between them – and turned to see Ade being punched. A fist slammed into his friend's face, then again, the wet, meat sound, brutal enough to carry through the tinny scratch of the disco music; hard on soft, slapping and real, a sound John hadn't heard in years. Gloopy red saliva sprayed from Ade's mouth, some of it spattering over the yellow T-shirt of a young girl who was freaking and trying to get out the way. There was space around the fight now, but too many people were standing between them for John to get through and help. He wasn't trying to. He'd frozen, his brain fluttering with possibilities like papers swept away in a breeze. Someone closer in grabbed the hitter's shoulder, trying to pull him away, and the boy shrugged him off, but slowed, first landing a deep blow into Ade's stomach. Ade fell on the floor, limbs folding in like a dying beetle. One of the other boys kicked him in the back. Within seconds it had already happened. Over, already: it had lasted barely longer than it took John to pretend he couldn't reach them in time. At that point John was aware of Eleanor looking at him and he knew he should be doing something and he was too afraid to and a million times too clever to, but even so he thought that he might die of shame. But, throughout, there was this other thing, a sensible voice, almost like his dad's voice, in his head, telling him to stay calm and shut up and wait till it was over. He could go in and do something, be brave and stupid. But he knew he'd only remember the stupid when it was over.

Ade coughed up brown phlegm, and spat. Eleanor looked white. John kneeled down, his face level with his friend's. The frantic disco beat was external and painful, people around them were staring. The boys who'd hit Ade had gone.

'Shit, mate, I'm sorry. I couldn't do anything.'

'Yeah,' Ade said. 'I know. Don't. Look, we'd better go to Warwick's.'

'Are you okay? Can you make it outside?'

'Yeah. It's not as bad as it feels.'

John lifted Ade's torso and sat with one knee folded underneath him and one leg straight, Ade's back resting against his chest.

'I should find some police or something,' Eleanor said. She was staring at John and there was something she wasn't saying that was all over her face. There was nothing he could do about it now. He'd done the wrong thing, but he'd done the only thing he could have done: the smart thing. She sat down on the floor with them. The bruised patches on Ade's face were starting to darken. The red-black mucus stitched his lips with twangy wet threads, which stretched and snapped as he opened his mouth to groan. He stood up like a baby, flailing and unsteady, but determined. John and Eleanor supported him on either side, leading him out. Ade made them stop when they were into the fresh air, and misjudging the distance of the wall he wanted to lean on, slammed heavily against it.

'Fucking hell,' Ade said. 'What made me think this was a good idea?'

'What went on in there?' John said. 'Was it about a pint?' His words were loaded.

'As opposed to what?' Ade snapped. 'A fucking gay thing, that what you think?' John flushed and glanced at Eleanor, guiltily.

'Where was your hotel?' he asked her. 'I mean, I understand if you want to just go. I can't come back with you, obviously. I could find you a cab.' He felt bad about abandoning her and not

243

being good enough, and angry at her for knowing it. There was nothing more to do. He was so focused on her that he wasn't really listening to Ade: which just made it worse.

'No, it wasn't a fucking gay thing,' Ade began again. 'It doesn't fucking have to be. Although the kid who kicked me – not the one who hit me – he'd looked, okay? That what you wanted to hear? It didn't have anything to do with it.'

'So what was it?'

'You seem to know, you fill it in. You know, there's no fucking reason ever, is there? He'd looked. So he thought he'd better point me out for a kicking. Or maybe I did spill the fucking pint. I don't know what happened. This doesn't happen, you know. Not to me. I don't get into fights. No one I know gets into fights. You tell me what fucking happened. You saw it fucking happen.'

'Can you make it over to that bench?' Eleanor said.

'Yeah. Probably,' Ade said. He eased himself away from the wall, transferring his weight on to John's forearm. His knees buckled when he was nearly at the bench. They both stumbled a bit and then tried again. When he was sitting down, Ade dragged the back of his hand across his mouth, and shouted, 'FUCK!'

'What?' John said.

'Fucking PAIN,' Ade said.

'Do you want a drink?'

'No.'

Eleanor smoothed her face and hair with both hands, and started to cross her legs, then changed her mind. Her back was curved and exhausted, her forehead cut with pain.

'I don't know what to do with myself,' she said. 'I've never been involved in a fight before.'

'Neither have I,' Ade said.

'I can't believe you didn't help him,' she said. John started. He felt sick, the instant quickening of his bowels.

'I wasn't near enough. I didn't even see until it was too late. They'd –' he began.

'I know,' Eleanor said quietly, her voice horribly mature. 'It's just you were out of there before you even . . . I'm sorry. No, I'm being stupid.'

John wasn't mad at her for saying it but angry seemed like the best way out of this. He turned round to defend himself again, more loudly, but saw her face in time: hurt and scared and tearful. Her teeth started chattering. She was just a little girl. He felt a surge of shame and regression and had to struggle against looking like she did. He didn't want to be the strongest person there, but knew he was supposed to be. He swallowed, realizing he hadn't swallowed in some time; it felt like he'd forgotten how to.

They sat still together until the sun rose, the three of them. It was an astonishing dawn: it looked like God. Eleanor was at least half-asleep on John's left shoulder and Ade leaned into his right, head forward; John couldn't tell if he was awake and didn't want to speak to him. The sky in the west was storm-coloured, and in the east pink-gold clouds folded over and over themselves, like cake mix curdled by eggs, the whole thing spilling into the sea. He felt steady again. Despite it all, he couldn't help being moved by the moment.

parties

There's an eerie corrupt-utopian dimension to photographs: people are always living it up inside them. They smile their mightiest smiles, although their eyes may roll anxiously to one side, concerned that they'll be caught not quite living it up enough. They touch more, flinging solid arms around warm shoulders, pressing flesh. So what if they're cold and aloof, and sad, in real life: all the proof in the world says otherwise. Photographs are all the proof there is.

Lainey found the pictures in a box file marked: Parties. She was alone in the office, but looked guiltily around her before she started to leaf through. Most of them looked recent, more or less. Dark pictures of people wearing black and grinning behind glasses of champagne. Pictures of Theo's teeth, upper and lower sets – grey-white, as if they'd never seen the sun – and Clare in velvet, toasting things, laughing. When they were friends. On the back of them, such clues as 'Launch', '1st Anniv', 'Golden Meteor Awards 98'. And a picture that didn't seem to belong there, with paler, subtler tones and a shinier look. It could have been taken in the late seventies or early eighties, something like that – Lainey wasn't too hot on fashion. But the line-up of girls was dressed in frilly, fussy blouses and garish make-up – jewel-coloured eyeliners, blusher in streaks pretending to be cheekbones. Second from the left, in an enormous hot-pink scoop-neck jumper that had slipped over one shoulder so that a slit of armpit showed, was a very thin Clare. Her eyes were heavily painted, her hair was big and spiky, her neck long and slender. Lainey brought the picture up to her nose. Perhaps it wasn't Clare. It could be her sister. She looked on the back for information, but it was blank. She screwed up her eyes. It was Clare, because she had a fairly unique smile – not that Lainey had seen it all that much, or at least she had never faced it directly – disciplined and self-conscious, the smile of someone who was never quite sure whether smiling might not be some terrible faux pas.

Lainey's heart quickened: she wanted more. Clare had only left ten minutes ago: she had time. But despite a mad urge to start pulling open drawers and really assaulting Clare's trust, Lainey was half-frozen by the space. Other people's empty houses were more silent. The quiet, shaken into touch now and then by the smothered rub of traffic passing close to the window, was spooky, like the way you thought dreaming felt when you weren't dreaming. She leafed through the file, which was full of differently sized pieces of paper, flyers, press releases. This time a folded packet of pictures. Lainey took it out. They were not as old as the thin picture, not as new as the pictures she'd already seen. Clare was already very fat, but it didn't yet suit her – unless seeing the very thin picture had just forced Lainey to redefine her. Now, when she saw her again in the flesh she'd see the thin Clare, see the fat as a large, strange extremity, no longer part of her. The pictures had been taken in summer. The sun was low and yellow, long shadows: a strange faded look to everything. Some of the people Lainey didn't know, there were a few she recognized – Saskia, the sub who'd come into the office once or twice, was there. It was a picnic; there were hampers and lots of bottles of wine. Binoculars: one of those open-air opera things. And something else. In every picture of Clare and Theo, and there were lots of them, more than a dozen, Theo was looking at Clare as if he were agonizingly, angrily in love with her. Clare didn't even seem to notice; her face was always turned away, laughing, talking, screwed with impatience. But Theo, throughout, was chasing her half-turned face, questioning her with a pained, insistent stare. Lainey hadn't seen this look before in anyone: it wasn't like she knew it, or recognized it, but it was unmistakable. He'd loved her.

Insight at this advanced level was narcotic; the cleverness felt fabulous: she wanted to reach more conclusions, and although she knew that all the evidence was there in front of her, it felt like a new talent. She wasn't normally good at reading people: that was something Chrissie did. She understood now why Chrissie liked to analyse – liked being able to look at people and see more than they told you, perhaps more than they knew themselves. And, not because she needed to confirm her suspicions, but because she trusted them and wanted to savour the feeling, she spread the pictures out in front of her on the hard blue sofa, and stared.

When the phone rang, Lainey jumped, actually shouting aloud. Clare, asking her if she fancied a sandwich. You know what, Clare was nice. Not as frightening as she would have people believe. Lainey smiled warmly into the receiver, dropping the stutter she sometimes affected when she spoke to her, a defence mechanism that she subconsciously hoped rendered her too pathetic for Clare to shout at. Whether or not they'd both been there at the time, Lainey had made small but significant discoveries about Clare, and she wasn't going to let her fall into the cold place again. She gathered up the photographs and smoothed their edges together, making the pile perfect before she slipped it back into the envelope.

Clare handed Lainey a tuna/mayo baguette. There was a white paper bag in her other hand as she headed for the stairs. Lainey wanted to keep her a while. She wanted to bond. She wanted to know more.

'Do you have a lot of work to do this afternoon?' she said.

'An article for the *Evening Standard* magazine,' Clare said.

'Oh,' Lainey said. 'About . . .'

'It's a profile. Of an author. Daniel Thompson – do you know him?'

'No.'

'Well. He was nice enough.' She turned to leave again.

'Are you not even taking time out for lunch?' Lainey said. It was an unambiguous invitation. Clare stopped. She inhaled audibly through her nose.

'I don't really have the time,' Clare said, and as she started moving again, it was clear that she wouldn't stop until she'd gone.

Lainey frowned and growled softly with frustration, but she was not ready to give up. She ate the sandwich and worked especially hard and waited. Hours later, Clare reappeared and said, 'It's four. You should really go home now.' She paused, and what she said next seemed all the more sincere for it. 'I do appreciate all the work you're doing for *Brazen*, Lainey. I think this last issue will be something we can be proud of.'

Lainey, for the hell of it, said, 'It must have hurt when Theo decided to set up a new magazine.'

'Theo can do what he likes,' Clare said.

'I mean, with you two being such good friends before. You must have felt, I don't know, betrayed?'

Clare didn't answer this time. Lainey searched for hurt in her small grey eyes, but they were flat and revealed nothing. Lainey, using the hugeness of her own tawny eyes, a space that men always found inviting, twitched her face with empathy and said, 'And the others going with him. I suppose loyalty would have been too much to . . .'

'The others must go with whichever magazine they think the most viable,' Clare said. 'And they apparently made the right decision. *Brazen* will fold, Theo's may not.'

'But you hope it does.'

'Lainey,' Clare said. 'Is there a point to this?'

'I'm not going to go and tell them what you said,' Lainey said. 'I'm not trying to find things out about you. I just wondered how you felt. If you wanted to talk about it . . .' Did it really matter if she went too far? 'I was just cataloguing the picture files, and I was just looking at some old pictures of you and Theo, and you seemed so – so friendly that I thought . . . I couldn't help trying to imagine what could have brought on all this. When he talked about you . . .'

'When did he talk about me to you?'

'Oh. Months ago. Not talked about you in a behind-your-back bitchy way. I just mean when your name came up. When he talked about you he said you used to be great friends. And then when I saw the pictures of you looking so close, I just wondered about now, and how it'd happened.'

Clare breathed out carefully and rolled herself back into the sofa. Lainey looked down, apprehensive. The editor started picking under her long fingernails with the nails of the other hand. She drew first her upper then her lower lip between her teeth. Lainey had to time her apology carefully if it was going to push Clare over the edge into vulnerability, and advanced girl-to-girl confidence.

'Go home, Elaine,' Clare said.

'Yes, sure. Okay. I'm sorry I pried. I was just . . . I suppose I felt sorry for you. And him. And everyone, really. It just seems so sad. Did you . . .'

'Thank you for all your work.'

'It's no problem at all. Same time tomorrow?'

'Actually, I think I can finish it from here,' Clare said. Her eyes delivered carefully measured formality. 'Thanks for all your work.'

'Oh. I see.'

Clare smiled. It was not a nice smile. Lainey stood up and looked for her bag. It lay under the desk, a sad empty thing with no work in it. As she bent to pick it up, she scooped into it the small school exercise book with the cover that said: Numbers.

'You know, fuck – off – Clare,' Lainey said, 'you cold fucking bitch. I'm *glad* they all fucked off and left you, you asked for it. Because you don't treat anyone like they're human. There's you and there's everyone else. It's like you're not even human – yeah, that's it, it's like everyone else *is* human and you're above them all. You fucking fat cow.' She turned to look behind her – she could still see the office window in the distance, and wondered if Clare was watching her talk to herself. When she'd got further down the street she had rethought things and in the new draft she said, 'Theo called me last night, actually, Clare, but I didn't want to hurt your feelings. He's said that now they've set things up he needs an editorial assistant. And we're all going to laugh about you and . . . oh, stop being stupid.'

The further away from Clare she got, the less anger she felt and the more . . . the more *admiration*. She couldn't help smiling, out of respect for Clare's frigid consistency. She stopped at a newsagent's and bought herself a scratchcard. No win. She leaned against the wall, which was hot from the sun, pulled back her hair in one hand and rested, tapping her lip with her little finger.

'You know, Clare,' she said under her breath, as she turned the corner, 'you may deserve everything you get, but maybe you deserve a little bit better, too.' She let a hand fall into the top of her bag, and fingered the edge of the book of numbers. Her eyes itched with uncried tears, but she blinked them behind her. With the flimsiest spring in her step and the reflected pride of someone who *had* pride pinkening her cheeks, Lainey walked away from *Brazen* for the last time.

'So John's over, is it?' Chrissie said.

'He didn't call me.'

'He should have called,' Chrissie said. 'Sorry.' She lowered her head to look compassionate. Perking up, she said, 'I suppose John's quite shy, that could have something to do with it.'

'There's no sorry about it, and I don't care if it's because he's shy, he didn't call me and that's pretty much that. It means you were right – *I* was right – to put an end to things. He just didn't care enough – not like care care, I mean give a shit, and I'm glad I found out before I made a fool of myself. So you don't need to feel sorry for me.' A tissue of bravado, but this was no place to be pitied. Soho Square at lunchtime: spilling over with pretty young things in trendy clothes. It made her feel like such a hick. 'Do you need to get back to work?'

'No, I'm fine. You? You at the supermarket again today?'

Lainey leaned into the iron railing behind her and stretched her bare legs out.

'Late shift. From four. God, I need a better tan,' she said.

'We should go on holiday.'

'You've just been.' Lainey lit up a cigarette. Smoking in the heat worked better. For a moment she lost her head, floated higher, felt sick, came back.

'You can never have too many holidays. Anyway, it was only for a few days. I thought you'd given up again.'

'It's been a rough few weeks. What was it like, being on holiday with Ivan? Like being married?' She felt naughty saying this, the sly teasing that only she could enjoy, but that wasn't why she said it. She genuinely delighted in watching Chrissie lie. Maybe 'lie' was too strong a word for something so artistic: Chrissie romanticized, and there wasn't anything very wrong with that, if it made her happy.

'Nothing like marriage,' Chrissie said. 'Nothing like my dad's marriage, anyway. No tantrums, no threats . . .'

No sex, Lainey thought.

'. . . just us, getting on. Sorry. Being smug. He's far too tidy. Deeply disturbed tidy. And he eats anything: squids and octopuses, things like that. You name it, he'll put it in his mouth. Which can't be a good thing.'

It became clear to Lainey as Chrissie talked how sensitive and generous her friend had been since John had left the frame. How sweet she was, and considerate. The brittle insight that had supplied sharp commentary for the duration of Lainey's last affair was nowhere. Lainey wasn't sure how to read that: as jealousy? Or could it be that Chrissie didn't think John had been good enough, that selfless concern had made her angry at him all the time? Lainey almost wanted to think this, that Chrissie's steely disapproval came out of caring too much – but she didn't believe it for a minute.

'You know,' Chrissie said, 'Ivan can be a pain in the arse, sometimes.'

Lainey bit her tongue. 'I'm sure he can. Look. Stop it. I know he's lovely. I don't resent you.'

'I know.'

'Listen, the reason I wanted to see you, I grabbed Clare's frequent-use phone book before she threw me out –'

'Frequent-use? You make it sound like shampoo.'

'Yeah yeah yeah, shush. I've got the numbers of the boys in the office. Question is, which do I call?'

'What do you mean?'

'Well, here are the choices . . .'

'Anyone famous in the book?'

'Not really. Just journalists.'

'Tell me a few. Have you got it with you?'

'Yes. But *listen*, Chrissie.'

'Can I take a quick look? While you're telling me.'

'For fuck's sake. Here.'

'Okay. Go on.'

'Right,' Lainey said, and tried to ignore the fact that Chrissie had probably stopped listening. She was always interested in the wrong bloody thing. 'The obvious one is Theo, to ask for a job with him.'

'Oh yes, do him. That's the one.'

'Well, I probably will,' Lainey said, 'but I'm presented with a really more interesting choice before then.'

'What? Who?' Chrissie was turning pages noisily and roughly. None of the nervous attention she'd paid to Ivan's CD sleeve. 'Jamie Gregory, I've heard of him. Don't like him.'

'The choice is Dom or Scott.'

'Remind me.'

'Scott's the sexy good-looking one. Skin like the last sip of a warm cappuccino before a long cold day. He wears his bollocks on the outside.'

'Right. He's the one who flirts – flirted – with you at the office. Go for him.'

'Wait. Dom was the clever one. The light one.'

'Light how?'

'In every way. Except' – and she put on an exaggeratedly grand voice – 'his intellect. I love the way he looks.'

'Pretty, is he?'

'No, the way he *looks*. At me. He makes me feel, well, I'm not sure. Dangerous. Or dirty or something.'

'Where does he wear *his* bollocks?'

'Well in.'

'Which one do you prefer?'

'Oh Chrissie, for fuck's sake, when will you learn, it's not that simple!'

'Remind me again,' Chrissie said, twisting her hair into a bun which she fixed with a Bic. 'How is it *not* simple?'

'I can only phone one.'

Chrissie opened her mouth to instantly refute this, but seemed to reconsider. She nodded.

'Probably true. But that doesn't make it less simple. You can't tell me you like them both equally.'

'I can only phone one, and I want it to be the one I'll have a chance with. I don't like them both equally. I like them both differently, in equal measures. I like the way Scott dresses, the way he talks, the way he is, he's gorgeous and he flirted – but I know he could do better. He's bound to know it too. Dominic doesn't know anything of the sort, even though he's lovely – he hasn't a clue. It's wrong to suggest this, because it's not true, but I can more easily imagine him being grateful for the attention.'

'Well, you've made the decision,' Chrissie said. 'You don't ask someone out because you think he's more likely to say yes.'

'Do you not?' Lainey said cynically. She was fishing slightly, but needed to hear it anyway. Chrissie, reassuring and schoolmarmy, widened her beautiful grey eyes with emphasis and veracity.

'You don't.'

They were back. This was how it had been before John, before the headache of over-involvement with each other. Allotted a silence to contemplate the Dominic/Scott decision, Lainey used the time to contemplate Chrissie instead. It was, she supposed, even possible that Chrissie had never had a real interest in her success. Not that Chrissie was a conscious saboteur, but her mood improved when Lainey's worsened. She enjoyed distress. Maybe she just enjoyed helping, but that wasn't good enough: it was wrong to enjoy anything when it only thrived in conditions that killed off everything else. Before, when they'd been halves of two couples and their short-cut closeness had seemed to become abrupt, staccato, it had been easy to conclude they'd reached the end of an artificially preserved friendship; Lainey had used the word 'outgrown' to herself. The night they'd taken that gloomy cab ride, streetlamps strobing the freeze of Chrissie's moodiness, Lainey had really thought they'd never be the same again. Yet here they were, the same again. Evolution had not been the problem, Chrissie had been the problem: Chrissie hadn't liked it when they were even.

On the face of it the best thing would be to end this stupid, static bind, with its consensual destruction. Only, if she did that, where would she go? Who would be there to tell her she could do as she liked, or she was being stupid, or to remind her there was still some way to go? Who else would let her believe she was different? There was another choice: stay. And if that seemed like masochism, there was a difference now. She had ammunition: she knew more about the fine balance of their affection than she had known before, and more about Chrissie than Chrissie herself knew. Thus equipped, she could even begin to have some fun.

an extra syllable

     The name: was it a coincidence? Eleanor. Like Elaine –
that was Lainey's full name – like Elaine but with more to it. A
step on from Elaine, an extra syllable. A serious Lainey. And
she'd called. He did it that way round, gave her his number
because it had been the thing to do after all they'd been through.
That way round, because he didn't want to sound like a sad old
fuck when he called her and heard her back away, pulling a face
to the person next to her, making unconvincing excuses. He
didn't want to take her number and never call it because he was
too afraid, hanging on to it just to hurt himself.

    But she'd called. This alone had made him suspicious – she
was making things too easy – but this time he wasn't going to ask
questions. He was going to take her somewhere nice, somewhere
good, and put it on Visa. I'd like to marry Eleanor, he thought,
carelessly. She brought out his flash side; he'd never used the side
before. He mentioned her briefly to Ivan.

    'I thought you were still into Lainey.'

    'Dah, that's over. Anyway, I'll see how it goes. I just wondered
if you knew anywhere that might be good for a first thing. Not
trying too hard, but flash enough.'

    'Is money no object?'

    'Money *is* an object.'

    'Yeah, I know somewhere.'

It wasn't the first time he'd been this excited, but it was the first time since he'd met Chrissie that he didn't expect someone to end up being wrong for him. Other girls he'd seen, there was always at least one thing on the surface that gave away how it would end. He knew they'd split over the way she wore lipgloss, or always tossed her hair. Eleanor hadn't had any surface flaws – other than being out of his league.

Lately, John had contemplated taking action. He'd started looking at Just For Men – a hair dye which was on a different aisle to waxes and gels. Eleanor was about twenty. He couldn't even remember twenty. He could remember before then, and since, but twenty! What was that even like? He tried to remember the girls who'd been around when he was twenty. They didn't go out with men who dyed their hair: they smoked joints and snogged men in dirty jumpers on dirty floors. He turned his head to study the new hairs that glittered like needles in his sideburns. In fact, apart from being evidence of degeneration, they looked all right.

'Are you seeing Chris tonight? Don't tell her, will you?' he said to Ivan.

'I'm not seeing her. Why not tell her? Leaving your options open?'

'No. I just don't need anyone to know. I can't tell you how good this girl is. The odds against me not making a fucking idiot of myself aren't worth looking at. Where are you going, then?'

'Just . . . into town, really.'

'A work thing?'

'Something like that. No, not really a work thing.'

'I'll be in Soho this evening, after my set. It'll probably be over around eleven. You don't know where you're going to be, do you?'

'Not really. We usually move around.' Ivan concentrated in the pause, and registered the need to offer something else. 'You could try the Slipper, on Wardour Street. We're probably going to be there for a while.'

'Yeah.' Unsure of whether Ivan was trying to put him off, but tentatively picking up from his suggestion a feeling that he kind of genuinely wanted him there, John made up his mind to probably not go along. 'Maybe I'll see you later, then.' The subtext of embarrassment attached them. Ivan smiled.

'Try,' he said.

John met Ade for a drink before he went to the comedy club. Ade was fine. He was with David, the bloke he'd brought to one of John's gigs months ago. They were sitting in one of those strange little dirty old men's pubs that John liked so much; you could hear yourself talk. Elsewhere in central London, shiny cloned renovations bulged with too many people hoping to get some.

'I picked my scabs and everything,' Ade said, 'I really wanted a scar.'

'Which was why you could be heard screaming: Not the face! Not the face! as you went down,' John said.

'Fuck off,' Ade said. 'I could have made a bit of a deal about you not fucking joining in, you big queer, but I didn't. Even though you were trying fucking hard to impress that teenager you were with. What happened to her after you took her back to her friends? Did you try it on?'

'Of course not,' John said. 'But she called me yesterday.'

'Jesus. What do you think she saw in you?'

'Potential. Listen, you coming along tonight? I've changed my name.'

'What, again?'

'Who are you this time,' David said.

'John Truelove,' John said, embarrassed saying the word to a homosexual.

'Is that funny?' David said.

'It's his name,' Ade said. 'It's his fucking name.'

'New material, new start, new honesty,' John said, trying to bury his sincerity with a joke voice. 'Just thought it might change my luck.'

'We were going for a dance tonight, mate,' Ade said.

'We don't have to,' David said.

'No. Go on. Go for a dance. In a way, it's always better when I don't know anyone.'

to be expected

She'd asked the Magic 8 Ball predictor, which was vague, but preferred Scott. Lainey poured herself some vodka and dialled the first four digits of either of their numbers, the dialling code. Then followed through with Chrissie's number.

'I'm going to phone one of them now,' Lainey said.

'Still haven't decided?'

'What do you think?'

'I've never met them.'

'That wouldn't usually stop you having an opinion.'

'And I do have an opinion. I don't want to take the blame, though.'

'You have an opinion! You didn't tell me that. Which one do I phone?'

'Laine. Shut up. You have to decide yourself. You have nothing to lose either way. Well, obviously I don't mean nothing. Maybe that's the key. Don't ask yourself what you have to gain, but what you have to lose. Which one would you be more able to stand never seeing again? And then call him.'

'You think Scott, don't you?'

'It's interesting you should say that. Why do you think I'd think Scott?'

'You think Dom?'

'Mackerras. Put down the phone. Pick up the phone again. And get on with it.'

'I'm going.'

They hung up together. Lainey added some cranberry juice and knocked the vodka back. She poured more. She thought about Dom, calm behind his computer: of his bright eyes, lit from behind by his shrewd, animated humour. The way he grazed the tension of the office with well-arranged one-liners, and softened the blows of Clare's and Theo's cheap shots at each other. The lustre of his observations. His sexy-wonky reticent smile. She called Scott.

'Yeah?'

'Scott, it's Lainey from *Brazen*.' She waited.

'Oh hello, Lainey. What's cooking?'

'Weird week, actually. I went into *Brazen* – Clare's putting out a swansong issue. We kind of knocked it up together.'

'Fucking hell. How's she taking the mutiny?'

'Not all that well. We pretty much fell out at the end.'

'She has a temper, but she doesn't really mean it, you know? Clare just likes to protect herself.'

'You always defended her! When you weren't taking the piss out of her. You know' – she laughed so he wouldn't be offended – 'you don't have to be nice to her now. You have a new boss.'

'Yeah, I took the piss, but I did that to all of you. The thing is, Clare was never as much of a bitch as Theo made her out to be.'

'Well, you can say that because she liked you. You were her favourite. You flirted.'

'I was her favourite because I was the only one there who was anything like nice to her – not even *nice*, *normal* with her. Theo was always pissed off with her, Dom treated her like a machine – even you, you were pretty detached and superior.'

'Never,' Lainey said, knowing he was right. 'She doesn't let people be nice to her.'

'Yes, she does, but the thing about Clare is she knows she's too clever to be pitied, and people always try to pity her. Because of the body thing. She's better than that. Clare's all right, and she's never needed that condescending sugar-coating that everyone gives her because they're a) shit scared of her and b) think she should justify herself or keep a low profile.'

'Well, yes,' Lainey said.

'I know I'm ranting. But it's true. I hope she'll be okay. I feel shit about leaving her, but I have to go where there's going to be work. Listen, why don't you come out tonight and we'll talk about *Brazen* times?'

'Tonight? Sure, yeah.'

'I'll buy you lots of drinks, we'll have a bitch about Theo and Clare, it'll be good.'

'Yeah,' Lainey said, dropping her fake indifference. 'I'd really like that. Okay, when, where?'

'You know the Atlantic, of course?'

'Of course.'

'So, shall we say eight?'

'Yeah. Yeah, eight.'

'Earlier?'

'No. Eight's fine.'

'See you there. Glad you called, Lainey.'

She called Chrissie back.

'Am I glad I did that.'

'You called Scott.'

'I did. How did you know?'

'It wasn't hard. You only ever really talked about Scott. He had enough character for me to remember him. Can't even remember the other one's name.'

'God, Chrissie, he sounded really pleased to hear from me. I'd hardly said anything and he asked me out. We're meeting tonight. At the Atlantic.'

'Not good,' Chrissie said, 'but perhaps he has his reasons.'

Lainey ignored her. 'He sounded really pleased.'

'Why wouldn't he? What are you wearing?'

'I haven't thought. Not jeans?'

'Not jeans.'

*

262

Lainey wore her only acceptable skirt, and heels. She'd been to the Atlantic once before with Chrissie, years ago, and was afraid the corners were going to confuse her: a deepish staircase led directly to a choice of bars. She went for the one with the people in. It was busy, but although she couldn't see Scott, it wasn't going to be hard to find him; the drinking area was deceptively small. He probably wasn't there yet: she was early. Lainey bought herself a Martini, not to be chic, but to get drunk quickly. The two suits beside her were getting louder, and she felt flimsy, squeaky. Unused to heels, her feet hurt already. She asked the closest suit if he'd mind moving his jacket and briefcase from the only spare barstool so she could sit down. The suit said, 'Where am I going to put my stuff?' She wasn't sure whether he was being provocative, or was genuinely offensive. She chose to play it straight, and then he could make his mind up about her.

'It's only a jacket. I'd really like to sit down.'

'I can't do that, I'm sorry.'

This kind of behaviour was to be expected of suits, but was none the less always surprising. Lainey sniffed and looked past them to the staircase, which delivered a steadyish pulse of new people, and no Scott. It was best that she stayed in one place, then he'd easily find her. She drank the last of her Martini, ate the olive, and bought another.

'You can't say that to the lady,' said the other suit. 'It's rude.'

'Perhaps you'd like to offer me your seat,' Lainey said.

'Ah, well, we had to come in very early to get these,' the other suit said, with the kind of greasy ease that indicated he thought rudeness was fashionable. Suits were turning out to be the last group of men to drop the nouveau-chauvinist pose, and it wasn't hard to see why. Less in tune with real fashion than other men, more contemptuous and frightened of women, they sheltered under the pack mentality. Take one of them away from his friends and he was forced to be normal, the rampant bravado withering into his best imitation of decency. They believed they were decent, inside, but resented having to be: they thought the

263

rest of the world didn't deserve their best behaviour. Together, they could make it known.

She tried to ignore them, but their conversation was all for her. That was often the way rich boys started talking to girls; they talked loudly about them, pushing for retaliation, but protecting themselves if there was none. They were bored: she was the first person to have spoken to them since they'd arrived. And she was pretty tonight, wearing girl clothes. If Chrissie had been there too, if anyone had been there, she'd have thought it her duty to snub them, but she was alone. Waiting. In such circumstances, attention of any kind became harder to reject. At quarter past eight it occurred to her for the first time that Scott might not be coming, and she slipped down on to the sides of her shoes, and finished her second Martini.

'Can we buy you another drink, to make up for the stool?' the other suit said.

'I'd rather have the stool,' Lainey said.

'Come on,' the other suit said. 'Let the lady have a seat.'

'Uh!' the suit said. 'What about my jacket?'

'What would you like to drink?' the other suit said.

'No, thank you,' Lainey said. She was taking a risk, letting her refusal go to another round, because the drinks here were fucking expensive, and she couldn't afford another Martini. But it wasn't as if they owed her a drink, even as obnoxious as they were, so she rode it out.

'Please,' said the other suit. 'It's the least we can do.'

'I'm more interested in the most you can do,' Lainey said. 'But all right. Martini. Not too dry.'

'Shaken, not shtirred,' said the suit, trying to inch his way in: an impression of a Sean Connery impression. She could tell that he didn't find her attractive. Actually, attractiveness was not the commodity he dealt in: she didn't look classy enough. The other suit was just bored, probably nicer, almost certainly the stronger one – the cooler one. The suit had submitted his Sean Connery to impress his friend, not her. While the other suit ordered the drinks, Lainey and the suit didn't say a word to each other.

264

'Are you waiting for someone?' the other suit finally asked, when she'd thanked him for the drink.

'Yes,' she said. 'And yes, I think I've been stood up.'

'You meeting at eight?' said the suit. 'It's only twenty past. You know what traffic's like in town at this time.'

'Yeah,' she said, looking around. 'How long are you supposed to wait in these situations?'

'Half an hour,' said the other suit.

'Maybe longer,' said the suit.

'Not if you're a girl, though,' Lainey said. 'You can't be expected to wait in a bar, alone, with all kinds of weirdos if you're a girl.'

Both suits laughed. She was used to more *bohemian* people, unused to audible amusement at a weak line. It embarrassed her. They were like little kids, the way they laughed more than they felt. It was office behaviour, as simple as that: in large spaces, subtlety could be missed, emotion had to be demonstrated. Faked, if necessary, and it almost always was necessary. She gulped the Martini to anaesthetize the cringe.

'Give it till half past,' said the other suit. 'Man or woman?'

'A man,' Lainey said, proud and ashamed of this. It was better to be meeting a man, but worse to be stood up by one. On balance, 'man' sounded better. 'So do you boys work around here?'

'In the City,' said the suit. 'London Wall.'

'The same company?'

'That's right: the Big Boys Male Escort Agency. No, actually, we were at school together.'

The most striking thing about men was that they realized they were – what would be the right word? – *expected* to be funny. Their duty, their role in modern society, was to amuse. There was nothing else for them now, since class had stopped meaning anything, breeding no longer mattered, money . . . wasn't everything, physical strength was obsolete. They'd almost run out of uses. It was strange: women hadn't changed, or didn't feel any different anyway – they still wanted Gregory Peck, or nearest offer – but society had reshuffled itself so profoundly that everything was different, and there was no way for men to assert themselves in it, apart from as entertainment. When they weren't being funny, or trying to be, when they were just saying things, they were always a bit ashamed, conscious of their failure to perform. Elsewhere, they swapped quips the way stags lock antlers, or threw them out like a peacock's tail. That was what made the thing John did even stupider. If the essence of modern man was his assumption of this humour assignment, what did it mean when one of them tried to make a living out of it? Was he saying that he was, in some significant way, better than other men? Was he just trying to earn money for old rope? Was it a serious search for approval made to look like a jumped-up stumbled-into party piece? Around her, a bar full of men shouting, trying to be heard. Whichever way you looked at it, men were sad fucks, and she'd waited long enough for them.

'I have to go now,' Lainey said. 'Thanks for the drink, and for keeping me company while I waited.'

'You can't go now,' said the other suit. 'It's your round.'

'You have to be kidding?' Lainey genuinely asked him, as she threw her cardigan over her shoulders and left them there.

Despite her decisive exit, Lainey didn't really feel stood up yet. She had Scott's mobile number in her bag, and called it from the phone in the Atlantic. He picked up immediately, shouting pleasantly down the receiver. He was somewhere loud, surrounded by loud people.

'Where are you?' she said.

'Who's this?' He smothered the mouthpiece noisily with his hand, and she heard him shout 'I don't know' behind it.

'It's Lainey. From *Brazen*. I thought we were going for a drink tonight.'

'Shit. I forgot. I am so fucking sorry, Lainey,' Scott shouted. He was pissed, really pissed. 'Shit shit shit. How can I make it up to you?'

'I don't think you can,' she said, but he was on the right lines. Being drunk was, for her, some kind of excuse.

'Will you call me tomorrow and we'll arrange something else?'

'Why don't you call me?'

'You know me, Lainey, I'm gonna forget.'

'You bastard,' she said, joking but hurt. 'I can't believe you've stood me up.'

'I'm really sorry,' he shouted. 'Listen, we'll speak soon but I've really gotta go now. We'll speak soon. Call me. We'll do something. Yeah?' He hung up.

If he'd cared even a little, she might have been able to call him again. If he'd shown even a slight interest – not remorse, she wasn't asking for remorse, just interest. But he was drunk, and having a nice time with other people, and he wasn't interested in her when she wasn't there. Maybe it was common sense, maybe an old Chrissie truism, maybe she was just growing up, but she knew that it was useless to chase after a man when he hadn't already taken you with him.

Lainey hadn't eaten that day, and the three Martinis hit her harder than she'd expected them to. She counted the measures on her fingers: it would be the equivalent of about seven gins. On an empty stomach, enough to make her wobbly. In fact, she was well on the way to legless, and the heels didn't help. She ended up getting a bit lost in Soho, which was never as frightening as it sounded. It wasn't hard to feel safe in Soho, no matter what time it was. The homeless people were younger here, frail, wrapped in coats and eiderdowns as if it were the middle of winter. The streets kept moving: busy with Japanese suits, pissed lads, a few trendier kids. She was somewhere near Brewer Street and thinking about asking for directions when she saw John's name on a blackboard outside a pub. The shock of staring made her trip, but she didn't fall. John Truelove. His real name, not the name he used. Had to be John, though; it was worth a look.

Lainey was carried through by a burning sense of injustice and a determined clarity. Even if it *was* the booze talking, she agreed with it. For the last few months she'd tried really hard, and it kept turning out wrong. People who meant well and people who meant nothing like well had been telling her things and meaning everything else. She'd been lied to and manipulated and fucked over. But she knew all the facts now: she was smart. John had never fucked her over. She was going to take him back.

John was standing by the bar with some men she didn't know. Even as pissed as she was, for a few seconds she was too afraid to go up to him. She'd never surprised him before, and the situation was unpredictable. She approached and waited to be noticed, and, just as it occurred to her that that might not happen and she'd have to do something else, he noticed.

'Lainey,' he said nicely, before he remembered to be embarrassed.

'Hi John,' she said. 'I saw your name outside. I was just sort of staggering around Soho and I saw your name and I thought it had to be you. Although you used to do this with a different name. Are you on tonight? Have you already done it?'

'You look nice tonight. Do you want a drink?'

'Yes, please. Um. Wine, please. White. Sorry, you were saying, have you already done your jokes?'

'My jokes?' he said, smiling. 'No, not yet. I'm on in about an hour, to do my jokes. What are you doing here alone?'

'I didn't come to see you,' she said. 'It must look like that, I know, but in fact I actually just got stood up, so I'm not as sad as you think I am.'

His smile got better. He paid for her wine and she drank a lot of it, hoping it would remind her of what she was going to say next.

'Listen, let's sit down and talk,' John said. 'You're staying for a bit, yeah?'

'Sure,' she said. She watched him raise his eyebrows to the men he was leaving at the bar, and followed him to some seats at the other side of the pub. 'Are you doing your, er, your thing upstairs?'

'My jokes?' He smiled again. 'Yeah. There's a little stage thing up there. You said you were stood up.' She could see that his concern was sincere, and kind, but he wore it with some pride, like a medal.

'Yeah. It wasn't a date, though.'

'Chrissie?'

'No. Well, it was a date, but not a proper boy thing, just someone I worked with.'

'How is work?'

'Work's shit,' she said. Noticing the effect her honesty had on him, she let his own awkwardness intimidate him. She watched him try to remember the appropriate catch-all condolence. 'How are you?'

'I'm doing all right,' John said, nodding. 'There's someone in from the radio tonight, I've been told, who's looking for new writers and stuff. So, you know. I'm hoping.'

Prospects *and* a frequent smile. What more could a girl want in a man? In a week of doing very stupid things, would fucking John again be all that mad? If it went wrong, she could just write it off as part of a stupid week. If it went right, if it went right . . .

'All night I've been thinking to myself, you phoned the wrong man, you phoned the wrong man. You see there were two. And I phoned the one who wasn't going to come and I've been thinking all night, I should have phoned the other one –'

'Laine –'

'No, there's going to be a point at the end of this, I promise. Do I sound really pissed? I am, but I know what I'm saying. So I'm thinking I should have phoned the other one, I got the wrong one and now I'm just thinking both of them were the wrong one and, you know, I ended it with you for *nothing*! No reason at *all*, and it was stupid of me and now – *now* – I think I've worked out that maybe the right one was the one that I'd already fucked it up with.'

He didn't say anything.

'I mean you.'

'I'm with someone else,' John said. Lainey felt the wine hit her head, which was still fluffed by the Martinis.

269

'How can you be? Tonight, you mean? You're with someone tonight?'

'No. Look, I didn't know when to stop you, because I wasn't sure what you were going to say and I didn't want you to think I was being an arrogant cunt. I mean I'm *with* someone. I met a girl in Brighton. I was down there for a gig. We just –'

'Already?'

'Yes. I'm sorry, Lainey.'

'Don't say sorry.'

'I know, sorry. For the sorry.'

'What's she called?' She was half-hoping he wouldn't be able to think of a name; because he was making it up.

'Eleanor.' It sounded made up.

'Eleanor. What does she do?'

'She's a student. At UCL. It's early days yet, but . . .'

Lainey covered her face with her wine glass, looked past him. 'Fucking excellent week this is turning out to be,' she said softly.

'I should go, really, I'm up in a bit,' he said. 'It's good to see you again. I mean it. And you're looking great. I mean that, too.'

'Well, of course you do,' Lainey said. 'You don't have to be involved with me any more. Of course you're going to think I look all right.'

'Don't be stupid. You look great.' He leaned to kiss her, and she backed away a bit, accepting it as if it hurt. 'If you want to talk ever, call. I like talking to you. I always did.'

He'd already risen when he kissed her, and made standing up the rest of the way a smooth, deliberate movement. Lainey didn't turn around to watch him walk past her. She could feel her heart beating in her rough, hot cheeks. She dipped her finger in the dregs of her wine and sucked it, trying not to cry.

stand–up

He could see her at the back. She looked a bit weepy, but had clearly been as pissed as fuck – he wasn't going to let himself be too flattered. In his experience, a lot of girls found him irresistible when they were too drunk to take advantage of, but conveniently forgot it later. All the same, he was anxious to be good. Not that he felt very bitter about Lainey, especially now, but when it came to letting people know what they were missing, you always hoped they quite minded missing it. The crowd had been pretty quiet so far, shy: the worst kind. But he was going to turn all that around. He eased them into it with a brief introduction, made fun of his name and his old comedy name, stretching the joke out nicely into the superficially sick reference to the recently dead celebrity. The audience made some noise, intakes of breath, oohing, and John said, 'Hey, laughter is just one of many responses. I'm not fussy.' Then he allowed himself a small faked snigger, as an example – in case they weren't sure how comedy worked, and went on.

'I don't know why you're expecting *them* to laugh at you. I'm the only one here you've slept with,' Lainey said.

This got a big laugh, some clapping, and John thought they'd probably heard his jaw drop. Beyond the dazzle of his spot, Lainey sat in a shadow, looking even redder than he felt; hot and distantly crazy. The audience was searching for her, trying to work out where the line had come from, the people next to her grinning and watching John for what he was going to do next.

'In fact, that's not even numerically true any more. Not this evening,' John said, and winked randomly into the crowd. One bloke gave a small deep cheer that carried well. Small titter. 'Thank you, sir. And er, thanks again for last night.'

Another big laugh. It was never the material that got audiences really going, it was the edge. The here and now. He tried to remember where he was; he needed the momentum to kick in before their good mood levelled off: the trouble was, they liked heckling more than the routines. When you went back into the set, they were always going to be a bit disappointed. To win round the female audience, he started to do his stuff about not liking women with big tits.

'What's your problem with them?' Lainey said. He watched heads swivel away from him again, and was afraid of what she was going to say next. 'Can't your big arse stand the competition?'

'Ladies and gentlemen, we have my ex-girlfriend in tonight.' There was some applause. A couple of women called out, he wasn't sure whose side they were on. 'I know this wasn't on the bill, so maybe you should think of her as a free gift. One given with every pint. Which was, if I remember, her successful opening line when we met.' They half-followed this. It half-worked.

'No, my opening line was: I'm sorry, sir, we only stock girdles for female customers.' She was getting better laughs than him.

'She works in a wholefood shop,' John said, annoyed because he only liked being the butt of jokes he'd set up himself. 'They don't even sell girdles. She saw me trying to lift some organic bread – I wasn't trying to steal it, just lift the fucker off the shelf.' He didn't get a laugh at all. 'It's, um, really heavy bread,' he petered out, drawing the shape of a loaf in the air, milking the laugh you got when jokes failed. 'Lainey. Sweetheart. Could you call my agent and we'll fix up a time for you to heckle me in private next week? This may come as a surprise to you, but I'm actually in the middle of doing some stand-up comedy at the moment.'

'It'll probably come as a surprise to everyone else here,' she said.

pre–post–structuralist
sex vibe

The doorbell buzzed, and Lainey woke and thought, Thank God; I don't have a hangover. Then she moved her head, and the poison asserted itself, tumbling heavily into her brain, *being* there like heavy grease in her stomach, and the pounding started, and the spinning.

'I can't get to the door,' she said, a croaky monotone. 'I'm going to die.' Despite being unable to hear her, the person at the door replied, with a longer, harder buzz. This one shook her to the core. She shivered violently and needed to vomit. The door handle was the closest steady thing after the bed, and she lunged for it – once she was up it was less bad, and she went to the window to see who was there. John was standing in the street wearing a white shirt. She thought about ignoring him, but he looked up and saw her.

'Lainey,' he shouted. 'Can I come in for a minute?'

'I feel terrible,' she shouted back weakly. 'And I look like it. No.'

'I don't care. It'll only be a minute.'

'Hold on. I think I need to be sick. I'll be with you. Hold on.'

She was glad to see him there and mad at herself for being so unprepared. Stumbling into the bathroom, she was confronted by the worst hair, mascara everywhere except her eyelashes, and a crusty patch that started from one corner of her mouth. Eyebrow hairs were growing back in places she couldn't even remember plucking them from. She started brushing her teeth, and the toothbrush made her gag. Good enough. The convenient proximity of all her bathroom fixtures, apart from the shower itself, was sometimes a blessing, and she moved her head only minimally to puke hard and deep, but with little substantial pay-off. The taste of gin and olives. She rinsed and went back to brushing her teeth, clamping the brush between her molars as she tried to do something about her hair. John buzzed again, the *cunt*.

'Shut up,' she said, and spat. With a little more toothpaste, she went round her teeth a second time. The hair was beyond hope. Her stomach heaved, she waited, and decided it wouldn't happen. She went downstairs to let him in.

'Did I wake you?' John said.

She yawned, nodding. 'It hardly matters. I look like shit. As you see. Does that matter?'

'You look fine. Can I come in for a minute?'

She yawned again, wider this time, shrugging. He looked a bit alarmed, and she thought it might have been because she looked like she was going to be sick again, and soon. It was a very long yawn. Her eyes were watering behind her glasses. She turned to head up the stairs, holding the door open behind her.

'Do you want . . . stuff? Tea, coffee? Sheep's milk?'

'No.' He sat down carefully on the corner of her bed. She knew the place must smell pretty bad, but she couldn't smell it. Her throat was blocked with residual smoke, a bitter grey fur that toothpaste hadn't shifted coating her palate. 'That was quite a heckling you gave me last night.'

'I can't remember?' she tried, begging him to let her forget, and smiled. He laughed.

'Do you want me to remind you?' he said. She shook her head. 'I didn't think so.' She yawned again, hugely, behind both hands.

'I'm not well,' she said.

'Who were you meeting last night?' he said. His eyes and his voice were kind, but that didn't mean a thing. It wasn't like people didn't fake kindness to get things.

'Oh, who even cares now? Someone I'm never going to see again. I picked the wrong man. As usual. Why are you here?'

'How would you like to write a sitcom?'

'What?' She hardly had enough energy to ask, the question was so stupid.

'How would you like to –'

'Yeah, I heard. I just didn't believe. You wake me up while I'm in the throes of death to talk shit at me.'

'That was strange,' the stranger with the green tie said. 'Was it as much of a surprise as it looked?'

'She's a mate,' John said. 'We didn't, like, plan it. But she was joking. Having a laugh. We do that sort of thing.'

'I could see that,' said the weird-looking man. 'I'm Steve Farnborough. I work for BBC radio. I've seen your set before, and I think there's a lot of good stuff in there. But we're not really looking for stand-ups.'

'Right,' John said. 'So . . .'

'So I wondered if you and your girlfriend had considered writing a sitcom. For radio. I know it's probably not something you've thought about before.'

'No, I have actually,' John said. 'I've got things I could show you.'

'Yeah, that'd be good. But I really liked the female-angle thing here, that sort of pre-post-structuralist sex vibe.'

'Oh, that,' John said.

'God, you're serious,' Lainey said. 'What makes you think *he* was?'

'He was. You're a writer, aren't you?'

'No,' she said, indignant. 'It's one thing I'm fucking definitely not.'

'Come on, Laine.'

'John, you're talking mad.'

'Well, what else are you going to do? We just need to spend some time together, bounce ideas.'

'Don't say "bounce ideas" ever again.'

'You work, I work, in between we see what happens. We've probably got more material than we think to go on.' Their eyes locked: they'd changed. They both knew more than they were letting on.

'Aren't you *with* someone now?'

'Eleanor. Yeah. Why should that be a problem?' How little you know women, Lainey thought. 'We can do this.' She didn't press further, not wanting to openly flatter herself that she'd be a threat.

'What's it about?'

'About twenty-five minutes.'

'We've got no chance, you're not even funny.'

'You are, though. What have we got to lose?'

Lainey looked down at her legs, which were bare, and goose-pimpled with stubble that hadn't quite made it through. John was looking at her face, his head on one side, a puppyish affectation that wasn't as winsome as he thought, but all the cuter for it. She'd had him before, and she could have him again. Was he for real, even, or was this a line – was he taking the sneaky way in? Long nights spent huddled over a warm script. She knew that if they tried to write together they were going to end up having sex, girlfriend or no girlfriend. She knew it. Possibly he knew it too. But last night's plan felt less obvious this morning. Hangovers had a way of collecting all the hindsight and putting it in order. She wasn't sure that John would be good for her now. But it could be fun finding out. Trying her best always backfired, so maybe doing her worst would work better. Eleanor could watch her own back; Lainey was tired of thinking.

'Which one of us is she like?' she said.

'What?'

'Which one of us is she like?'

'Who? Eleanor? It's not like that. She's not like either of you.'

Lainey noticed that although he needed to check that she was talking about Eleanor, he didn't ask who 'us' was. She reached behind John's head for the Camel Lights on the television. He blinked, bracing himself, as if he'd expected her to hit him, and she stifled a laugh. She lit up and inhaled. She hoped it would help her make up her mind.

'Chrissie,' he said.